D0823956

A
FRAGILE
THING

ALSO BY KEVIN WIGNALL

A FRAGILE THING

KEVIN WIGNALL

This is a work of fiction. Names, characters, organizations, places, events, and incidents are either products of the author's imagination or are used fictitiously.

Text copyright © 2017 Kevin Wignall
All rights reserved.

No part of this book may be reproduced, or stored in a retrieval system, or transmitted in any form or by any means, electronic, mechanical, photocopying, recording, or otherwise, without express written permission of the publisher.

Published by Thomas & Mercer, Seattle

www.apub.com

Amazon, the Amazon logo, and Thomas & Mercer are trademarks of Amazon.com, Inc., or its affiliates.

ISBN-13: 9781612185804
ISBN-10: 1612185800

Cover design by @blacksheep-uk.com

Printed in the United States of America

A
FRAGILE
THING

Chapter One

Capri, Gulf of Naples — 2009

The yacht looked sleek and understated, a brushstroke of white against the vast blue, a thing of simple and enticing beauty owned by one of the most dangerous men Max was ever likely to meet.

Their boat skimmed across the water toward it, too fast, the driver showing off, so that even the shallowest waves on this flattest of seas seemed to lift them into the air before dropping them back down.

They slowed as they closed in and the sides of the yacht looked higher now, and Max could see a few of Vicari's men standing sentinel here and there along the decks. Seeing them made him wonder if he should have brought some of his own team.

Francesco seemed to read his thoughts because he said, "It's better it's just the two of us. If you'd brought bodyguards it would have shown weakness, not strength."

"I know."

"You're business partners; you have to remember that. Equals."

"I know."

Max smiled, and could see now that for all his reassurances and his decades of experience, it was Francesco who was nervous. And maybe that was *because* of those extra decades or because Francesco was Italian and knew precisely the kind of danger that Luciano Vicari represented. For his part, Max's nerves were more those of excitement, and he knew it wouldn't be wise to make a habit of this, but even so, meeting a Mafia boss of this stature felt like one for the memory bank.

As they pulled alongside, a member of the crew, dressed in whites, appeared at the top of the steps. He waited there and saluted when Max reached him.

"Welcome aboard, Signor Emerson. If you follow me, Don Vicari is waiting for you."

"Thanks." He threw a glance over his shoulder, but Francesco's smile suggested he didn't share Max's amusement at the novelty of it all.

They followed the crewman along the side of the yacht and out onto a large open deck, a lounge area looking across the pool, which seemed suspended over the deeper blue beyond.

There were two men sitting there, one of whom Max immediately recognized as Vicari. He was wearing a white suit over a black shirt with an open collar, his dark hair slicked back, and glasses that were tinted blue rather than opaque. Max knew he was fifty-two but he didn't look it in person.

The crewman was about to speak, but Vicari saw them and rose to his feet, holding his arms out in welcome.

"Signor Emerson! Welcome." He spoke English with a slight American accent.

Max smiled as he approached, and said, "Don Vicari, it's good to finally meet." Vicari embraced him and then Max stepped to one side. "I think you've met Francesco before."

"Of course, welcome again."

As they greeted each other, Max looked at the other man, who was now getting to his feet. He was wearing a bathrobe that was tied but hanging loose, exposing the yellow swimming shorts beneath and a belly that looked as if it had been inflated. He had thin reddish hair that had been expertly teased and shaped to cover his head. Max guessed he was in his late fifties, although he was in such poor shape that it was hard to be sure.

Vicari turned now and said, "Signor Emerson, this is Senator Robert Colfax. Senator, Max Emerson."

Colfax stepped forward, holding his hand out and smiling with an air of superiority and a well-rehearsed warmth. "Good to meet you, kid. I've heard a lot about you."

There was something in his manner that Max didn't like, as if he were talking to some teenage intern.

Max felt his humor drain away, but before he could reply or even shake hands, Vicari said, "Senator, why don't you go inside and find something to do. Signor Emerson and I have business to discuss."

It was obvious from his tone that Vicari wasn't happy, and Colfax looked unsure how to respond. He smiled awkwardly and lowered his hand again, the look of a man who was struggling to see what his mistake had been, and nervous about how much he'd upset his host. "Sure. I'll leave you to it."

He walked off the deck and Vicari waited until he'd gone before saying, "He should have treated you with more respect. You're twenty-seven, no?"

"That's right."

Vicari smiled. "I was the same age when I achieved my current position. Very young. But people soon learned."

A crewman came out onto the deck pushing a trolley laden with champagne and glasses.

"Please, won't you both take a seat, and we'll toast our first year in business together."

"Thank you, Don Vicari."

They sat opposite each other, with Francesco off to one side, and Vicari smiled as the champagne was poured.

"I hope you'll call me Luciano, and I can call you Max. You may be young, but I consider you an equal—we're business partners—and when it comes to investing, you have a golden touch."

"Thank you."

It all seemed slightly surreal. Yes, Max was already rich and powerful, but here he was on first-name terms with someone a lot richer, for now at least, and definitely more powerful.

Vicari watched as Max and Francesco were handed glasses of champagne, then accepted one himself and said, "To business!" They raised their glasses, repeating the toast, and sipped at their drinks. Vicari looked at his glass and nodded with approval. "I lived in America for a while, when I was young, in New York City and Connecticut."

"That's a coincidence—my mom was born in Connecticut and my dad grew up in Nassau County, Long Island."

He cursed himself even as he spoke, wondering why he'd seen fit to share his genealogy with someone like this. Max knew how to make money, but he still had a lot to learn about how someone in his position was meant to act.

And yet, to his surprise, Vicari looked genuinely impressed. "Amazing. I love Long Island."

"Me too. We used to go a lot when I was a kid."

"But you've never lived in the US, no? Only ever Switzerland?"

"And Italy."

"Naturally. But you must still feel a connection—so much of your business is in America."

"A fair amount of it."

Vicari nodded, apparently giving a lot of thought to the matter, and as friendly as he was, Max could see something in him that hinted at the very real danger lurking beneath the surface geniality. He could easily imagine how terrifying it would be to end up on the wrong side of this man—he seemed so relaxed, and yet there was something taut in the air that surrounded him.

Of course, that was part of the thrill. Max didn't have any friends his own age, and didn't really have friends at all since work had taken over his life, but right now he wished he did, or that he and Stef were still together, so that he could go back and say, "You'll never guess who I met today." Not that Stef would have been impressed by something like that.

Vicari looked down at his champagne but, after considering it, put the glass aside. "Your American business is actually why I wanted to meet with you today. It's better that we don't meet too often, better that we don't know too much about each other's business, but I heard you've been having problems with a big property investment in Colorado, and I want to help if I can."

"You have good sources, Luciano, but you don't have to do that."

"It's what friends do."

Max nodded appreciatively, but was wondering how Vicari even knew about Colorado—he was impressed, but concerned too, because they'd gone to great lengths to keep their involvement secret.

"Tell me more about this local politician . . ."

"Hayden Manning. Not just a politician: he's a businessman, environmental campaigner. The team sounded him out early on and he was onside, but now he keeps blocking it, no matter what we do, no matter what we offer. It's reaching the point of being a problem."

In reality, it was far beyond that point, and Max had woken in the night a few times in recent weeks, trying to figure out a way of appeasing Hayden Manning. For Max, it was the first serious setback he'd had since setting up Emerson five years ago, but with so much invested he knew it could easily prove the last, unless he found a solution.

"So I imagine the money you've invested is worthless unless Manning withdraws his opposition."

"Pretty much. We could handle the loss, and it won't affect you, but I can't pretend it wouldn't be a real setback."

Vicari nodded, as though Max were the one who'd raised the issue and asked for his counsel.

"I have a problem too just now. Senator Colfax." He paused, acknowledging his distaste at having to bring the Senator back into the conversation, and nodded at Max as though they had some mutual understanding. "The Senator is in a position to help with some very important deals we'd like to secure in the US, but he'll only do it if we can guarantee that his fee stays out of reach of the authorities."

Max saw where the conversation was heading, but couldn't resist saying, "How much are we talking about?"

"Fifty-four million dollars." Vicari let that sink in, the fact that it was a small enough amount to be hardly worthy of note. "So, I was thinking, maybe we could solve each other's problems, just this once. You handle the Senator's money for me, and I'll deal with your road-block in Colorado."

Max didn't need to ask if Vicari was confident he could do that, and the thought was so immediately appealing, the prospect of wiping out all the stress of recent weeks with just one word, that he had to force himself to stay silent and consider it properly.

For one thing, although he'd been investing Vicari's money this last year, he'd been a step removed from the laundering process itself. Handling a bribe for a US senator was something else, the kind of thing that could come back to bite him if he wasn't careful.

Then there was the question of how Vicari intended to deal with Hayden Manning. Max could feel a charge of adrenaline running through him, because there was only one likely answer to that question. There had been times in the last few weeks when he'd felt like killing Manning himself, but that had been fantasy. This was real, even if it didn't feel like it—with Max's say-so, Vicari would kill a man who had a wife and three or four children, a man Max had never met, someone with regular hopes and fears and beliefs.

"You've taken me by surprise, Luciano. I'll need to discuss this with Francesco, if you don't mind."

"Of course. That's as I'd expect." Vicari stood and so did Francesco. "I'll leave you alone. Help yourself to more champagne, and call if you need anything."

Once Vicari had left, Francesco took his place facing Max. Neither of them topped up their glasses.

"So, Francesco, how did he know about Colorado?"

Francesco smiled. "I might have had a little chat with his lawyer. I didn't mention it to you because I wanted your response to be spontaneous."

"Did you, now?" But he smiled too, because, as ever, Francesco's judgment had been right and Max probably would have failed miserably at pretending to be surprised. "So, what do you think?"

Francesco had obviously hoped to solicit some sort of help from Vicari, but now that the offer was a reality, he seemed uncertain. "You know, Max, our arrangement with Vicari is set up specifically so that we're on the right side of the law. We could still do the same here, but getting involved with a crooked US senator is a more dangerous game." Max nodded. "That said, I'm not sure it would be wise to refuse this favor, whatever we decide to do with the other half of the bargain."

Max laughed a little, even with the seriousness of what they were discussing.

"Francesco, it was really the other side of the bargain that I wanted your opinion on."

"Yes, I know." Francesco tried another smile himself but his heart wasn't in it. "I've puzzled so much about why this Hayden Manning changed his mind at the eleventh hour, why he refuses all negotiation. I even wondered if it was some kind of grudge, but there's no way of tracing the Greenwood development back to Emerson, let alone to you. So maybe it's principles alone, and you have to respect that, but this man's actions will cause real damage—to the company, to you personally. It's why I raised the issue with Don Vicari's lawyer, but now I'm faced with the question, is it enough to sanction his death? And I can't answer."

"How serious is our situation?"

Francesco looked reluctant even to reply. "If we keep growing at the current rate, particularly with the money coming on stream from the new Russian clients, within a year we could just about take the hit, but until then it leaves us in a very exposed position. There's no question we need Colorado to happen. I can't pretend otherwise."

Max was annoyed with himself, that he'd overextended or under-researched, or failed to allow for someone like Hayden Manning changing his position at the last minute. He'd never make that mistake again, and he still wasn't sure that this was the right solution, but he was determined he wouldn't allow the last five years to be for nothing.

"Okay, let's do it."

Francesco looked surprised, although not unhappy. "You're sure you don't need more time?"

That was one thing Max didn't need. It was a simple decision, and time would only complicate it. "No, it's like you said, we've given him chance enough. He's attacking me and he's attacking my business, and I'll take the blows, but I will not let Hayden Manning destroy Emerson. Let's do the deal."

Francesco nodded but stayed where he was. "You know, Max, five years ago, when I told my colleagues you'd offered me a job and I'd accepted, they thought I was crazy, throwing my career away on someone fresh out of school. But I knew, and I never saw your youth, only your talent. So now I have to remind myself, and you, that you *are* still young. I'll back you one hundred percent, whatever you decide, but I don't want you to make a decision here today that you'll come to regret."

Max appreciated the sentiment, and it was the first time that Francesco had ever mentioned Max's age, but the way he saw it, this was a binary choice before him—Hayden Manning or Emerson Holdings.

"Francesco, if I allow this man to destroy my company, I'll regret it for the rest of my life."

"I know that." But he looked somber. Then, after a moment or two, he looked more hopeful. "And of course, we're not killing him. We've tried our best and now we're washing our hands, that's all."

They both knew that wasn't true, but Max could see it meant a lot to Francesco, for his own sake or maybe for Max's, to defend the action they were taking here.

"Exactly. All we're doing is asking someone else to solve our problem for us. How they do it is up to them." He waited a beat, and added, "So you agree?"

"It has to be your decision, but yes, I think we have no choice."

Max stared at him, finally tilting his head and raising his eyebrows, as if to ask what he was waiting for.

Francesco smiled and stood, but before he could move, a crewman came out of the door and waved in acknowledgment. Francesco remained standing and looked around at the view from the deck, settling finally on Capri. "This is really quite something."

He wasn't wrong there, and it made Max see that these were the kind of trappings they should have too.

"You know, Francesco, maybe you should buy yourself a yacht, when Colorado's sorted, keep it down in Genoa or somewhere like that."

"Maybe. And what about you, Max? What gift would you buy yourself?"

Before Max could answer, Vicari came back out and said, "Well? Do we have a decision?"

Max stood too. "We do. I'll want Colfax's fee bundled up with the regular investment funds so the specific amount isn't visible, but that's my only condition. We have a deal."

It seemed a wondrous thing, somehow, that a man would die because of those few words.

Vicari nodded with what looked like genuine respect and approval, and shook Max's hand. And Max wondered what it meant to have the respect of a man like Vicari, not just for his investment acumen, but also for a decision like this. He knew one thing—he no longer felt like he was merely acting the part.

They sat again and talked for a while longer. Colfax never came back out, but as Max and Francesco were leaving, Max could hear the Senator somewhere inside, laughing in a way that seemed to suggest some sexual activity. It was a disturbing sound in itself, but more so because the Senator was the only one laughing.

For the first time since boarding the yacht, Max was filled with unease. He carried Manning's fate surprisingly lightly, a death that felt like it was really nothing to do with him, little more than the ceremonial washing of hands that Francesco had described.

But part of that bargain was aiding the man whose ridiculous attempt at seductive laughter was spilling toward them as they left. And hearing it, Max couldn't help but think that he'd been too confident in his assurances, and that the decision he'd made here today would sooner or later come back to haunt him.

Milan, seven years later

Max was a little bit in love, or wanted to be. It was her dancing alone that did it and when the knife appeared his stomach tensed, and as it plunged into her he held his breath, even though he'd known that this was how it ended.

When the lights went down he closed his eyes, savoring that moment of peace, the almost mystical intimacy of the theater, and then the applause stuttered into life and built until it filled the auditorium and Max joined in with it.

Renaldi turned to him with a look of expectancy and said something, although his words were drowned out by the surrounding noise.

Max said, "It was beautiful," and Renaldi put his hands over his heart in appreciation.

As they were walking out, Renaldi said, "I'm so pleased you enjoyed it, Signor Emerson. It means so much to us to have such a generous benefactor, and so young. It makes me very optimistic for the future."

Max was generous, there was no doubting that, but he hardly felt young. "I'm just glad I can make a difference."

"Oh, that's without question. Such a difference."

At the after-party, Renaldi introduced him to the dancers, but the spell was broken now, and close up and without the makeup and costume, the female lead looked nothing like Viola. Max complimented them all and they thanked him politely, and he felt as invisible to them as he had in the dark of the dress circle.

Renaldi had known Viola and was keen to introduce Max to some of the other dancers in the company, perhaps thinking he'd guarantee Max's sponsorship if he could find him another girlfriend. Max got left with one of them, a sweet girl called Jen who was from Toronto, but they didn't find much to talk about beyond places they knew in common, and Max excused himself, probably to her relief as much as his—he noticed her across the room a short while later, laughing and relaxed with one of the male dancers.

Max edged gradually toward the exit, talking to people who knew him or remembered seeing him back when he'd been dating Viola, and collared by others who knew only that he was a generous benefactor. He wanted to escape, and wasn't even sure why he'd agreed to come to the party in the first place.

The last to intercept him was one of Milan's city councillors, keen to explain the aims of a foundation he was in the process of establishing. It was obvious why the councillor was talking to him and Max felt like telling him he'd contribute as long as he didn't have to hear the sales pitch, but when his phone vibrated and he saw it was Francesco calling, he took the opportunity to escape.

"I'm so sorry, but I have to take this."

"Of course." The councillor looked put out. "Perhaps later . . ."

"Yes, or send some information to my office. Excuse me." Max answered the call. "Francesco." He couldn't hear his reply. "Just a second, let me go somewhere quieter."

He stepped out onto the roof terrace. There were a few people smoking, looking out over the city night and the illuminated cathedral, but he walked off to one side and stood in the shadows before putting the phone back to his ear. "Okay, I can hear you now."

"Max! How was the ballet?"

He smiled. "It was good, and of course it has the added benefit of amusing you."

"It doesn't amuse me . . . Well, it does amuse me, but only because of the way you got involved. I mean, you became a benefactor because of Viola, but you're not together anymore."

"She moved to New York—it's not as if we stopped liking each other." Although perhaps he had to admit it hadn't gone very much deeper than that, and just as this evening's dancer had reminded him a little of Viola, so Viola had reminded him a little of Stef—he didn't need counseling skills to know that was no foundation for a relationship. "Anyway, I'm sure you didn't call to hear about the ballet."

As he spoke, the smokers went inside, a brief burst of the party noise as they opened the door and closed it again. He was alone out there now.

"You're right, of course." There was a weighted pause. "Marco and Lorenzo haven't felt the need to mention this before, but I think you need to know now. I'll tell you more when I see you but someone working in the building of our Luxembourg office has been trying to access our computer systems—unsuccessfully, I might add. Lorenzo and the German are out there at the moment. It might be something and nothing . . ."

"But?"

"But it's possible there's a link to a certain US politician we once met."

"I see." He didn't need to ask which politician. He'd met a few in the last twelve years, but only Robert Colfax would warrant Francesco calling at this time in the evening.

"Yes. So, I was thinking, on the way back to the lake, you could have Roberto stop by here and I'll give you more idea of what we might be dealing with."

"Okay. I'll be leaving soon. Give us maybe half an hour, forty minutes."

"I'll see you then."

Max ended the call and stood for a moment, thinking about Colfax and how he'd somehow known this day would come. They'd rid themselves of one politician who'd been intent on ruining them, only to replace him with one who'd looked like ruin personified.

The door opened and there was another brief burst of noise before two people came out onto the terrace and closed it again behind them. They probably couldn't see Max where he was standing and they were only silhouettes themselves as they walked over and stood at the balustrade looking out over the city.

They weren't smoking, just standing with their arms linked, talking quietly, a sweet and playful closeness about them. Max could see now that it was the young dancer from Toronto and her male friend, wrapped up in each other, both part of the same world.

Two more people came out, and he took the opportunity to move from the shadows. The party was even livelier, the chatter and laughter developing a slightly manic quality. He politely brushed off the councillor and someone else Max didn't even recognize. He managed to avoid being seen by Renaldi too. It wasn't his most natural environment, and hadn't been even when he'd been dating Viola, but right now, after one simple phone call, he felt more keenly than ever that he really didn't belong here at all.

Chapter Two

As Roberto drove him to Francesco's house, Max sat in the dark in the back of the car, thinking about his one brief meeting with Robert Colfax: that grotesque physique and ridiculous hair, the oily confidence that had been so quickly undermined by Vicari's displeasure.

The memory was bright and fresh in his mind and yet it simultaneously felt a lifetime ago—a lifetime in which he'd built Emerson Holdings into the multi-billion-dollar company it was today. He'd changed too, fully becoming the person he'd imagined himself to be that day on Vicari's yacht, and the agreement he'd made had been integral to that.

Two weeks after their meeting, Hayden Manning had failed to return home from a hunting trip, and a day later his jeep had been found abandoned in the woods five miles from his Colorado home. They'd presumed he'd fallen somewhere on one of the trails, but his body had never been found. Little more than a month later, the Greenwood development had received the go-ahead.

On the anniversary of Manning's disappearance, a local paper had been the first to link it to Greenwood, suggesting Manning might have been the victim of foul play, vaguely pointing the finger at the Las Vegas Mafia.

Thereafter, the Las Vegas Mafia had been a feature of the theories about Manning that peppered the Internet, although the Greenwood element of the story had dropped off the radar. It would have been almost impossible to link Emerson Holdings to Greenwood anyway, but within two years Max had taken his profits and moved on, and he'd never invested in Colorado again.

Meanwhile, three months after the meeting with Vicari, Max had diverted fifty-four million dollars from an investment fund, channeled it through London and the Caribbean, and eventually paid it into a company incorporated in Delaware, a company that was ultimately controlled by one Senator Robert Colfax.

That was the complex web they'd set about creating that day on Vicari's yacht. In the years since, Max had become accustomed to hearing speculation regarding Manning or Greenwood, or Vicari's business dealings, and it had never troubled him. But he'd sensed from the beginning that Colfax was the danger, the one person capable of inadvertently unraveling everything they'd so carefully constructed, and he feared this might be the start of that.

Roberto turned through the gates and up the drive to Francesco's house. Alessandra opened the door even as Max was getting out of the car.

"I'm sorry to disturb your evening, Alessandra."

She waved her hand dismissively. "Come on in—he's in his study. Roberto, don't sit out here, come into the kitchen and have coffee with me." Max kissed her. "You smell nice. How was the ballet?"

"Beautiful." He said it without thinking—it was already as if he hadn't been there.

He walked through to Francesco's study, where he found him sitting in one of the armchairs, staring intently at a tablet. He put it to one side and stood. "Sit down, Max. I'll get you a drink."

"No, I don't want to keep you."

"Nonsense." Francesco closed the door and poured them both a drink as Max sat down, then handed him a glass and sat himself.

"Thanks." It was brandy. Max took a sip and held it in his mouth for a few seconds, letting the flavor build through the heat. "So, what have we got?"

Francesco nodded, acknowledging the business at hand. "For the most part, it's the kind of thing that happens and the team doesn't bother you with it. For about six weeks we had some sustained attempts to hack our systems, all unsuccessful, then they stopped. A week or so later, we noticed some strange activity in our Luxembourg office, computers being turned on during the night, failed attempts to enter the system. It turned out the building had just hired a new night watchman."

"I'm guessing he wasn't just bored and fooling around."

"No, and he's no ordinary night watchman. He's a dual national, Saul Goldstein—American, but also with a Maltese passport. And Lorenzo says the pattern is suspicious. For example, last week, Wednesday through Saturday, he tried the same terminal each time, got as far as the drop-down menus, but again, only one attempt each night."

Max instantly saw the significance of that pattern. "He's thinking if there's only one failed attempt, the system won't flag it up."

"Exactly, but our system flags every failed attempt. He can't know that, and as we sit here I imagine he's trying again."

Max nodded. If Lorenzo and Klaus, or "the German" as all the others called him, had flown out there, it suggested they thought it was serious, and that they might need to step in.

"So what's the connection with Colfax?"

Francesco picked up his tablet and tapped away at the screen as he spoke. "The German pulled the security footage from the lobby. It didn't show much. Goldstein spent most of each night reading. But one night just over a week ago, our man made a call on his cell phone. The sound quality isn't great, but we've studied it and we're confident of what he's saying. You'll hear him mention that it's taking longer than he expected, then he responds to something from the other person and tells them to concentrate on Colfax."

Francesco handed him the tablet. Max looked down at it, saw the guy behind the desk, young and wearing a collar and tie. All Max could really see of him from this angle was dark, curly hair.

He pressed play and almost immediately heard him say, "It's gonna take longer than I thought, but don't sweat it, I'll get there." Goldstein listened to the response, but as he did so he leaned back in the chair and looked up, directly into the camera. It seemed to physically bring him up short and his voice was much lower when he spoke again, as if suddenly conscious that he was being recorded. "No, I got this. You concentrate on Colfax . . ." Max couldn't make out the final few words, and wondered if he'd only understood the others because Francesco had planted them in his mind ahead of time.

"What does he say at the end?"

"He says, 'You concentrate on Colfax—that's where the story is.' So maybe he's a journalist. Lorenzo thinks it's a possibility. On the other hand, Marco thinks he might be working for a competitor."

"Why would a competitor be interested in Colfax?"

"I imagine he means the kind of competitor who might want to put you out of business."

"I see." Max handed back the tablet. "Could he be Government?"

"I think it unlikely. He doesn't have the right look. They've asked the hacker in Torino to do a search on him anyway."

"Which hacker in Torino?"

"Do we have more than one?"

Max smiled. "I just like hearing you say his name."

"*Crazy Mouse*—are you happy?" Francesco laughed a little himself. "I mean, what kind of person calls himself like that? Crazy Mouse!" Becoming serious again, he said, "We have everything covered, but I'll still be happier once we know exactly who this Goldstein is and what he's up to."

Max felt the same. Why, after seven years, had a young guy called Saul Goldstein started digging with some determination into the possible links between Emerson Holdings and Senator Colfax? It was a question that should have made him recoil, but it drew him in instead, like an imminent accident he couldn't tear his eyes away from. "Maybe I should meet him." Francesco looked intrigued and Max said, "They could pick him up, give him the choice of coming out here to see me or going to the police. I'm guessing he'll choose the former. That'll give Klaus the chance to go through his apartment, see what he can find. And whoever he is, it might just rattle him enough to tell us the truth."

"It could work." Francesco didn't sound convinced, but Max could see that he had a similar curiosity about Goldstein. They'd both been there on the yacht that day; they'd both been party to what had been agreed, even if it had been Max's decision alone. "I'll arrange it with Lorenzo."

"Good. And now I won't keep you any longer." He finished his drink in one gulp and stood up.

Francesco put his drink aside and stood too.

Max noticed a picture frame on his desk and picked it up to look at the photograph: a beautiful little boy with a dimpled smile.

"Is that Claudio? He's so big."

Francesco smiled, a grandfather's pride. "That's from the summer. He'll be three in two weeks."

"About the same age as my nieces. So I guess they're getting big like Claudio too." Francesco nodded, his smile falling away into regret, but he didn't say anything. "Sorry, I didn't mean to bring up the subject of my exile."

"Partial exile. Your parents are good people. And your brother and sister, they simply misunderstand the nature of our business."

Max nodded and put the picture back on the desk. For most of the three years in which he'd been effectively cut out of his family's life, he too had seen it as a misunderstanding, and a willful one at that. Tonight, though, knowing that Saul Goldstein was in an office a few hundred miles north of here, knowing something of what Goldstein was looking for, Max wasn't so sure there'd been any misunderstanding at all.

Chapter Three

Domenico took the plane to Luxembourg on Tuesday afternoon and met up with Lorenzo and Klaus. The three of them picked up Saul Goldstein at his apartment just after he got back from work first thing on Wednesday morning.

They gave him the choice of going to the police or explaining himself to the boss of Emerson Holdings and he'd jumped at the chance of the latter, or, at least, of avoiding an interview with the police. Lorenzo and Domenico flew him to Milan, kept him for a few hours at Lorenzo's place to unsettle him further, then brought him to Max's house on Lake Maggiore early in the evening.

They took him to the library and then Lorenzo called in on Max's office, where he was sitting talking to Francesco.

"Boss, whenever you're ready, Saul Goldstein's in the library."

"Thanks, Lorenzo. Did he give you any trouble?"

"Not much."

"You check his cell phone?"

"He didn't have one—said he'd left it in the apartment. I'm sure the German will find it."

"Good. And how does he seem?"

"Scared, I guess. I mean, taken from home, private plane to Milan. Given some of the people we deal with, I guess he thinks we're gonna kill him."

Max nodded and looked at Francesco. "And yet he still preferred to come here rather than go to the police. Let's see what he has to say for himself."

They walked together to the library, where they found Marco and Domenico standing, and Goldstein sitting on one of the leather sofas. He looked younger and cooler than he had in the security footage, in his mid- to late twenties, casually dressed in jeans and a checked shirt, that mop of dark curls—Max could imagine him working in a hip bar or as a barista, charming the girls with his folk-singer looks.

Goldstein got to his feet as they came into the room, and Max noticed his hand was bandaged. He didn't need or want to know how that had happened. Max gestured for him to sit again, which he dutifully did. Max sat on the sofa facing him, while Francesco took a seat off to one side.

Marco, Lorenzo and Domenico remained where they were, and Goldstein glanced up at them, then back at Max, his eyes never settling anywhere.

"Do you know who I am, Saul?"

Goldstein twitched at the sound of Max's voice, his nerves shot, and cleared his throat before replying.

"You're Max Emerson."

"My men tell you why you're here?"

"Sure, but I don't know anything about hacking. I only got that job to help stretch out my trip to Europe—you know, earn a bit of extra money. And I know it looks bad, me trying to access the computers in your office, but I saw a guy log in and I thought I got the password. All I wanted to do was Skype my girlfriend back home. I know it's stupid. I just wanted to speak to her, that's all."

"Why isn't she traveling with you?"

21

"Excuse me?" Max didn't repeat the question. "Er, she . . . she has a job. She's a designer for a fashion company in Tribeca. They've got a new collection showing next month, so she couldn't spare the time."

Max looked at Lorenzo.

"How long since you picked him up?"

Lorenzo looked at his watch. "Twelve hours."

He turned back to Goldstein.

"Twelve hours and that's the best story you could come up with—that you came close to accidentally hacking our secure systems so you could Skype your girlfriend?"

"Mr. Emerson, if it sounds weak, it's because I didn't make it up. I . . ."

"What do you think we plan to do with you, Saul?" Goldstein looked afraid of responding, as though he'd been set a lethal riddle. "If you think we'll hurt you, you're wrong. That's not the kind of organization we are. What we will do unless you tell me the truth is hand you over to the authorities. I guess the FBI would have jurisdiction over this . . ."

Marco said, "That's right, boss—some of the networks he tried to access are American."

Goldstein looked from Max to Marco and back again, alarmed and confused.

"So, we hand you over to the FBI, and then you can wave goodbye to your girlfriend because under US law the crimes you've committed come with a very long prison sentence."

Max's real fear had been that Goldstein might be FBI himself, but his panicked expression offered all the reassurance Max needed on that front. He looked so afraid that Max wondered if he'd had a run-in with them before.

"Last chance, Saul: What were you doing and who are you working for?"

At first it looked as though he might not answer, and his voice was full of defeat when he did speak.

"No one. I'm not working for anyone. I'm writing a piece for *The Atlantic* about money laundering. I'm not commissioned but my cousin's an editor there. He said if I wrote it, he'd get it in the magazine. Then a friend who works in a hedge fund recommended I check out your business."

"Which hedge fund?"

"Padbrook."

Max noticed Francesco become more alert. Padbrook had been involved in the Greenwood development in Colorado, although Max couldn't remember their exact role or whether there was any cause for concern at them being mentioned now. He'd never worked with them since.

Max wanted to ask Goldstein about Colfax and where he tied in to all of this, but he knew he couldn't be the first to mention him. If he really was a journalist, that would be like Max handing him a guaranteed scoop.

"What's your friend's name?"

"Joel. I don't know his second name. He's a friend of a friend. I met him at a party and we got talking, that's all."

"What did he tell you?"

"He told me he'd heard about this holding company, Emerson, with more money under management than any hedge fund he'd ever worked on, easily over a hundred billion, hundreds of IBCs spread across the world—massive property and financial holdings, the whole lot." He glanced up at the others again, then back at Max. "I started to ask around . . . but then someone told me to be careful, that you handle money for a lot of really dangerous people: here in Italy, in Russia and Kazakhstan, other places too. I wanted to find out if it's true, if there's a story in it—like, investment banker to the world's Mafia, that kind of thing."

There'd been a time when Max would have been flattered by that description, even though it wasn't meant to be complimentary. But not anymore. He imagined it as a strapline on a magazine or newspaper feature, seeing it as other people would see it, as his parents would see it, and anger came in on the back of that thought.

"The answer to both questions is no. It isn't true, there isn't a story, and we'd sue *The Atlantic* out of existence if it published one."

Goldstein looked unnerved, his short-lived volubility deserting him.

"You called someone on your cell phone last week while you were at work. Who was it?"

"My cousin, the editor. He's been doing some background checking for me."

Max remembered the security video and Goldstein spotting the camera, lowering his voice. His answer made sense, and fit with what was on the tape, but was that because he'd preempted this question being asked?

"What's your cousin's name?"

"Elliot. Elliot Goldstein, but please, don't involve him in this. He was trying to help me out, but . . ." He ground to a halt, a hopelessness about him.

A brief silence followed, and then Marco said, "He's lying, boss."

"I'm not! I swear, even the other stuff. I live with my girlfriend in Tribeca. I'm trying to make it as a writer, dreams of a Pulitzer, all that lame stuff. That's all, I swear. I'm just a regular guy trying to get a break, and I'll admit, I messed up, but man, this isn't what I . . . I don't know—I don't know what else I can tell you."

Max could see it all, perhaps even too clearly. He could see this guy and his slightly bohemian girlfriend, their cool little apartment, lazy weekends in bed, going out for coffee, full of dreams. Above all, full of dreams. He could see it all and envied him, if it were true, and maybe even if it weren't.

He wasn't sure why he should envy anyone, particularly someone who was struggling. Max had achieved more in his twenties and early thirties than most people could ever dream of, and had accrued the kind of wealth that went beyond wealth, and yet still he envied the things he did not have, including the simple existence painted by Goldstein, full of hope and ambition and not much else.

Max wanted him gone.

"Okay, here's what's about to happen. My men will take you to the airport and they'll put you on the next available flight back to Luxembourg, either tonight or first thing in the morning. And with any luck, I will never see you or hear your name again. Now get out of my house, and consider yourself lucky we're not the kind of organization you think we are."

Goldstein nodded, looked at Lorenzo and stood. "Thanks, I guess."

Max barely offered an acknowledgment, and Lorenzo and Domenico walked Goldstein out. But just as he walked through the door of the library, Goldstein threw a last look back at Max, and for just that fraction of a second he looked transformed. He'd been so meek, so earnest and eager to please, so afraid, and yet for that briefest moment he looked calculating, full of hatred—a look so intense that it unsettled Max, almost to the point of telling them to bring him back.

But then Marco sat down on the sofa where Goldstein had been sitting, and Max turned to him and said, "You really think he was lying?"

"Maybe not about the girlfriend, but I don't believe he's a writer." Max thought back again to his imagined version of Goldstein's idyllic domestic set-up, a fantasy that was quite possibly itself built on a lie. "I think he's a hacker working for a competitor or a hedge fund. We'll see what the German digs up, and I'll talk it over with Lorenzo, but we'll check out the backstory too: the guy at Padbrook, the cousin at the magazine. We'll get back to you, boss."

"Thanks, Marco. And good job by the whole team."

"Thanks, boss."

He got up and walked out, and Francesco waited until he'd gone before looking at Max and saying, "I know what you're thinking, but Padbrook were third tier. Even at the time they didn't know Emerson was involved with Greenwood, so I don't think we have to be alarmed about that."

Max nodded, acknowledging the point, not quite believing it.

"He was well informed, though."

"Like Marco said, probably a hacker for a competitor, trying to discredit us. At worst, a freelance journalist. Either way, our system worked, we caught him, and now we move on."

Max accepted the point without really believing it. He kept thinking back to Saul Goldstein's expression as he'd left the room, that brief vicious stare, and feared they'd all missed something, that there was more to Goldstein than any of them had reckoned for.

The only consolation was that Francesco's other point was undeniable—their security systems had worked, and Marco and his team had done their job. The world was probably full of individuals who'd like nothing more than to ruin Max Emerson's day, but their systems *had* worked, so it wouldn't be Saul Goldstein, and it wouldn't be today.

Chapter Four

Max spent an hour or so on Friday morning playing tennis with Matteo Buonarroti. He had twenty years on his host, which was probably the only reason he beat him—Matteo had been a handy player in his time.

They sat with cold drinks afterwards, looking out over the gardens and the lake. Paolo, Max's boatman, was talking to one of the gardeners down near the jetty, their chatter and occasional laughter softly audible. The pale Belle Epoque facade of Max's house was visible in the sunshine haze on the opposite shore.

"I can understand why your ancestors chose to build here—it's the best view on the lake."

Matteo laughed a little and said, "Of course, your house didn't exist when my ancestors built here."

They turned at the sound of light footsteps as Lucia Buonarroti came out onto the terrace.

"Max, you are coming to the party next Wednesday?"

"He's coming to the party."

"I do hope so. It's really quite shocking that you've lived here two years and you haven't met Isabella yet."

"How could he meet her when she's in New York?"

She slapped her husband lightly on the shoulder as though he'd said something mean, and smiled at Max. "I'm glad you're coming, anyway. I'm sure the two of you will be great friends now that she's moving back."

Matteo sighed heavily as his wife walked away again.

"When's she arriving?"

"Tomorrow. I have to warn you, Max, Lucia is a born matchmaker, and she's convinced the two of you would be perfect for each other."

"Well, I'm flattered that she'd think so."

Matteo shook his head. "You're a serious man, Max, and Isabella . . . She's an angel, but serious? No."

"I thought she was completing her master's degree."

"In art history! It's just been an excuse to live in New York, and all at my expense. Honestly, at her age."

Max laughed. As far as he knew, Isabella was only in her late twenties. He reached over now and shook Matteo's hand.

"I'd better go, but I'll see you next week, if not before."

"I look forward to it. And we should try to get one more game in before summer ends."

Max nodded, but looked up at the late-September sky: a cloudless powdered blue—it felt as though they had a few weeks yet.

◆　◆　◆

Paolo cast off as soon as Max was on the boat and they started across the lake. They were midway across when Max realized his phone was vibrating in his pocket, taking a few seconds to notice it against the boat's engine and the gentle rock and sway of the water. He answered quickly before it rang off, only seeing as he did so that it was an unknown number.

"Hello?"

"Mr. Emerson?"

"Yes."

"Mr. Emerson, I'm sorry to disturb you, but my name is Catherine Parker and I'm calling you from the embassy in Rome." Her voice was southern, with a languid quality to it, captivating enough that it didn't occur to him why anyone would be calling him from the embassy. "I wonder if I could arrange to meet with you. It's very important."

Her accent was charming, but it was only ever going to get her so far, and those final three words put him on his guard.

"How did you get this number, Miss Parker? This is my private cell phone."

"I'm not entirely sure. I . . ." She seemed surprised by his objection. "Maybe I should have made it clear to begin with, I'm calling from the embassy in Rome, but I'm a Special Agent with the Federal Bureau of Investigation."

Max felt his hackles rise and immediately thought of Saul Goldstein. They'd all been convinced he wasn't government, but the FBI didn't call out of a clear blue sky, and he doubted Catherine Parker was seeking investment advice.

"Well, that probably explains why you consider it normal to invade my privacy. If you want to talk to me, I suggest you call my office."

"It's because this matter is private and confidential that I called your cell. And as I said . . . it is very important."

"Thanks for the concern, but call my office in an hour."

He ended the call and only noticed now that his heart was racing. He had nothing to fear from the FBI wanting to talk to him, not on its own, but it felt as though some planetary alignment was taking place, even if he couldn't see the pattern that was forming.

Max went up to his room when he got back, showered and changed, then headed down to the office.

"Good morning, Rosalia. Have I had any calls?"

"Yes, your sister called earlier."

He started to smile, an instinctive reaction, but it didn't get very far.

"She tried your cell but I told her you were playing tennis. She wanted to check some dates—should I call her back?"

Rosalia sounded hopeful, but Max shook his head. "It's my mom's birthday next month."

"Oh. I see." *Checking dates* was a code of sorts, for making sure Max wasn't there when the rest of the family was visiting. Lottie was always at pains to say how nice it would be to see him, but it would only cause friction between Max and Henry, so it was better like this for the time being, until things were different. *For the time being* had been three years. "I'm sorry, Signor Emerson." Rosalia's words were weighted with the injustice she felt on his behalf.

"Thank you, Rosalia. Anything else?"

She looked between her notepad and the screen in front of her.

"Monsignor Cavaletti's office called. He was due to come on Monday to update you on the restoration, but he can't make it so I've booked him in for Wednesday at the same time. There are some invitations on your desk to consider, and flowers in your office from the Manfredis, thanking you for the dinner party."

"Okay, thanks." Max checked the time. "I'm expecting a call from an American lady at the embassy—you can put her through. And do you know if Francesco and Marco are about?"

"Yes, I think so. You want them?"

He nodded with a smile and strolled through into his office, walked over to the display of flowers and looked at the handwritten note, then crossed to his desk and started glancing through the invitations. It all felt slightly surreal—he no longer needed to play the part of Max Emerson of Emerson Holdings, but now he played this part, turning up at dinners or parties, playing tennis with Matteo

Buonarroti, attending openings and charity functions, making polite conversation: an imagined version of the wealthy businessman's social life, all surface and no depth.

Max heard Marco's voice in the outer office and a moment later he appeared in the doorway.

"You wanted to see me, boss?"

"Yes, come in, Marco. Take a seat." They sat down opposite each other on the leather sofas. "I just wanted you to be here. I had a call when I was coming across the lake . . ."

Max stopped because he heard Francesco speak to Rosalia before breezing into the office.

"Take a seat, Francesco." As Francesco settled himself, Max continued. "I was just about to tell Marco: I had a call on my cell earlier, from an FBI agent from the embassy in Rome. I didn't know they even had people overseas."

"Neither did I. Did he say what he wanted?"

"She. Special Agent Catherine Parker. And I didn't give her a chance. I told her to call here." He checked his watch. "Any minute now, in fact."

Marco had taken the news in silence, but his thoughts became clear when he said, "I'm convinced Goldstein wasn't FBI."

"Has Klaus come back yet?"

"No, he's still out there." Marco looked preoccupied. "You know the German, he does his own thing. I think he'll be back next week."

They heard Rosalia speaking and then Max's phone started to ring. He picked it up and sat down again as Rosalia put Catherine Parker through.

"Mr. Emerson, I hope this is more convenient, and I'm sorry for any invasion of your privacy. It was not intentional."

"Apology accepted, Miss Parker. Now, what can I do for you?"

He was conscious of sounding more abrupt than he'd intended, and she seemed to pick up on it too, her voice becoming more formal and measured when she spoke again.

"As I mentioned earlier, Mr. Emerson, I'd like to meet with you if that's possible, to discuss an issue that's of a very sensitive nature, relating to the financial affairs of Senator Robert Colfax."

It was like the first jolt of turbulence on a flight—Max felt a sudden sickly hollowness in his stomach.

"Naturally, I'm happy to offer the FBI any general advice I can, but I've never heard of Senator Robert Colfax, so I'm not sure what I can add there."

He noticed Francesco and Marco become slightly more alert at the mention of the Senator's name.

"We both know that's not true, Mr. Emerson."

He smiled, regaining his equilibrium.

"Well, if you're going to accuse me of lying, it's probably better you do it to my face. If you have my cell number, I'm sure you have my address—how about Tuesday at three?"

"I'll be there, Mr. Emerson, and—" He ended the call.

He looked at Marco and said, "Has Crazy Mouse come up with anything on Goldstein yet?"

"No, we didn't tell him it was urgent, but I can ask him to prioritize now. Also, I wouldn't have bothered you with this, but the German's watching Goldstein's apartment—it's the reason he's still out there, because Goldstein hasn't been back yet."

Francesco looked at Marco. "You think it's connected?"

"He wasn't FBI, and he seemed nervous when you mentioned handing him over. So maybe he has form, the FBI has him under surveillance, and now they want to find out if it's true that there's a link between you and Colfax."

Francesco said, "Or it could just be a coincidence." Max and Marco turned to him and he shrugged in response. "It does happen." Neither of them responded.

The final element of the planetary alignment was in place. It was Colfax, and hidden behind Colfax was Hayden Manning and a combined collection of truths that even now could achieve what Manning had so very nearly done seven years earlier.

Chapter Five

Special Agent Catherine Parker arrived fifteen minutes early. Her driver was taken into the kitchen and she was shown outside. Max kept her waiting until the appointed time and then walked through from his office.

He hesitated at the doors out onto the terrace. She was standing at the balustrade, a blonde in a pale-gray suit, looking out over the lawns and across the lake to the far shore. A warm breeze was cutting in off the water, catching strands of her hair.

It seemed to impair her hearing too, because she didn't turn as he walked across the terrace and appeared to be caught off guard slightly when he said, "It's a beautiful view, isn't it?"

She turned and smiled, but saw who she was talking to and quickly shifted her expression into something harder.

"It is, and a stunning house. Doesn't it bother you at all, that it's paid for by the proceeds of crime?"

Maybe Max's own abruptness on the phone the previous week had encouraged Catherine Parker to take a tougher approach herself, but he smiled, admiring her bluntness—all the cards on the table, all at once.

"Well, you certainly believe in getting straight to the point. Max Emerson. Pleased to meet you." He held out his hand and she shook it, her grip firm, her palm a little moist—maybe she was just nervous, despite the front, and that was why she'd been too blunt too soon.

"Special Agent Catherine Parker." She took a badge out and showed it to him. "Thank you for agreeing to see me, Mr. Emerson."

He didn't look at the ID—he knew who she was. But he noticed a leather document folder she'd placed on the balustrade and did wonder what might be in that.

"You're welcome, but you're also a little off your patch, wouldn't you say?"

"It's a misunderstanding a lot of people have. We're a domestic agency, but our reach is global."

"Nice slogan—you should put it on your letterhead."

She looked unsure how to respond and he wondered if she had any sense of humor at all. He was distracted by a noise behind him and turned to see Laura emerging with a tray. He watched as she placed it on the table.

"Please, why don't we take a seat. It looks like we have Bellinis."

"Just juice for me, if you don't mind."

Laura stopped what she was doing, looking up, but Max said, "If you insist, but your driver's being taken care of in the kitchen, and I doubt someone of your standing would give away state secrets after one Bellini."

Her face hardened another notch.

"Nor would someone of my standing be coaxed so easily into having a drink she does not want."

Max held his hands out, saying, "Miss Parker, I'm just being sociable. Whatever you think of me, and it's clearly not much, I had no need to agree to this meeting. I was just hoping to make it as friendly and productive as possible."

She stared back at him for a moment before yielding. "I'm sorry, you're right. Yes, a Bellini would be great, thank you." Laura continued with the drinks as smoothly as if someone had briefly pressed the pause button and knocked it off again. Max showed Catherine Parker to her seat as she continued, "I'm cranky. I stayed in Milan for the night and didn't sleep at all well."

"Are you based in Rome?"

"Yes. Yes, I am."

Laura finished pouring the drinks and stepped back.

Max smiled at her. "Thank you, Laura, that's all for now." He raised his glass. "Good health."

Catherine Parker nodded uncertainly, but raised her own glass and took a sip.

"So, what can I do for you, Miss Parker?"

"I suspect you have a pretty good idea already, Mr. Emerson. We believe Senator Robert Colfax used his position to influence a number of contracts between US concerns and criminal elements overseas— in particular, the Mafia organization controlled by Luciano Vicari. In exchange, we think he received a payment of somewhere between forty-eight and fifty-four million dollars."

Max continued to meet her eyes but didn't respond, and after a second or two she seemed to find his gaze unsettling.

"That's the basic outline, although this is bigger and goes deeper than you could imagine. But we need proof. More specifically, we need the money trail—we need to know where it is and how it got there."

There it was, out in the open, and already it seemed less threatening. Max supposed it was no great leap to assume Emerson might have channeled the money, but the fact that they weren't even sure of how much Colfax had been paid suggested there was a lot of guesswork involved.

That didn't mean he could afford to be complacent. For one thing, he still didn't know if there was a link to Goldstein, or if Colfax's misdeeds would be the end of the story for either party.

"That's all very interesting, Miss Parker, but you still haven't told me what *I* can do for you."

She didn't look impressed. She took another sip of her drink and looked out at the lake. A small sailboat seemed to catch her attention, its canvas billowing and straining against the wind. Beyond that, one of the ferries was cutting across to Stresa.

She was still staring out when she said, "I'm authorized to say that if you give us what we want, we can offer you full immunity in exchange."

She turned back now, driving home her seriousness, and Max felt a slight spike in his blood, of guilt and fear and high alert, the nagging sense that things were never as well hidden as people hoped. The only reason he knew she couldn't be talking about Hayden Manning was that they were unlikely ever to offer immunity for such a crime. So she was talking about financial crimes, and here he felt on stronger ground.

"I don't need immunity from you or anyone else. I own a financial services company, one that keeps firmly within the legal framework of the jurisdictions in which it operates."

"Jurisdictions?" Catherine Parker shook her head in apparent disbelief. "You operate in tax havens, Mr. Emerson—the kind of places no legitimate business would operate."

"Really? Delaware, Wyoming, the US Virgin Islands—are you suggesting they're not legitimate?"

She smiled grudgingly, an admission of the misstep, but when he smiled back at her, she became serious again.

"Have you ever actually met Vicari? Do you know anything at all about his business?"

"I know about mine. I know I don't breach client confidentiality."

"Admirable, I'm sure, until you consider who those clients are."

She picked up the document folder, unzipped it and took out a sheaf of large photographs, looking at the one on the top of the pile before placing it on the table.

Almost instantly it started to lift in the breeze, so Max put his hand on it to hold it down. It was a young woman, sprawled awkwardly, naked but for pale-gray leggings, her breasts and torso scarred and sliced, her face almost completely shot away.

"Her name was Maria, nineteen years old, working as a hairdresser but going to night school in the hope of becoming a nursery teacher. When her father was killed, she gave evidence to the police against one of Vicari's men. The trial collapsed, but they still did this to her."

He wasn't sure how this tale of ruthless retribution was meant to make him consider breaking the confidentiality of Colfax and, by association, Vicari, but before he could respond, she'd placed three or four more photographs, one after the other, an older woman, two young men who in death were locked in an oddly tender-looking embrace, another young man whose throat gaped open, a woman with a neat bullet hole in her temple.

Max saw them and didn't see them, viewing them with the same mix of repulsion and grim fascination as he did similar footage on TV or photographs in the papers. Finally, she put down a picture of a young boy smiling at the camera, dark-haired and large-eyed.

"We're not sure of his real name, but he was a refugee from Libya and we think he was eleven or twelve when Vicari's people sold him to a pimp in Rome. For the next year, he was raped and abused by countless men. He was no more than thirteen when he threw himself in front of a train."

It reminded Max of a conversation with his brother five years earlier. One of Henry's big corporate clients had asked him if he were any relation to the Max Emerson who was investing Mikhail Leonov's billions for him. Henry had been furious, reeling off a similarly gruesome litany of Leonov's reputed crimes, as if Max were somehow complicit in them.

It was the hypocrisy more than anything that was the same, Henry never prying too far into the practices of his own corporate clients, the FBI really caring nothing for the smiling boy in this photo or the thousands of others like him.

"It's very sad," said Max, shaking his head. Catherine Parker looked hopeful—a look that riled him. "So what are you doing about it?"

"Excuse me?"

"You heard. What are you doing about it? What are the politicians in Rome doing about it, or the politicians back home, or in London, or the union officials who probably signed off on Colfax's deals? Why aren't you going after them instead of Colfax? More importantly, why aren't you going after them instead of me?"

"Those pictures." She pointed at the photos, her anger barely contained. "That's where your wealth comes from."

"It's where all our wealth comes from. If it weren't, somebody would've done something about it."

She shook her head, looking frustrated.

"No. And you know what, Mr. Emerson, it might not be fair that we've singled you out, but as far as we're concerned, you're the weak link, and the Bureau won't stop until you give us what we want."

"It'll never happen."

Max was confident of that, and not just because of the darker secret that was obscured by Colfax's money. Catherine Parker had to know that if he started working with the authorities against his own clients, he'd quickly end up featuring in a gruesome photograph of his own. But before she could respond, his phone started to ring.

He looked at it and turned it off even as he said, "I'm sorry, I didn't realize it was still on."

"That's okay. If it's important, I don't mind . . ."

He smiled, shaking his head. It was his brother-in-law Nicolas. Max had missed another call from Lottie and still hadn't responded yet, so now Nicolas was trying, and he almost took some perverse pleasure from the fact that their plans for his mom's birthday would be on hold until they could be sure Max wouldn't turn up and spoil the party.

"I feel bad, Miss Parker. You've come all the way up here from Rome, had a terrible night's sleep, and even if you didn't know it yourself, I'm sure your superiors must have realized that it was pointless. Even if I knew anything about Robert Colfax, I wouldn't be able to help you. If Robert Colfax were my biggest enemy, I still wouldn't." As if seeing the obstacle, she picked up the photographs and slipped them back into the folder.

"What about if there's a way of helping me that wouldn't compromise your principles, and wouldn't imperil you in relation to your other clients?"

Max found himself distracted by her use of the word "imperil"—it sounded too old-fashioned, too quaint for what they were talking about here.

"What do you have in mind?"

She once again appeared to see some hope in his response, but then deflated a little and said, "I don't know. I just wanted to see if you'd be open to such a suggestion, if I can work something out."

"By all means, feel free to give it a go, as long as you know it's unlikely I'll ever be able to help you."

"I'm not so sure about that. But let me offer you a friendly warning too. It's true what I said: the Bureau's determined to pursue this matter and they will not leave you alone until they get what they want. For me personally, I'm just trying to find the best outcome for everyone, including you."

He nodded, acknowledging her attempt at the clichéd iron fist and velvet glove, and stood. She got to her feet too. She seemed surprised that he was signaling the end of the meeting, but he wasn't sure what else they might have covered—he doubted she wanted a tour of the grounds.

But just as he thought he had the measure of Catherine Parker, her face lit with a smile and she put one hand on his arm as she pointed at the terrace with the other. "Look, the cutest little lizard!"

Max could see another four from where he was standing, and was used to seeing them scuttle away whenever he walked across the terrace or around the grounds. But there was something charming in her enthusiasm, a glimpse of someone beyond the professional Catherine Parker he'd just encountered.

It also told him, of course, that she wasn't based in Italy. She'd flown out specifically to pursue him, which probably said something about how much the FBI wanted this and how much more of a problem it might become.

"*Lucertole*—that's what the Italians call them. I think maybe they're just wall lizards."

"*Lucertole*," she said, trying out the word, making a decent fist of the Italian inflection.

She only seemed to notice now that her hand was still resting on his forearm and she looked apologetic as she took it away, the hint of a blush on her cheeks. If she was playing him, she was doing it well because all at once, within that moment, he found her immensely attractive.

Domenico stepped out onto the terrace, and Max smiled and shook Catherine Parker's hand, saying, "It's been a pleasure, Miss Parker, and though I doubt there'll ever be much room for serious negotiation between us, I do hope we meet again."

"Yes, I'm sure we will, and like I said, Mr. Emerson, we won't give up on this."

He nodded, smiling, although the edge of steeliness had returned to her features. "Domenico will show you out."

Domenico gestured for her to follow, and the two of them left the terrace.

Max stayed for a minute, walking to the edge of the terrace, watching the pale-gray outline of a Guardia di Finanza patrol boat approaching along the shore. It cut in closer and was within shouting distance as it passed. Someone waved from up top and Max automatically waved back. He could see then that it was Mercaldo, and the young lieutenant gave him a relaxed salute as the boat's engines fired up and it sped off along the shore. And Max smiled, thinking it was just as well Catherine Parker hadn't been there to see that.

Absentmindedly, he took his phone and turned it on, then stared back out at the lake, the wind warm on his face. The sailboat Catherine Parker had contemplated earlier was still tacking against the wind, the water a sparkling blue. Max had one of those rare moments of sensing how lucky he was to be here, and he couldn't understand why he struggled to feel it the rest of the time, why it was never quite enough.

His phone started to vibrate and ring in his hand and he looked down and saw with frustration that it was Nicolas again. Max looked back up at the lake, not wanting to answer. Then he thought he should, in case something was wrong, in case it wasn't about arranging dates, but that Lottie was unwell or had been in an accident.

It was unlikely, of course, and in truth Max knew exactly how the conversation would pan out. But at least it was Nicolas so he wouldn't have to listen to Lottie's slightly hollow expressions of sorrow and regret. He still didn't want to hear it, but he answered all the same.

Chapter Six

"Nicolas, what can I do for you?"

Nicolas was audibly relieved in response, saying, "Thank God, Max, I've tried to call your cell a number of times."

"I only had one missed call . . . Why, what's wrong? It's not Lottie?"

"No. No. Charlotte's fine. Upset, but . . . I don't know how to tell you . . ."

"So just tell me."

"It's your parents, Max. I'm so sorry. They were killed, in their car."

"What are you talking about?"

It was a stupid question, and yet he hadn't been able to stop himself asking it. His parents were dead—what questions could there be but stupid ones?

"They . . . they went off the road. Yesterday lunchtime, but we only found out for sure this morning."

Max had just been given the worst news, and yet it was this detail about the timing that weakened him physically, so much so that he put a hand out to lean on the balustrade. They'd been dead twenty-four hours. How could that be? He thought of the random collection of things he'd done in that time, and in some way he felt even less of a son that he'd continued living his life, that he hadn't picked up at some subconscious level that he was adrift, that the people who'd brought him into the world were no longer in it themselves.

"What do you mean, they went off the road? Where? How?"

It was still hard to believe he was talking about something real—that this wasn't just a matter of establishing facts. It was as though he were standing on the edge of a precipice, desperately trying to look everywhere except down.

"It was an accident, Max. They were on their way to visit us. You know your mother didn't like tunnels. It was a mountain road. It seems . . . Well, we don't know for sure."

It was true, she didn't like tunnels, and his dad would go to great lengths to avoid them for her, not always easy in a country like Switzerland. It was one of the many little details and idiosyncrasies that had apparently been lost in an instant. She had not liked tunnels. A bubble of grief welled up inside him, pushing into his throat, in danger of overwhelming him.

"Does my brother know?"

"It was Henry who told us. He asked me to call you."

"He could've called me himself." There was a prickle of irritation, and Max knew he'd be even more the black sheep now that his parents weren't there to defend him. He clung onto that feeling, determined not to allow Nicolas to hear him upset. "How's Lottie?"

"She went to bed. She took it very badly."

"Of course. Is there anything I need to do?"

Clearly the answer was no. They'd only found out *for sure* this morning, which meant they'd had an idea yesterday and had known *for sure* for at least a few hours, yet Max was being told only now, such an afterthought had he become.

"I don't think so. Henry said he'll take care of everything. I'm sure he'll be in touch as soon as he knows more."

"I'm sure he won't, but thanks for letting me know, Nicolas. And look after Lottie."

Max ended the call even as Nicolas was replying. He turned off his phone, unsure why except as some sort of instinctive response to the news that had just come through it. Then he turned it back on, thinking he might be wrong and Henry might call—it was unlikely perhaps, and Henry wasn't the type to see the death of their parents as a reason for overcoming the rift between them, but Max left the phone on anyway.

He walked down the steps off the terrace, crossing the lawns to the stone balustrade at the water's edge. The sailboat was far off now, and was soon obscured from his sight by one of the white passenger ferries crossing between them.

A memory crashed in from his very early childhood, of being on the deck of a paddle steamer on Lake Geneva while two sailing dinghies raced each other nearby. His dad had said, "Look at the boats, Max," and had hoisted him up, holding him tight but standing his feet on the railing—a feeling of such exhilaration and controlled danger, with the wind in his face and the water churning and rushing past below his feet.

"Look at the boats, Max." He heard it as clearly as if his dad were standing behind him now. A sob broke free, rising up suddenly from deep within, and tears filled his eyes, and he cried, for the first time in many years. He stood there and cried and felt more alone than at any time in his life.

After a while he dried his eyes, composed himself, breathed. He turned and walked back to the house, feeling some vital part of him had been torn out, the importance of which he only realized now that there was a strange and unsettling void in its place.

He went up to his bathroom and washed his face, then stared at himself in the mirror. He felt both too old and too young to be an orphan, but here he was, orphaned all the same, and there was no time left to prove to them that their fears were unfounded, that Henry was wrong about him, that they could be proud.

They'd visited not long after he'd bought this place and they'd loved it, but sitting on the terrace that first day, his mom had asked him casually if the company owned the house. "Not *the* company," he'd said. "I set up another company specifically to buy it." His dad had looked pleased by that but his mom's concern had lingered, as though she'd feared the house and everything else could be taken away from him at any moment.

It was a sign that Henry had continued to whisper in her ear about how risky Max's business was. That day, though, Max had been relaxed about it, confident he could allay their fears in time, little knowing that time would run out long before he'd had the chance to do so.

He made his way back down to the office and as Rosalia looked up he said, "Rosalia, I've had some bad news. My parents have been killed in an accident—a car crash . . ."

She looked startled at the words, shaking her head in confusion, and then burst into tears: a response so raw that it made him feel that his own sadness at the news had been inadequate somehow. Rosalia had met Max's parents on their couple of visits here, but that was the extent of it.

"Now, Rosalia, don't upset yourself."

She tried to respond, but Max couldn't make out her words. He comforted her, then went through to his own office and poured her a brandy. He poured himself one too and carried them through. He sat her on the little sofa, then pulled a chair across and sat opposite her.

"I'm so sorry, Signor Emerson." She took a timid sip of her brandy. "You'll want me to cancel your appointments? The Monsignor in the morning, and the boat for tomorrow night?"

Max nodded automatically, without really being sure what would happen over the next few days. He usually dictated what happened and when, but his parents took priority now, and that was all in Henry's hands.

"Of course, if you call the Buonarrotis, give them my apologies and, yes, you can tell Paolo I won't be needing the boat."

"And Monsignor Cavaletti?"

He couldn't attend a party at a time like this, but Cavaletti was different, and Max wasn't sure what he'd do with his morning otherwise.

"No, I'll see him as planned."

"Good." Rosalia smiled, perhaps thinking it would help for Max to see a priest. "If you let the household staff know what's happened, but tell them I don't want any fuss. And could you tell Francesco, and say I'd like to see everyone at six in the library."

She nodded, but said, "The German isn't here."

"No, I just mean everyone who's about."

"I'll get onto it right away."

But she sat and so did Max, and they both sipped at their brandy. Only when she looked in danger of crying again did she finish her drink quickly and stand, going back to her desk. Max stood too, but without any conviction—he felt he should call someone, but he saw it viscerally now, that for all the trappings of his life, there was no one for him to call.

Chapter Seven

They were all in the library when he got there, standing as if they were themselves waiting to go to a funeral. Francesco stepped forward immediately and shook his hand.

"Max, I know you won't want any fuss, but let me express on behalf of all of us, and all the staff in the house, how sad we are to hear this terrible news." The others nodded in agreement. "You're family to us, and your pain is our pain."

"Thank you, Francesco. Thank you, everyone. I just wanted to let you know that I'll be spending some time in Switzerland over the next few weeks—I don't know the details yet—but I'm sure you can manage everything in my absence, and I'll still be in touch. That's all. I just wanted to let you know."

The truth was, he'd just wanted to pull the sticking plaster off in one go and get their condolences out of the way, and he'd guessed they'd probably prefer it that way too. A terrible thing had happened to Max, but not to Emerson, and they had a business to run.

Marco stepped forward and shook his hand, saying a few words and making his way out of the library. The others followed suit, leaving one by one until only Francesco remained.

He looked satisfied that things had been done properly, the appropriate respect shown, and said, "I'll be eating with you this evening."

He could see Max ready to object. "Alessandra insists, and if my wife insists, I'm not going home until I've eaten."

Max nodded, giving way.

"Good, I have a phone call to make, but I'll see you in a little while."

"Thanks, Francesco. How did the call go with Leonov?"

"Leonov is always happy." He put his hand on Max's arm, telling him with that simple gesture to forget about business. "Max, the next few weeks will be difficult, but we're here for you. I meant what I said."

"I know."

Francesco smiled and left him alone, and Max looked around the library, a room that hadn't been used for its real purpose in the two years he'd lived here. He walked over now and took one of the books off the shelves, the first time he'd even done that.

The library's contents had been included in the sale by Oblomov, the previous owner, and Max saw now that the leather-bound volume he was holding, perhaps a novel, was in Russian. He shook his head, bemused, as he closed it again and placed it back.

He found Francesco in the dining room later, talking amiably to Laura, but he smiled at the sight of Max and said, "Good, I'm hungry."

He sat and so did Max as Laura poured the wine.

Once she'd left them alone, Francesco said, "So how did it go with the FBI?"

The meeting with Catherine Parker hardly seemed important now, but Max knew that it was, and that he had to remain focused on it.

"As we expected, they want us to hang Colfax out to dry. I told her we couldn't do that, even if I knew what she was talking about. I don't think she'll give up, and of course, in the vaguest possible terms, she implied life could become difficult for us if we don't cooperate."

"Interesting. I wonder what she has in mind."

"Nothing, she was bluffing, and she knows there's nowhere to go— we don't break any laws."

Francesco nodded, looking much less certain, and there was that ever-present understanding between them, that even if they hadn't broken any laws as a company, a law had been broken on their behalf. After a brief weighted pause, Francesco said, "Max, you don't have to do anything wrong for governments to make life difficult." He slid his glass a little way across the table, then slid it back, the look of someone contemplating a chess move. "I'll ask Lorenzo to find out how badly they want Colfax. Also, if Colfax has been talking out of turn, I'll see if we can find the details. But in the meantime, tread carefully, and if she asks to meet again, maybe you should agree, just to be seen to be playing ball."

Oddly, Max liked the idea of seeing Catherine Parker again, despite everything.

"Do I really want to be seen playing ball with the FBI?"

"As long as it's hardball, why not?"

"Okay, but obviously it's unlikely to be in the next couple of weeks."

Francesco nodded gravely. "Who do you want to take you to Switzerland?"

"I'll go alone. I could be coming and going quite a bit."

He realized as he said it that he still imagined himself being involved in his family's affairs, when in truth they'd probably only want him there for the funeral itself, and even that grudgingly.

As if picking up on that thought, Francesco said, "I can understand that, but let me take advice from Lorenzo and Marco when it comes to the funeral itself. After all, a funeral is in the public domain, so whether you like it or not, there is a security issue."

"Okay, but I want to avoid it if I can. My family doesn't have the best view of me as it is, without me turning up at my parents' house with an armored limousine and bodyguards."

Francesco stared at him for a moment but didn't answer, and as he picked up his wine he said only, "Your family's wrong."

"I like to think so, but if they are, they're in good company. The FBI thinks I'm a crook too."

"The FBI investigates a lot of good people, often without them knowing. We have to take it seriously, no question about it, but it signifies nothing. And you have to accept, any business that's grown as quickly as yours will attract scrutiny, from the FBI, from people like Goldstein, from competitors. The important thing is, you have the right team in place to deal with them."

"I believe it."

Laura came back in with the food, and Francesco made a seamless shift into a lighter tone. "Alessandra thinks you need to find a wife."

Max noticed Laura smiling and that made him smile in turn.

"You talk about me with Alessandra?"

"We rarely talk of anything else."

Francesco kept a straight face, but Max and Laura both laughed and the conversation remained on lighter topics now, notably the Buonarrotis. It seemed Francesco had something in common with Lucia Buonarroti, in that he too thought Isabella might be the ideal candidate to fill that role of potential wife—a good match, and an advantageous one too.

It made her sound like a prize in a fairground shooting gallery, and Max had no doubt that she was glamorous and beautiful, but he wasn't even sure that was what he wanted right now. Nor, if she had any sense, would Isabella Buonarroti be interested in a man like him: at odds with the FBI, "investment banker to the world's Mafia," and an embarrassment to his own family—or at least to those who were still alive. For all his wealth, Max wasn't convinced he was much of a prize at all.

51

Chapter Eight

Max had feared he wouldn't sleep but did and woke up rested the next morning. As he lay there, he remembered his parents were dead, but it was already tempered now by the knowledge that they'd been dead the previous morning too, without him knowing about it, without it affecting his plans in any way. It somehow went to prove that he could get through this day as well, and the day after and the day after that.

This was the future now, and the future he'd previously imagined or taken for granted was gone. He'd perhaps always known that he'd lose them one day, but one day far off, after a long and gentle decline, not like this. This was what he'd failed to imagine, but it was now his truth.

The sun was still shining but the wind had intensified, so he met Monsignor Cavaletti in the large drawing room overlooking the lake.

Cavaletti took Max's hand in both of his, nodding with sympathy but saying nothing. And he remained silent until they'd both taken their seats. "I sometimes think the loss of a parent is the hardest thing. We can understand the terrible grief of losing a child or a husband or wife, but we take our parents for granted, so we're losing something we didn't even know we had until the moment of losing it."

"Wise words, Monsignor, thank you."

Laura came in with the coffee, and they waited until she'd left before resuming.

The Monsignor sipped at his and said, "If you'd like me to hear your confession before I leave, I'd be more than happy to accommodate."

"I'm sorry?"

He smiled. "It's a strange thing, but in times of grief, people often find it helps to reconcile themselves with God."

Perhaps this was the moment in which Max was meant to admit that he'd sanctioned the death of a man who'd threatened his business interests. But there was no guilt there. Yes, he feared its exposure, he regretted that he'd left a wife without a husband and children without a father, but he felt an almost total disconnect with the death itself. There had been an intractable problem and it had been dealt with on his behalf—that was the sum of it.

"Monsignor Cavaletti, I was raised a Catholic, but I'm not what you might call practicing. And even if I were, I have nothing to confess."

The old man looked taken aback, perhaps revealing what he really thought of Max's wealth, even though he was happy to accept his generosity—he obviously thought Max had plenty of reasons to confess, even without knowing about the murder of Hayden Manning.

"We all sin, Max, in thought as well as in deed."

"So let me put it another way: there's nothing in my life for which I feel I need forgiveness."

"Then perhaps you're right. But the offer remains, should you experience a Damascene Conversion."

"Thank you, I appreciate that. And to the matter at hand, I take it the rest of the funds arrived in good order?"

The Monsignor clasped his hands together in a show of gratitude, and said, "Not only arrived, but work will begin next Wednesday. Naturally, you're going to be preoccupied in the coming weeks, but as soon as you have the time, you must visit and see how they're getting on. The church will be closed to the public during the restoration, as you can imagine, so perhaps best to have Rosalia check with my office first."

"I'd like that." He thought forward to a time beyond the funeral, maybe beyond these other distractions too, imagined submerging himself in a world of frescoes and Renaissance painters and historical sites.

"And you think it's definitely a Gozzoli fresco?"

"We're certain of it. We were almost certain already, the only doubt being a question of whether Gozzoli ever came this far north. But the expert we've hired turned up some very interesting evidence. Gozzoli visited his cousin and stayed for most of 1458, despite many calls for his services elsewhere. The cousin lived very close to the church of San Michele, so this is what we now believe—Gozzoli painted his procession of the Magi here in San Michele, before going to Florence the following year and starting work on the Magi Chapel. It's an amazing discovery. And thanks to you, it will be available in all its glory for the world to see."

"I'm glad I can make a difference."

Cavaletti smiled at him and nodded, but didn't respond at first, sipping his coffee again before finally speaking. "My offer of confession was well intended, but not the right thing."

"I didn't mind you offering at all, and I'm sure I'll be taking stock in the days ahead, but confession isn't what I need right now."

"Perhaps not, but you're right about this being a good time to consider your situation. Not to make major decisions, of course, but to begin the process of asking . . . what you really want in life. That would be my question to you, Max—what do you want?"

It took Max a moment to realize it wasn't a rhetorical question, that the Monsignor was waiting for an answer, and he knew the answer he had wouldn't offer any satisfaction. Yes, he wanted something else, but it was something always out of sight beyond the horizon, so that all he could do was keep pressing on.

"I don't know what I want. I'm not sure I ever knew."

The Monsignor looked bemused, glancing out at the lake, then around the grand room in which they sat.

"Yet you're so driven. If you didn't know what you wanted, what inspired you to build all of this?"

"I'm not sure I know that either. I guess I always thought I'd know what I wanted when I found it. So maybe that's what this is, just my way of searching."

"And a lucrative search it's been. But you should never forget: success and wealth are empty vessels, and if you make the search about those things alone, it's only emptiness you'll find at your journey's end."

"Are you telling me money doesn't buy happiness?"

"Not quite." He smiled at Max's teasing. "It's true, of course, but it's also true that poverty doesn't buy you a good meal."

He laughed and patted his stomach, not taking himself too seriously. Max smiled too, and reached forward to pour more coffee, but he knew Monsignor Cavaletti's advice had been more than the truism Max had reduced it to. After all, why was he funding the ballet and church restorations and countless medical causes if not to mask the emptiness at the heart of everything he did?

He'd spent the years since university building this vast empire, for the sake of building it alone. And he wasn't sure what he had lost along the way, but he felt as though he'd lost something—a purpose or a reason, or simply sight of the dream that had fired this journey in the first place.

He'd been telling Cavaletti the truth. He couldn't remember what he'd wanted when he set out, and he still didn't know, and felt no closer to it now than he had twelve years ago.

Chapter Nine

Despite the talk with Monsignor Cavaletti, Max worked for a couple of hours after lunch, checking the latest from Gupta in Mumbai, speaking to the London office, studying the remoter reaches of the markets as he often did.

Every time his thoughts sank back toward his parents he made himself busier, and for the most part he did a reasonable job of not dwelling. It was the silence he found harder to ignore. He kept expecting another call, from Nicolas or Lottie, maybe even from Henry, and it seemed extraordinary to Max that they could have nothing more to tell him.

Even aside from providing more details about the accident, there had to be things to discuss, plans to make, and he found it hard to believe that he'd be excluded completely from all of them, but no call came. His business had led to his exile from his family and now it seemed the business was almost the only thing he had left.

Midway through the afternoon there was a knock on the frame of his open door, and he looked up to see Klaus standing there. He understood why the others insisted on calling him the German, because with his tan and blond flat-top he looked like a stereotypical German baddie in a movie. And whereas the others all wore dark suits, almost in competition with each other to see who could look the sharpest, Klaus wore tight black jeans and a leather jacket.

"Come in, Klaus." Max shut the computer off and headed over to the chairs.

"Boss, I'm very sorry to hear about your father and mother."

"I appreciate it, Klaus, thanks." He shook his hand, then poured them both a drink and invited him to sit. "What did you find out?"

"Marco told me that Goldstein admitted to being a journalist."

"Freelance, but yes."

"I'm pretty sure he's lying about that."

That backed up Marco's instinct, and piqued Max's curiosity.

"The apartment—I found lots of notes scribbled here and there, but it didn't make me think of a journalist . . ."

"Intelligence, law enforcement?"

Klaus shook his head, saying, "No, not that either, but somebody very professional in his own way. Firstly, I found no electronic device at all, not even the cell phone he used that night, which suggests he keeps them in a separate location. Secondly, I went back to the office. Marco told me what Goldstein said about seeing someone log in to that terminal, but it's physically impossible. I thought maybe he might have used keylogging, but that wouldn't get him past the drop-down menus. That was when I found the camera."

"Go on."

"Very sophisticated, hidden in the cubicle frame, and he was unlucky, because he put it there at night, but during the day the light from the window caused a small amount of glare off the screen for a camera in that position—it's why he kept getting one of the letters wrong and why we caught him. Otherwise, he could have been into our system."

That was a concern.

Max said, "I've asked for the hacker in Turin to look at our systems again, but . . ."

"That's good, boss, but we need more. I told Lorenzo he needs a more thorough review of physical security in all our offices. But I also want to look more into who Saul Goldstein is. The equipment he used in the office—it's too sophisticated for a freelance journalist. My real concern is he's a professional hacker working for a competitor."

"Did he ever come back?"

"No, but you can't read too much into it. Some clothes, some toiletries—there wasn't much else in the apartment for him to go back for. Like I said, he probably has a safe house." Klaus knocked back the remainder of his drink and stood. "Leave it with me, boss. One way or another, I'll find out what Goldstein was really up to."

Max stood too and walked Klaus through to the outer office, but as he thanked him Rosalia took a call.

She covered the mouthpiece and said, "It's Monsieur Duret?"

Max nodded. "My parents' lawyer. Put him through."

Klaus waved a silent goodbye and Max walked back into his office and picked up the phone.

"Max, what can I tell you—I'm so sorry."

"Thank you, Monsieur Duret, and thanks for calling."

"I would have anyway, as a natural courtesy, but there are things to discuss, as you can imagine." Apparently changing the subject, Duret said, "Your brother is here today—he was in Geneva when he took the call. He identified the bodies."

"Good God." Max sat back down where he'd been a moment before and picked up his glass, draining the brandy that was left in it. For some reason, perhaps only because no one close had ever died in an accident before, it hadn't occurred to him that someone would have had to identify them. He felt a rare flash of sympathy for Henry.

"Yes, a terrible thing."

"How did he seem?"

"The same as ever. As you know, I never really knew Henry and Charlotte the way I knew you, so it's harder for me to tell. He seemed to be taking it well, but I can't be certain."

It was true, Duret had known Max nearly his whole life, but not the others. Henry had been eleven and Lottie eight when Max was born— an unexpected addition after a couple of miscarriages. And Henry had already been at boarding school by then, with Lottie following a few years later.

Max often wondered if that had been the original source of their resentment: that Max alone had gone to a day school near the family home in Vevey, that Max alone had been fully part of their parents' world for all those years. They still talked a lot about their schooldays and how much they'd enjoyed them, but who knew what anger burned within those reminiscences.

Duret allowed a pause to creep in before saying, "Henry's flying home to Vienna in the morning, and coming back in a day or two."

Max didn't pick up the measured tone at first and said, "Well, I'm sure he'll have everything covered."

"Naturally; he has a lawyer's mind, after all. But there are some things I would like to discuss with you, Max, preferably alone, before the others come."

"Monsieur Duret, I'm not in the will, we both know that."

"No, but nevertheless, there are still *certain* things . . ."

It was obvious Duret didn't want to discuss it over the phone, so rather than exchanging riddles, Max said, "Okay, if Henry's flying home tomorrow, I'll drive up in the morning and call you when I get there."

Even as he said it, he knew it was a response to the lack of communication from them, to their apparent determination not to involve him even in this. A little bit of him relished the fact that he was forcing his way back in, with Monsieur Duret's help, whether the others wanted it or not.

"That would be perfect. I'll be ready to come out to the house as soon as you call." Another brief pause. "Max, you know the business of the will . . ."

"I know, Monsieur Duret, and it hardly matters anymore. I'll call you tomorrow."

"I look forward to it."

Max ended the call.

It had been Henry's idea, the last time they'd all been together as a family, three years ago, just after Lottie's twins had been born. There had been a few tense conversations between him and his brother that weekend, but over dinner on the last night, Henry had suggested how prudent it might be, in the light of "Max's continuing activities," to remove him from the will and any trusts, to ensure there was no chance of the whole family being dragged in if Max ever faced a damaging lawsuit or even prosecution.

Their mother had smiled in that deceptively sweet way of hers and said, "It's good that we think about these things—after all, none of us will be around forever. But we have our own lawyer, Henry, so you have no need to worry yourself." She'd turned to Henry's son then, and said, "Felix, would you like to come help me and Madame Bouchet with the dessert?" And that had been it, end of discussion.

But Max had known it wouldn't be the end of it, that Henry wouldn't relent. He'd even been pretty certain that Henry would have discussed it with Lottie beforehand, building up in her mind the danger of being associated as a family with someone like Max. Until they got their way, he'd thought, things would never return to normal.

The next day, after the others had gone, he'd spoken to his parents, telling them Henry had been right, that it was best to safeguard the inheritance of the others, the grandchildren in particular, and he'd reminded them that it was hardly as if he needed the inheritance himself. Reluctantly, they'd agreed.

So it had been at his insistence, and yet still it hurt and he was never sure why. Maybe it was because he'd feared they would have come around to Henry's view on their own, and that was why he'd intervened, to make it easier for them. Or maybe it was because Henry had felt the way he did in the first place—he remembered idolizing his brother and sister when he was young, remembered the excitement when they came back from school for the holidays, and yet now here he was, the kind of person they both felt they had to be protected from.

But in the end, his gesture over the inheritance had made little impact anyway. Things had never returned to normal. He'd had no contact from Henry in the three years since, and no real explanation for that radio silence. He'd heard from Lottie and Nicolas, of course, before every parental birthday, before Christmas or summer gatherings, all the things he'd once been an integral part of.

It was the world he'd be forcing himself back into from the next day onwards. And he was intrigued to know what Duret wanted to discuss with him, what might be so sensitive that he didn't want the others to be party to it—but whatever it was, Max doubted it would ever be enough to bring him back into the fold of his already diminished family.

Chapter Ten

Francesco wanted to eat with him again but Max insisted this time and ate alone. It was just one more reason he was pleased to be driving north in the morning. Hopefully, by the time he returned, the team would have stopped worrying about him and everything could go back to normal.

After dinner, he strolled out onto the terrace, then across the lawns and along the lakeside. The wind had dropped considerably and, unlike in high summer, there was a coolness to the night air now, a welcome change.

He was conscious of reaching the point where he'd stood and cried the previous day and increased his pace involuntarily, as if to avert some hidden danger.

He stopped a little way along and looked out across the lake, the lights littering the far shore, some of them blinking and flickering like candle flames. He could hear the engine of a boat somewhere out on the dark water, although he couldn't see it. And he could hear music too, coming to him in brief waves on the breeze.

After listening for a little while, he knew which part of the shore the music was coming from, and perhaps he could also hear snatches of voices and laughter now, because it was coming from the Buonarroti house, the party in full swing. Had he been there, he'd have been miserable and wanting only to leave, but it seemed a decent metaphor for his life right now that he was standing here alone while the party continued without him.

Unexpectedly, it brought a memory to mind of a similar night many years ago, in the garden of Stef's parents' house on the shores of Lake Zurich. He couldn't remember why they'd been alone there that weekend or even when exactly it had been because they'd been a couple for two and a half years, nearly their whole time at university.

He remembered only that it had been the same kind of night as this, the beginnings of a chill in the air and the lights across the lake and the sounds of a party going on a little way along the shore. They'd talked of finding the party and crashing it, but had decided against it in the end because they were there with each other—what did they need of other people?

He thought of her now, just as he'd thought of her often in the last twelve years, almost as a touchstone: the place to which he always returned, by which he judged everything. It had even been what had first attracted him to Viola, that in some intangible way she'd reminded him of Stef.

It wasn't even as if he were still in love with her, but there was undoubtedly a longing of sorts for that time, and he missed her now and again and found himself wondering where she was, who she was with, and he knew if he'd had her number right now he'd have called her, for all the wrong reasons, simply to hear her voice.

Maybe it was just grief, finding a different way to the surface, and perhaps he no more wanted to speak to Stef than he wanted to be at that party. There were only two people he really wanted to speak to right now, a conversation that would never be within his power again.

Max turned slowly and walked back to the house. As he passed through the main hall, he could hear Laura and Domenico talking in the kitchen, their voices carrying in the evening stillness, soft and calm and so comforting that he almost walked through to them. Yet ironically, his appearance would have ended that lulling conversation and seen them both jumping up, eager to do his bidding, so he left them in peace.

It was early but he went to his room, packed and then went to bed, wanting already to be on his way. He fell asleep quickly, but woke a few times, and more than once thought he could hear the sounds of the party drifting across the lake. Perhaps he could, but it was more likely his dreams spilling into wakefulness.

When he woke for the last time and saw a chink of daylight, he checked his watch and saw he'd slept for nearly ten hours. He jumped out of bed, as though late for an appointment, and was on his way within an hour, even before Rosalia had come in for the day.

◆ ◆ ◆

It was another beautiful morning, the warmth already in it, but Max was heading north, and by the time he stopped at Simplon to stretch his legs, he could feel how much cooler it was on this side of the mountains. Mist was still clinging here and there on the slopes above.

He stopped again at Sion and stayed half an hour. He got a coffee, bought some flowers for Madame Bouchet and chocolates for Thérèse, her niece. And he was surprised to find himself slightly nervous as he got back in the car to drive the final stretch.

Max had been back on many occasions, and even in the last three years, despite the best efforts of his brother and sister, he'd been up to visit his parents two or three times. But this felt different somehow.

His parents wouldn't be there, of course, and at some point in the next week or so, maybe in the next few days, he'd see Henry and Lottie again after all this time. And because of the way they were with him, it also felt as though he'd be saying goodbye to that whole part of his life once and for all.

Here he was, sinking back into his past one last time, because the final tethers linking him to that past were lost. The house would belong to Henry and Lottie, and whether they sold it or not, the family itself would reform around them, excluding him completely. Yes, in so many ways, this felt as though it might be a final bow.

Chapter Eleven

The reunion with Madame Bouchet and Thérèse was even more highly charged than he'd expected, and he became tearful again, not so much from the intensity of their sorrow, but from their overwhelming joy and relief at seeing him, welcoming him back, as if everything would be fine now that Max was here.

It was as though they saw him as the true head of the family now, and yet simultaneously he felt once more like a child with a scraped knee, comforted and coddled and pulled into the warmth of the kitchen. Thérèse wasn't much younger than her aunt and neither woman had changed as far as he could tell—seeing them brought his childhood back just as much as this house did, these gardens, the oak in which the remains of a tree house could still be found. Sitting there with their competing musical voices and their smiles and tears, he almost expected his parents to come in any second to see what the fuss was all about.

They wanted to feed him, and even when he told them he wasn't hungry they still brought bread and ham and cheese, poured him a small tumbler of red wine, "just for now," as if he'd only delayed the onset of a much larger meal. It reminded him of every time he'd come home from university, with Madame Bouchet feeding him up as if he'd been starving in a garret.

Afterwards Max took his bag up to his old room, no longer the room of his youth, although there were still some old college textbooks and even favorite childhood novels on the shelves. Yet when he walked to the window and looked out across the lawns to the trees, he felt he'd never been away, the familiarity deeply ingrained, sitting always just under the surface.

The world looked more autumnal here than on the other side of the mountains, and although the trees obscured the lake at the moment, within weeks the leaves would fall and that tantalizing strip of blue would appear far below. A part of him wanted to be able to stay here to see it, to see the landscape slip away into winter with all the promise and excitement he remembered from his childhood.

He wouldn't be here to see it, though, and he knew he'd probably never visit this house again once the funeral had taken place. Perhaps that was as it was meant to be, and with that thought, he called Duret's office to let him know he was here and ready to see him.

Max spoke only to his secretary, but Duret was true to his word and within half an hour his car came up the drive. Max went out to meet him. Duret was another person who'd always seemed old to Max and yet looked no older now, with a robust, well-fed gravitas about him.

They shook hands and Duret said, "You've grown."

"Monsieur Duret, I'm thirty-four, I stopped growing some years ago."

The lawyer laughed, but his expression turned regretful as he looked up and said, "Such a beautiful house. What will you do with it now?"

"That's up to Henry and Lottie. I guess they'll sell, but who knows, maybe they'll keep it for vacations."

Duret raised his eyebrows, apparently in no doubt as to what would happen, that Henry and Lottie would sell the place as soon as it was appropriate. Now that he was back here, Max hoped it wasn't the case, but that was his sentiment, not theirs.

"Come, why don't we go to Jim's study?"

"After you," said Max. "Would you like coffee or a drink?"

"Thank you, no, and I won't be very long—though, of course, I'm at your disposal any time you wish."

"I appreciate that, although I imagine you'll have more dealings with Henry than you will with me." Thérèse emerged into the hallway as they walked through, but Max was quick to head her off. "We don't need anything for now, Thérèse, thanks. We're going into Dad's study."

She nodded, saying, "It hasn't been touched."

Having said it, she looked slightly embarrassed, perhaps fearing she was being too precious, but Max smiled, letting her know that he understood. This house and this family had been a big part of her life, and of Madame Bouchet's, and they wanted to protect it as it had been for as long as possible. He sensed it now, in the atmosphere of the rooms, like a held breath.

His dad's study was the same: the computer on the desk, a yellow notepad and pen, waiting for him to come back and boot up, as if the markets themselves were still waiting for him to return. Max smiled, remembering being mesmerized by his father's mysterious world of companies and commodities. This was where it had all started for him.

Max and Duret sat opposite each other on the two leather armchairs and then Duret reached into his jacket and pulled out an envelope.

"Your father asked me, if anything happened to him and Patricia, to read this letter to you. It's from both of them." Max nodded, assuming it dated from the time the will had been amended, but Duret seemed to sense his misunderstanding and added, "This was a little over two weeks ago."

He looked grave now, letting the words sink in before slowly pulling the letter free from the envelope and opening it out. He stared down at it, then reached for his reading glasses and appeared to gather his thoughts, taking a deep breath before he started to read.

To our dearest Max,

There are too many things we'd like to tell you, and so little time. Maybe you wouldn't want to hear them anyway. But the thing we must say is how heavily the changing of the will has weighed on our hearts in the last three years. We thought of changing it back on so many occasions without telling you, and didn't only because we did not want to go against your express wishes. It also made us rest easier knowing that you are set fair financially, and we hope that your exclusion from the estate will help to facilitate a thaw in time, between you and your brother and sister. But please know, whatever Henry or Charlotte or anyone else thinks, we are prouder of you and your achievements than you could ever comprehend, and it's been one of our greatest joys to see our beloved boy turn into the finest of men.

Max's throat tightened instantly, tears filling his eyes, not only for the unqualified love they'd expressed in those words, but for the fact that he hardly felt worthy of it—he wished he could believe he was the finest of men, wished he could prove them right, but he knew that he fell far short of what they'd believed.

Duret looked up. "Would you like me to pause?"

Max shook his head. Duret smiled and looked down again, taking a moment to find his place before resuming.

I remember when you were a teenager, it was one of your pet theories that I wasn't just in finance, that my past suggested something more mysterious, that I must have been a spy. Maybe you think this is the moment I tell you that you were right, but you were wrong, Max. I really was just in finance. However, it is true that on one occasion in my younger days, I was indeed asked by the US government to act as a middleman in some complex negotiations, the nature of which I'm not allowed to disclose even now. It wasn't as exciting as it sounds, and would be worth no mention at all were it not for one fact—that I married the CIA officer who handled me.

"Mom was in the CIA?"

It seemed extraordinary. It was true, Max had always suspected his dad, just because of all the exotic places he'd traveled to in his career, the people he'd met. But his mom had been such a serene presence, so understated, and even as he thought it he guessed that was exactly how an intelligence officer was likely to be.

Duret said, "Perhaps I should let them answer." He looked back at the letter and resumed reading.

Yes, you always thought it was me, but it was Mom who was the spy—she tells me I shouldn't use that word, but what other word can I use? She was good and effective and most certainly made enemies, and that's the real reason we're writing to you now. If Monsieur Duret is reading this letter, it means we're both dead, and if we're both dead, even if it looks like an accident, you need to know there's a better-than-average chance we were murdered.

Duret looked up briefly and nodded, as if to reassure Max that he'd heard him correctly.

Your mom was reluctant to tell you this, making the reasonable point that it wouldn't change anything and would only fill you with anguish. But I know you'd want the truth, now of all times, and so does she. If you're in any doubt about the circumstances of our deaths, you can contact the embassy in Bern and ask to speak to someone called Brad Kempson, and he'll know where to take it from there. And ask Madame Bouchet for the letters. I'm sure Monsieur Duret will tell you more about your early years, but you were such a precious gift to us, one for which we'll remain eternally grateful.

All our love, Mom and Dad

Duret stopped, looking overcome himself, and as he folded the letter and put it back into the envelope he appeared older than he had before reading it.

He handed the envelope to Max, who nodded his thanks, but then cleared his throat and said, "Was it an accident?"

"I think so. They were driving from here to Lyon, to visit Charlotte and Nicolas, but you know your mother didn't like tunnels . . . The mountain road they were on, it's known I think—there are sometimes accidents."

"I'll want to go up there, just to see for my own benefit, and maybe speak to the police who . . ." Who what? Who'd retrieved the car, who'd recovered the bodies—police who were unlikely to see it as anything requiring an investigation.

"Of course. If you come by the office in the morning, I'll get the details together for you. It was across the border, near Morzine."

"Thanks. What did Dad mean about getting the letters from Madame Bouchet?" Duret shrugged, nonplussed. "And what did he mean about my early childhood?"

71

This time Duret smiled affectionately, clearly thinking back to the early days of his involvement with the Emersons. "It's true what the letter says: your mother was in the CIA. I never knew very much, naturally, but I think her job was quite . . . dangerous? Sometimes. It's why they decided to send Henry and Charlotte to boarding school as soon as they were old enough."

"She was still in the CIA when I was a kid?"

"Only fully until you were three, and even then less active than she had been. You were so unexpected. The miscarriages your mother suffered, I'm certain her work played a big part in them, and after the second, Patricia believed she wouldn't be able to conceive again. It's why you were so cherished, why they were determined you wouldn't board, that you'd go to the international school here. They even regretted sending Henry and Charlotte away, but when they'd made the decision things had been so different."

"Do Henry and Lottie know about this?"

"Not as far as I'm aware. They were so young. Perhaps Henry had an idea his mother worked for the government, but Jim and Patricia went to great lengths to protect all of you from the truth."

Max sat for a moment, taking in the enormity of it all. There were so many things—the suggestion that they might have been murdered, his mother's secret career, the real reason for the miscarriages, for Henry and Lottie going to boarding school, and the reason Max hadn't—but almost the hardest to assimilate was just how much they'd been through in the years before his birth.

He'd always imagined Henry and Lottie had resented him because they'd gone to boarding school and he hadn't, that they'd thought him the favored child. Would it have made a difference if they'd known the real reason for them being sent away? And would it make a difference now? It mattered only if they hadn't known the truth, and the more he thought of it, the more unlikely that seemed.

"From what you're saying, Henry would have been fourteen when Mom left the CIA—even if he was away at school some of the time, he'd have known, I'm sure of it."

"Does it matter?"

Max shook his head, because whatever the source of the grievance, Henry had found other reasons to dislike him in the years since.

"Let me give you a piece of advice, Max, and I know you'll ignore it, but I give it all the same—speak to this man, Brad Kempson, but then let it go."

"Monsieur Duret, for better or worse, I operate in a world where people who do bad things don't always pay the consequences. But if someone killed my parents, I'll find out, and I will absolutely make them pay for it."

Duret smiled, an expression that suggested he'd expected no other answer, and said, "I know they said it in the letter, and I think they wished perhaps they'd said it more to you directly, but they were so very proud of you, Max, and wished only, well . . ."

"Wished only what?"

"That you were happy. You know, I think they hoped to see you married, a family, but happy most of all."

"Well, there's time for a family. And I'm happy enough."

"Good."

He wasn't fooled, Max could see that. And he wasn't even sure himself why happiness eluded him, why he constantly felt hungry for something that was always unseen and out of reach.

"But now I should go. Have you heard from Henry at all?"

Duret stood and so did Max as he said, "Not for three years. I expect he'll speak to me at the funeral."

"Or before, I hope. I think he flew home to Vienna just for a day or two, and will perhaps come back with Alexandra and Felix. I think perhaps Charlotte and Nicolas are coming too. There are things to discuss, naturally."

"Naturally. So I'm sure they'll be thrilled to find me here."

"It's your home too, at least for now." Duret smiled at some memory. "I remember when I first became your father's lawyer, just before he bought this house, so you were maybe two or three at the time, and I remember thinking, such a wonderful family, such gifted children, such energy: the Emersons!"

"They gave us the best of childhoods, there's no doubting that." It was a pat response, but there wasn't much else Max could say—maybe they'd remained a wonderful family, but it didn't feel that way to him.

Monsieur Duret nodded but also said no more, and Max showed him back to his car.

◆ ◆ ◆

When Max came back inside, he found Madame Bouchet in her sitting room. She was dozing in her armchair but stirred as he knocked gently on the doorframe and stood to usher him in.

"Madame Bouchet, there were some letters . . ." He didn't know how to easily explain it further, but she knew immediately what he was talking about. She nodded, a frown creasing her brow as she walked across to the bureau and opened a drawer.

As she came back, she pointed to the other chair and waited until he was sitting before handing him three envelopes. She sat herself then. "They came one week, then another, then another. The last one was two weeks ago."

Max opened an envelope. It was a single sheet of paper with a line of printed text in the middle reading, "We never forgive and we never forget—the time of atonement is at hand."

He started to open the second, but Madame Bouchet said, "The same. All three the same."

So instead, he looked at the envelopes. One was addressed to Patricia Howard, her maiden name, the other two to Patricia Emerson. They were date-stamped one week apart, and had all been sent from the same place, Vienna. He knew it had to be a coincidence, but he relished the prospect of sharing that little fact with his brother—that their parents had received threatening letters in the weeks before their death, letters that had all been sent from Henry's home city.

Chapter Twelve

The next morning, Max drove into Vevey to pick up the details Duret had promised him: the location of the crash site and the police unit that had dealt with it. Duret was talking to a client when he got there but his secretary handed an envelope to Max. He didn't wait to speak to the lawyer again, and didn't open the envelope until he was back in his car. The map had been printed off the Internet, with the details for the police station printed on a separate sheet.

Seeing the road marked, the D228 above Montriond, Max felt a small surge of love and sadness. It was true that his mom had been afraid of tunnels, and he wondered now if that fear had been a relic of some past mission or just an irrational fear she'd always had, but his parents had also loved the mountains—walking in them, driving in them.

Max could see from this map that it was exactly the kind of route they'd have relished, not to avoid tunnels but just for the drive. His dad did most of the driving, but Max couldn't imagine either of them losing control or driving carelessly enough to crash. Or at least, it seemed unlikely enough to be worthy of a closer look.

He set out, heading west along the southern shore of the lake before turning south into the mountains. The autumnal tones of the previous day had shifted and this morning he drove under a clear blue sky, the light dazzling, the mountains crisp and sharply defined.

It was late morning by the time he reached the D228 and slowed. It was a narrow road, and although he didn't see many other cars, there were quite a few cyclists testing themselves against the climb.

Max had imagined an entirely mountainous road with precipitous drops, but these were tree-clad slopes, rising and falling steeply on each side of a snaking narrow road. He drove along a stretch with rocky outcrops and trees rising up on one side, and a low wooden crash barrier on the other, the slope falling away so steeply that the tops of the trees were only just above Max's eyeline.

And it was here, on a sharp bend, that he saw the simple barrier had been broken. Police tape now stretched across the gap. Max reversed along the road until he found a section where it was wide enough for him to pull over to the side under one of those rocky outcrops.

He got out of the car and stood for a moment, surprised at the stillness, the air disturbed only by birdsong. He'd seen a couple of other cars but couldn't hear any now, not even in the distance. He walked back to the crash site, feeling the incline and the camber beneath his feet. It had seemed easy enough to handle in the car, and walking it only reinforced that feeling—this wasn't an inherently dangerous road.

When he reached the broken barrier, he stopped. He'd thought of clambering down the slope, but it fell away steeply enough here to make climbing down something of an undertaking. He could see one smaller tree that had been snapped and small pieces of debris that he presumed had come from the crash. The wreck itself was gone, which was a relief.

Max could easily understand, looking at the drop that was green and shade-dappled below him, that such a crash would have killed his parents. But unless his dad had suffered a stroke or heart attack at the wheel, Max didn't believe for a second that he'd have left the road here.

He heard the slightest noise over his shoulder and was surprised to see a cyclist in full gear coming up the incline toward him, already quite close, powering away, his legs turning faster than the bike's progress seemed to merit. Max smiled and only realized now that a bleakness had settled upon him standing there, enough that this unexpected human presence left him heartened.

Max nodded at him, and the guy nodded back as he took the bend, but he stopped then, and after a second climbed from the bike and wheeled it back to where Max was standing.

The cyclist looked back down the slope and said, "You speak English?"

Max noticed he had a Dutch flag on his shirt.

"Yes, I do."

The guy kept his helmet on and his sunglasses, so Max could only see the bony jaw, slightly prominent white teeth and pronounced Adam's apple, along with tufts of sweat-slicked hair hanging down from the back of the helmet—his entire appearance was defined by the cycling outfit, like someone who'd just stepped out of a spaceship.

He pointed at the barrier and said, "My friend was here, just after. He called the police. He tried to get down the slope to the wreck, but it was no good. He was pretty upset about that, but they said the people were dead already in the crash so that made him feel better."

Max nodded and looked back down the slope. There was no way the police could have known if it had been instant, although he guessed it was a possibility looking at the drop. They'd probably just been trying to make the eyewitness feel better.

"Was your friend cycling too?"

"Yeah, sure—we come every two years, from Utrecht in the Netherlands, but it's the first time anything like this happens."

"Did he see anyone else on the road?"

"Yeah, sure. A truck—you know, like a recovery truck."

"No, I mean before the accident."

The guy smiled, his teeth dazzling. "That's what I'm saying. He told the police. The car, it passes him—and then less than a minute later, the recovery truck, going too fast for a road like this."

A recovery truck, going too fast for a road like this, but it wasn't the truck that had crashed over the side.

The cyclist said, "You knew the people?"

"No, I'm from the consulate—the people in the car were American."

"Oh, that's too bad, to die on vacation. So, I say goodbye now."

"Bye, and thanks for your help."

The Dutch guy got back onto his bike and continued along the road, his legs turning over easily, the bike crawling away from Max at little more than walking speed. Max stayed for a while longer, looking at the drop over the edge and at the landscape beyond.

Unexpectedly, he thought of Hayden Manning as he stood there. He didn't really know anything about him or even what he'd looked like, and he knew nothing of how he'd died, but he thought of the abandoned jeep and wondered if it had been in a lonely spot like this.

Max didn't know how old Manning's children had been, but he imagined one of them now, grown up and wanting answers as to why their dad had disappeared and where his body was—maybe wanting revenge too. If Max's parents had been murdered, he had to question what position he was in to condemn the person responsible, when Max himself had left those children without a father.

But as he walked back to the car, he shook the thought off. Hayden Manning had made himself an adversary, threatening Max's business, and given the people whose money might have been lost in the process, threatening Max's life too. Manning had picked a fight and Max had been ruthless in making sure he won it, that was all.

What had happened here on this lonely mountain road was different. Even with the CIA background, his parents hadn't been enemies to anyone for at least thirty years, but somebody had driven them off this road, and he saw no hypocrisy in wanting that person to pay for it.

He waited a while before driving on, collecting his thoughts, and no other traffic passed in the minutes that he sat there. He thought he'd pass the cyclist again when he drove on, but he didn't, and regretted that he hadn't taken his name or the name of his friend.

He drove to the police station in Morzine and spoke to the officer on the desk, whose face remained blank as Max said, "I'm here about the accident on the D228."

Not so much as a raised eyebrow was offered in response.

"My name's Max Emerson. The people in the car were my parents."

The officer finally offered an expression, but it was one of confusion. He cocked his head to one side and said, "But . . . their son was here. I spoke with him, and I was with him when he identified the bodies. He talked about a sister—she lives in Lyon, no? Her husband works for Interpol?"

"Yeah, that's right."

The officer raised his eyebrows, as if Max had confirmed his right to be confused.

"But he mentioned no brother. I even heard him say, in the morgue—to himself, you know—'Now there are just the two of us.'"

Max made an effort to take it in his stride, but it hurt, and his expression must have shown it because the officer immediately looked embarrassed for repeating the comment. What stung most was that his brother had said it to himself, suggesting Max's exclusion from the family wasn't just a stand for Henry, but a state of mind.

"That sounds like my brother. But I am their son—I have my passport if you need proof." The officer looked as confused by the offer as he had been by Max's original claim.

"There's no need, unless . . . What is it you want, Mr. . . . . ?"

"Emerson, same as the people in the car. I've just been to the crash site. I met a cyclist there and he said his friend had reported seeing a recovery truck driving very fast."

The officer shrugged, the shrug of a man who felt his professionalism was being questioned. "We told this to your brother. No one else saw the truck. And the cyclist, his description was very vague, but it's plausible. Our early inspection suggests the car of your parents was hit from behind, quite hard. So, we're appealing for more witnesses, and we search for the truck, but . . ."

"So you think it was deliberate?"

"No, it's impossible to say. Maybe the driver was going too fast, he didn't stop in time, or he was distracted. Who knows? He left the scene, but sometimes people do this after accidents, and we don't even know the truck was responsible. Perhaps there was another car the cyclist did not see. We're looking into all possibilities."

"Okay. Thank you for your help."

The officer nodded, then he smiled awkwardly and said, "And I'm sorry. If I had known there was another son . . . but I didn't."

"It wasn't your fault. Thank you."

Max stayed in Morzine for lunch, piecing the accident together in his head as he ate. His parents had passed the cyclist, then less than a minute later the truck had followed, going too fast—the driver maybe realizing he had to catch up with them on the right stretch of road. His dad would have seen the truck bearing down on them in the rearview, but he wouldn't have had anywhere to go. The only action open to him would have been to increase his own speed, inadvertently making the job of the truck driver easier.

It had been intentional, Max knew that in his gut. Even if he hadn't been left the letters, having seen that stretch of road, he'd have come to the same conclusion—if they'd been hit from behind, it had been done on purpose, and with only one purpose in mind.

He wondered if Henry would see it that way, but then his thoughts snagged on what the policeman had said and he smiled. The sting had lessened and he felt superior now in the face of Henry's pettiness. To wish Max wasn't part of the family was one thing, but to deny his existence even at a time like this was so extreme as to be almost laughable.

He wondered too what Henry and Lottie's planned itinerary was for the next day or two. If Duret was right, they were all coming back to Vevey today, with many things to discuss, and the last thing they expected was for Max to be there. But as the old lawyer had said, it was still his home as much as it was theirs, for the next week or two, at least.

Chapter Thirteen

It was late afternoon by the time he got back. There were two cars parked outside the house: a jeep that he presumed belonged to Nicolas, and a rental that Henry had probably picked up at the airport.

As he walked in, Madame Bouchet came out of the kitchen and waved him over with the air of a conspirator.

"You don't want me to mention the letters?"

"No, not for now."

"They're all in the drawing room." She rolled her eyes, the meaning of which was lost on him, but made him smile all the same. Even when he'd been little, she'd had a way of conspiring with him, as though it had been them against the adult world. "Come into the kitchen."

He followed her in and found Thérèse sitting at the table with a pale blonde adolescent who was eating a sandwich. It took Max a moment or two to see that it was Felix. He was fourteen or fifteen now, and he'd grown a lot bigger in the past three years but had lost his childlike cuteness—he was thinner in the face, his eyes slightly unfathomable, even his bone structure giving him a look of aloof seriousness. He'd been a sweet little kid, but he looked every bit like Henry and Alexandra's son now.

Max smiled and sat down at the table. Madame Bouchet brought him a tumbler of wine and looked ready to offer him food.

"I had lunch in Morzine. It wasn't good, but I can wait for dinner now."

She didn't look impressed, neither by his account of Morzine's restaurants nor by his determination not to eat for the rest of the afternoon. The boy finished what was in his mouth and Max said, "Hello, Felix. Do you remember me?"

"Of course. Hello." He looked at Max for a moment, uncertain, perhaps nervous, then returned his attention to his sandwich and took another tentative bite.

Max looked at Madame Bouchet and Thérèse, who both seemed on tenterhooks, the pair of them no doubt full of misgivings as to what this reunion would be like. Max smiled, offering what reassurance he could, and drained the glass before standing up.

"Well, I'm sure they can't wait to see me."

Max walked out and along the hallway. He could hear his brother and sister laughing about something and stopped at the closed door of the drawing room. It was Henry talking, with Lottie joining in, and it only took Max a second to know they were talking about their schooldays. He'd have known it even without hearing the words, so familiar was the rhythm and timbre of the various school stories they told.

He opened the door and stood, a moment passing before they realized he was there. Henry and Nicolas were both standing, Henry in an expensive but conservative navy suit, an upright patrician quality to him, his hair now flecked with gray, Nicolas also in a suit but looking slightly more crumpled, a posture that veered naturally toward slouching.

Lottie and Alexandra were sitting opposite each other on the sofas, next to their respective husbands, the differences between the couples just as marked in the two wives. Lottie still had something of a little girl about her: an eagerness, a softness, an innocent desire for everyone to get along and for everything to be alright. Alexandra, who'd given up a ridiculously aristocratic surname to become Alexandra Emerson, sat with a straight back, her blonde hair held firmly in place on top of her head, her pale features giving nothing away. They were all holding long drinks, gin and tonics, he thought. But even from here, he could see that Nicolas and Lottie were halfway down theirs, whereas Henry and Alexandra's looked untouched in their hands. Nicolas turned first, and nodded a minimal greeting. Henry turned to see what he was looking at, and it was immediately clear that Madame Bouchet and Thérèse hadn't mentioned he was here—Max doubted Henry would have been more shocked if his own parents had walked into the room, although he'd have probably looked considerably happier.

But then Lottie saw him and any thoughts Henry might have had about how to deal with this unwelcome intrusion were cast to one side.

"Max!" She scrambled off the sofa, putting the drink down on the table, in tears already as she ran across and threw her arms around him. He laughed a little, perhaps with relief, even though he knew her joy wouldn't last, and certainly wouldn't be enough to smooth things over, and held her as she sobbed into his chest.

He took the opportunity to study their reactions. Nicolas had a look of weariness and relief about him, the look of a man who'd been overwhelmed by the scale of his wife's grief, happy to see her crying in someone else's arms rather than his own. Alexandra, after a brief turn of the head, was facing forward again, barely acknowledging Max's presence or the spectacle of Lottie crying. Henry stared at him, his face full of calculation, trying to work out what Max was doing here.

Max patted Lottie on the back now and said, "Okay, let's sit down."

She nodded, reluctantly pulling away, and retreated back to where she'd been sitting.

Max sat at the other end of the sofa, looking up at his brother as he said, "Nice to see you all—I wasn't expecting you."

"What are you doing here?" The coldness of Henry's voice and the intensity of his stare suggested there wasn't much hope of a reconciliation.

Lottie said, "Henry, please . . ."

"No, Lottie, he has every right to ask." Max looked back at his brother. "It seems my parents died. It probably galls you, but they never stopped being my parents and I've remained welcome here over the last three years, just not when any of you were here."

"Naturally, they were willing to forgive the shame you've brought on this family, but I'm not, and your welcome here died with them. So I ask again, what are you doing here?"

Before Max could answer, Alexandra stood and said, "Henry, as unpleasant as the situation might be, Max has every right to be here at a time like this, and I'm sure that for one week we can all be civilized with one another." Max couldn't quite see her face where it was turned toward Henry, but her tone was challenging enough, and after a moment Henry yielded, nodding at her. Alexandra turned her chilly gaze on Max now, and he thought how useful it would be to have someone like her on the payroll. She offered a strained smile and said, "I'm very sorry for your loss, Max, and it's good to see you. We'll be dining at seven. I hope you'll join us."

He nodded, and she put her drink down on the table and walked out. Henry followed her, taking his drink with him, but he still wasn't quite finished and turned to look back at Max from the door.

"Don't talk to my son." He left, closing the door behind him.

Nicolas sighed heavily and collapsed into the sofa where Alexandra had been perched. Max leaned forward and picked up Alexandra's almost untouched drink, taking a gulp even as he sat back again.

He looked at them both and said, "Well, that went pretty well."

They both laughed in response, and Lottie reached out and put her hand on his, her eyes still full of tears. But she looked happier now, and that made Max happy—maybe it wouldn't last, but it was something.

Chapter Fourteen

"Where are the girls?"

Nicolas said, "With my parents."

Lottie added, "We'll bring them to the funeral, of course, but we thought, well . . ." She looked at Max again and her brow creased. "What *are* you doing here, Max? You must have known it would upset things."

"I didn't know you were all coming so soon, and I had some business to discuss with Monsieur Duret."

"But I thought—"

"You can relax, I'm still not in the will. I had some other business."

Lottie wasn't ready to move on and said, "I never wanted you out of the will. It was a spiteful thing for Henry to do. I know they said it was your idea in the end, but it wasn't—it was his."

Max felt like asking her if she'd argued his corner, but it was a pointless discussion. Besides, he had to admit in his own mind that it had been the right thing to do. Emerson was no more immoral than most other businesses, but there was no denying it attracted a greater risk than the average financial company, and not just because of the decision he'd made seven years ago.

"Lottie, I know Henry had his own reasons, but as it happens he was right: it is safest for me to be legally at a distance from the family. And I really don't need the money."

She produced a fragile, dismissive laugh. "For Heaven's sake, Max, none of us needs the money." She looked at him then, a look in her eyes that was almost pleading. "You'll be good, won't you?"

There it was. She was still the older sister, eight years older, mothering him almost as much as if he'd been her own child. The bond between the two of them had always been closer than that between Max and Henry, if not quite as close as the bond between Henry and Lottie—the original family, the children whose experience had been almost the same, measured by the same markers.

And yet she was asking him to do something that was impossible. It had never been Max's behavior that had been the problem, but his way of making a living, and he could hardly change that for the sake of a weekend. He wondered sometimes if he'd not called his company Emerson Holdings, might that have made a difference, but he suspected the stigma would have been there anyway.

"I'll try my hardest, Lottie." He sipped at his drink again— Alexandra's drink—and said, "Is it really so scandalous? I mean, really, outside the bubble of this family, does anyone really care how I make my money?"

He thought of the Buonarrotis, eager for him to meet their daughter—generally eager for him to be part of their social circle. But he also thought of Monsignor Cavaletti's surprise that Max felt he had nothing to confess. Did that suggest a different truth, that these people all liked his money, but that they were all equally aware of the sleazy world that underpinned it?

A little of Lottie's happiness seeped away as she mulled the question and Max hated that he'd done that to her, at a time like this.

"I worry about Nicolas, about how it could affect his job if something went wrong with you."

Nicolas shook his head, but Max sensed there was some truth in it. A high-ranking official at Interpol probably didn't have much to gain from a brother-in-law with the kind of business Max controlled.

"You talk about something going wrong with me, but what if something went wrong for Henry? What if one of those juicy corporate clients of his sued him, or if he got accused of malpractice, or even sent to prison?"

"Henry wouldn't ever allow himself to be in that position."

"And nor would I, Lottie. I know I'm a lot younger than both of you, that you always looked on me as the baby—spoiled . . ." She tried to object, but he waved it aside. "The thing is, I know what I'm doing. Yes, I deal with people I wouldn't necessarily sit down to dinner with, but the rest of the world deals with them too. And I never break the law. I never do anything that could result in a scandal."

Even as he said it, he thought again of Hayden Manning, of Colfax and the FBI, thought again of Saul Goldstein. Technically he operated within the law, but at best he was only ever one hacked password away from a scandal.

Lottie squeezed his hand and said, "I hope that's true, just . . . I hope it is. I'll see you at dinner." She stood up. "I just wish you and Henry could be friends again."

"I'll try."

She smiled and walked out, although in truth Max was thinking that he and Henry had never been friends—the age gap had been so great, and although his older brother had seemed an Olympian figure to Max as a young boy, Henry had never quite warmed to the new baby in the way Lottie had.

Once she'd gone, he looked at Nicolas and said, "Is it a problem for you?"

Nicolas half shook his head, half shrugged, giving the impression that Max's business was of no concern at all to him and his career. He sipped at his drink, which was almost finished, then looked at Max again. "It's difficult for Charlotte."

Max was confused. She'd worked for the World Health Organization until having the children, and he couldn't imagine his work would have affected her role there—if it had really come down to it, she could have probably pointed to the health charities that Emerson Holdings supported. He could only assume Nicolas meant it was difficult because of the animosity that had built up in the last few years.

"You mean because of Henry?"

"No, Max, because of you." He could see Max didn't understand, and looked exasperated. "You know my brother was a heroin addict. He almost died, more than once, and thankfully he got through it. He'll never be fully healthy, and there's always a risk of him going back, even now, but he survived. The thing is, when he was an addict, there was this constant tension within the family. We were always waiting for the phone to ring, always waiting for something to go wrong. You don't even know you have the tension, but it's there, all the time. If I'm honest, even now, and he's been clean for over ten years, it's still there, a little."

"And you're saying that's how Lottie is with me?"

"I'm saying that's how everyone is with you, even your parents. I know enough of the world to be confident of your claims, but I also know enough to understand that their fears are well founded: you handle money for criminal organizations—the same organizations my colleagues and I are trying to put out of business. Your clients are some of the worst people, and it doesn't matter how much you say you stay inside the law yourself, you will always be defined by the people you do business with."

Max didn't have a response. He'd certainly never been compared with a heroin addict before. But he hated to think Nicolas was right. It was bad enough to think Lottie had been on edge all these years, thinking Max's business dealings might tarnish them all, but to think that his parents might have felt like that was worse, a gnawing, hollow discomfort.

It wasn't the impression they'd given in the letter they'd left for him, of course, but it would have been typical of their unconditional love for him that they'd have refused to acknowledge the tension he might have caused, the anxiety, the embarrassment. He wasn't sure he'd have ever changed course for them, but he wished he'd known how serious their misgivings had been.

Perhaps sensing that he'd caught Max unawares, Nicolas seemed to have a change of heart and said, "I'm sorry, Max, maybe I'm being too harsh. It's been a tough couple of days, you know."

Max nodded, and at the same time felt his phone vibrate in his pocket. He took it out and saw that Francesco was calling. He rejected the call and looked back up at Nicolas.

"You're not being too harsh, and I'm glad you told me. There's not a lot I can do, because I'm not changing my business, but it helps me understand, at least."

Nicolas smiled, regretfully, and pointed at the phone in Max's hand, saying, "Well, I'll leave you to deal with your phone call."

He stood, collected Lottie's glass and walked out of the room. Max sat for a moment longer. It had sounded so lively in here from beyond the closed door, a family taking this opportunity to reflect on their past together, and within ten minutes the room was deserted and silent. He had to accept they had a point—what *was* he doing here?

Chapter Fifteen

Max walked out into the gardens, walking most of the way across the lawn to the trees before returning Francesco's call.

"Max, I'm sorry to disturb you, but you said you'd get back to me on the Nevada positions."

Max was annoyed with himself, because he'd looked at this and had meant to speak to Francesco before leaving. "My fault, Francesco. I looked at them and I'd rather err on the side of caution. Wind them up, use channel two, and park it all in London."

"I'll get onto it right away. There is one other thing. Lorenzo found out that Catherine Parker is head of a team of three agents, and one of them is currently in Palermo trying to set up a meeting with Luciano Vicari."

"He'll never agree to it."

"No, and I've been in touch with his people to reassure them. But at the same time, it gives us some indication of how much the FBI want this."

"Enough to hire a hacker to do some fieldwork for them?"

"No, I don't think so. Lorenzo, Marco and Klaus are all in agreement—Goldstein's a professional, but not that kind of professional."

"Even so, I want to redouble the focus on everything being watertight."

"It's all in hand. In fact, you could stay up there longer if you wanted to."

"I think three days will be enough, for me and for them. See you Monday, Francesco."

"See you Monday, Max. Be safe."

"You too."

Max ended the call and turned back to the house. Felix was standing at the top of the lawn, staring in his direction with an unsettlingly vacant expression. Even standing still, there seemed to be a slight awkwardness about him, although Max guessed that was just his age.

Max waved at him and started walking toward him. The boy waved back but looked fidgety now, and Max wondered if he'd been instructed not to talk to his uncle.

He didn't bolt, though, and Max said, "How's it going, Felix?"

"Fine, thank you."

Max nodded, looking at him, then up at the windows, although he knew Henry and Alexandra were probably in the guest room they always used, on the other side of the house.

"Your dad doesn't want me to talk to you. Which is fine. I'm not likely to be part of your life anymore, so I don't really need to get to know you."

Felix nodded, and Max could see from that small gesture that he *had* been instructed to avoid Max. Yet he'd come out here and stood watching Max make a phone call, waiting until he'd finished. Maybe it was just the age he was at, full of curiosity and the beginnings of defiance.

"How old are you, Felix?"

"Fourteen."

"Dangerous age." Felix raised his scarily pale eyebrows. "I'm kidding."

"Oh." He nodded, and Max wondered if he was used to talking to adults at all, other than his own parents, who probably didn't provide much of a touchstone for the average fourteen-year-old. "Papa says you're a criminal."

Max smiled, imagining Henry's embarrassment if he'd been party to this indiscretion. "I haven't broken any laws. Your dad, of all people, should know that means I'm not a criminal."

"He says you're the scum of the earth."

Max laughed, not least because the phrase sounded so strange in Felix's slightly gauche accent with its hint of German underpinning it. "I might be on shakier ground with that one." He laughed again, amazed rather than injured by the comment. "Does he really despise me so much?"

Felix didn't know how to respond, but offered a weak smile then and said, "I don't have a brother."

"No. I guess you have lots of friends, though."

The answer was apparent just from the expression, Felix's face a mix of panic and self-reproach. But then he asked Max in return, "Do you?"

"Of course." And right now that didn't feel like a lie, even though his real friends were all people who worked for him. Maybe that was true of most people in their thirties anyway, the world narrowing down to work and family—or just work in his case. "Mainly people I work with, but when I was your age I had a lot of friends. Don't you have any interests, ways you could meet people?"

"I play piano." He lowered his head slightly. "And I compose."

Max wasn't sure where to start with that, but he was saved when the French doors opened from the drawing room and Alexandra came out. Felix turned, on edge, but she smiled at him.

"Papa thought it might be nice if you help him choose the wine for dinner. Would you like that?" He nodded, without much enthusiasm as far as Max could see. "He's in the kitchen with Madame Bouchet."

Felix lowered his head and walked away, and Alexandra watched him go before turning back to Max.

He decided to head off any reproach and said, "I know. Henry doesn't want me talking to him, but he's my nephew. I can't just ignore him."

"And nor should you. It's silly of Henry, childish." She stared momentarily across the lawn to the trees—she was beautiful, but icy, the kind of woman who'd look good in a photo shoot but wasn't easy to warm to in person. She turned back and offered her version of a wry smile and said, "My great-grandfather was a fraudster, sent to prison on two separate occasions, lost most of his estates, but it didn't cause any lasting damage to the standing of the family, and didn't stop my grandmother marrying well. Of course, I understand Henry's . . . unhappiness at the rather sordid nature of your business activities, but all families have their black sheep, and I see no reason why we can't behave civilly to one another."

"Well, good luck with that."

Alexandra laughed, her face briefly lighting up, reminding Max of the way Felix used to be as a child, a reminder that in turn made him feel sorry for the way the boy was now.

"So, I meant to tell you, the priest will be joining us for dinner."

"Father Anselm?"

"You know him?"

"A little. He wasn't the priest when I was a kid. I think he came here when I was at university."

"Yes, that would be about right. We asked Monsieur Duret if he and his wife would like to join us, but they already had other plans. We'll see him tomorrow."

"Of course."

For the reading of the will, though; Max wouldn't need to be there for that. Alexandra nodded, and tried a smile, then turned and walked back into the house.

Max took his phone and found the number for the embassy.

As soon as he got a response, he said, "Good afternoon. Brad Kempson, please." He realized only as he spoke that it was late in the afternoon and a Friday.

"Who's calling?"

"Max Emerson."

"Hold the line."

A moment later a male voice came on the line and said, "Mr. Emerson, you're calling for Brad Kempson?"

"I am. I appreciate it's quite late in the day."

"Actually, he's not in the office today anyway. Can I ask you the nature of your enquiry?"

"I was told to call him, that's all. If you could give him a message. I'm the son of Patricia Emerson, or I should say Patricia Howard . . ."

"I see."

"Yes, and, er . . . Well, I wanted to meet with him, if I could. I'm on this number all the time. I'm in Vevey until early Monday, then back later in the week, but I can meet with him any time it's convenient."

"I'll certainly pass the message on, Mr. Emerson, and it goes without saying, I'm sorry for your loss."

"Thank you, I appreciate that. Bye."

He ended the call and slipped the phone back into his pocket, then headed back into the house. And it was only then that something occurred to him about the tone of the man he'd spoken to at the embassy: definitely circumspect, but perhaps also the tone of someone who'd been expecting Max's call.

Chapter Sixteen

When Max got down for dinner, he found Father Anselm sitting on his own in the drawing room. The priest looked up and smiled, then more broadly as he saw it was Max.

"Max! I didn't know you'd be here."

"No, I seem to be surprising a lot of people with that. How are you, Father Anselm?"

"Very well indeed." He looked well, plump and red-cheeked with small glasses, a boyish quality about him even now, although Max guessed he had to be sixty. "Of course, this has been a terrible shock."

"Of course." Max looked across the room and noticed the champagne glasses and a bottle in the ice bucket. "Can I get you a drink?"

"Very kind of you, Max, but Madame Bouchet is bringing me a little aperitif."

Max nodded but walked over and poured himself a glass. As he turned back, Madame Bouchet came in and handed the priest a tall glass, something that looked like vermouth on the rocks. As she left again, she looked at Max and rolled her eyes.

Max raised his glass to Father Anselm and said, "Good health."

"Good health, indeed." The priest took a gulp of his drink, the way a thirsty child might. "I'm hoping for the funeral to take place a week on Tuesday. It would have been sooner but there were some minor issues to work through."

"That sounds fine to me, Father Anselm, although I guess you really need to discuss it with Henry."

"Yes, yes. I have spoken to him briefly."

They fell into silence, and Max was just beginning to wonder where the others were when he heard voices approaching and all five of them came into the room at once. Nicolas poured the drinks as Henry apologized for keeping Father Anselm waiting and reintroduced him to everyone. He acted as though the priest had been on his own until now.

Lottie told him about the twins. Then Alexandra talked about Felix's piano-playing and composition, the boy smiling and responding to the priest's comments, the appearance of someone who was used to being shown off like this, used to making formal conversation with authority figures. He looked simultaneously adept and miserable.

Madame Bouchet appeared again and Henry smiled, every inch the head of the family as he said, "Well, if everyone's ready, I think it's time for us to move through to the dining room."

They made their way out, Father Anselm talking animatedly to Felix and Alexandra about Monteverdi, Nicolas talking to Henry about golf, Lottie smiling and nodding at all of them, not really listening but wanting to appear interested.

Poor Lottie, thought Max—she'd put her career on hold while she brought the children up but looking at her now, three years on, somehow less substantial, he wasn't sure that had been such a good idea.

He stood for a moment after they'd gone, finishing his drink, enjoying the renewed silence. The sun had set, and he pushed the doors open and stepped out onto the terrace, taking a hit off the chilled air, feeling the lake out there beyond the trees, feeling the mountains, feeling a deep love for this place that was as much a part of him as his own genes.

He turned then and walked back in and through to the dining room. The others were talking, none of them apparently noticing his delayed arrival, no one commenting as he took his place at the bottom of the table, opposite Henry. Alexandra was to Max's left, Felix to his right—it was as though they'd hemmed him in.

Father Anselm was saying, "So it is a little later than I would have liked, but a week on Tuesday does look like the earliest we can do it."

Lottie said, "That could actually work for us, Father. There are relatives in America who'll want to come, so it gives them time to arrange travel."

Max was distracted by the thought of these relatives—there was an uncle who couldn't fly because of some ear defect, a couple of aunts who exchanged Christmas cards but little more, a handful of cousins Max had seen once every two or three years in his childhood, but no more than that. He couldn't really imagine the airlines experiencing a rush for tickets.

Henry smiled at Lottie, a quizzical expression that suggested he was thinking much the same as Max, but then he turned back to Father Anselm. "It will be a Requiem Mass."

"Of course," said Father Anselm, although he didn't sound so sure.

The other adults at the table nodded, but Max said, "Really? You think that's what they would've wanted?"

"I imagine it's the very least Maman would expect, and Papa would have wanted it too."

"Well, Dad went to our church but he was raised Episcopalian, and I think Mom would have preferred a simple funeral service—she'd have thought about the people coming who aren't Catholic."

Father Anselm made a show of accepting the point, but Henry seemed to have made up his mind.

"It will be a Requiem Mass. I'm sure you'll allow those of us who are still in full communion with the Catholic Church to be the judge on this one."

Max smiled, but turned to the priest, saying, "I have to admit, Father Anselm, I'm not a regular churchgoer, but I live a good life, as far as I'm able."

Henry offered up an almost comical scowl, but Father Anselm seemed oblivious to the conversation's undertones and said, "The Lord sees what's within your heart, Max, and that's always more important."

"That's exactly what Monsignor Cavaletti said to me earlier this week when he heard my confession."

"Oh! I met Monsignor Cavaletti once at a conference. Such an entertaining man."

"Then I'll mention you to him next time we meet."

"No, I wouldn't bother—he's unlikely to remember me, but he was such a character."

As the exchange went on, Max could see Henry eagerly waiting to jump in with the obvious question.

"*You* made your confession?"

"It's as Father Anselm says, Henry: it's what's in your heart that counts. And I'm sure greater sinners than me have made confessions. I'm sure greater sinners than me have even heard them."

Father Anselm shrugged in acknowledgment of the final point. Nicolas laughed a little, and then so did Felix as he realized Max was talking about the clergy. Henry remained unmoved.

"It will be a Requiem Mass, and that's settled."

The door swung open, and with perfect timing Madame Bouchet and Thérèse brought in the food. The dinner went off peacefully after that, with the gravitational force of the conversation pulling toward Henry and Father Anselm at the other end of the table.

Alexandra engaged in some fairly stilted polite conversation with Lottie about the twins, and with Felix about school and his music, talking as if the boy were a nephew she was showing an interest in rather than her own son. She made a similar effort with Max, asking him about the weather on Lake Maggiore and about the previously mentioned Monsignor Cavaletti. Other than that, Max felt pretty much like a spectator.

It was only when they were eating dessert that Felix, very much his mother's son, turned to Max and said, "Do you care for music at all, Uncle Max?"

Max was conscious of Henry lending an ear all of a sudden.

"I do, and it's something I've been wanting to become more involved in recently. I support the ballet in Milan."

Alexandra looked at him with surprise. "Really? Do you go?"

"When I can. In fact, I was there just a few days ago, at the premiere of the Carmen Suite from the Bizet, but by a Russian composer . . ."

"Yes, I know the piece you mean, by Shchedrin. Interesting."

Max didn't need to spell out why he'd become interested in the ballet, and was also conscious that he was lying to them more than he needed to this evening—he had nothing to gain, and was really just involved in a game of spite with his brother.

Alexandra smiled with something approaching warmth as she said, "I loved ballet as a girl. I don't think I'd have ever reached professional standards, but then I grew so tall, it made little difference."

"Perhaps I can write a ballet." They both looked at Felix, the boy immediately looking uncertain under their gaze. "It would be interesting, I think, to see the music interpreted in that way by other people."

"I think it would be interesting too, don't you, Max?"

Henry didn't give Max chance to respond, saying, "Felix, perhaps before the end of the evening you could play something for Father Anselm."

The priest smiled, although he was unable to hide his alarm.

"Alas, I'll have to be leaving quite soon. Thérèse has kindly offered to drive me home, and I have an 8.30 mass in the morning. Another time, I hope?"

"Of course, Father, and we'll be staying now until the funeral, so I'm sure there'll be other opportunities."

After the priest left, they moved back into the drawing room, except for Felix who went to help Madame Bouchet in the kitchen, probably as a means of escape. The other four had cognac. Max poured himself a stiff scotch.

Once they were all sitting, Lottie returned to the comment Henry had made at dinner, saying, "We'll be going back on Sunday, for the twins. But we can be back here as soon as you need us."

Henry smiled at her. "Don't worry, Charlotte, everything's covered. There might be more to do afterwards—the house sale and things like that."

She nodded, her face dropping a little at the mention of the house sale.

Max said, "You're selling up?" Henry turned and offered an expression that asked simply what it had to do with him. "It's a shame, that's all. This place is a part of our history."

"Yours more than ours. Charlotte and I were already at boarding school when we moved here. We never quite had the same connection with the place as you did."

There was the resentment, barely beneath the surface.

"And what about Madame Bouchet and Thérèse?"

"I'm sure there'll be some provision for them in the will, and who knows, whoever buys the place might want them to stay on. The simple fact is, the house is the biggest part of the estate so it has to be sold. Given its size and the land and the position, the agent thinks it'll fetch at least twenty-five million francs, so it would be ridiculous to do anything except sell."

Lottie had lowered her head, either at the mention of the money, or of the agent.

Max said, "You've had the place valued already?"

"Yes, we have, because we lead busy lives and we didn't want this to happen but it has, and there are things to be done. The agent came earlier today while you were off doing whatever you were doing—it's why we came here today, to meet with the agent, just as we met with the priest this evening, just as we'll meet with Monsieur Duret tomorrow." The implication in everything Henry said was clear, that these things, these meetings, concerned them but not Max. He'd been removed from the will but in Henry's view he had been just as neatly excised from the family itself. Max even understood now why Henry hadn't mentioned a brother to the police officer in Morzine, because he really seemed to no longer believe he had one.

"I was visiting the crash site. That's what I was doing today." Henry looked like he'd been slapped in the face, the others in varying degrees of shock. "I visited the crash site and I went to the police station in Morzine. It wasn't an accident—they were pushed off the road."

Henry said, "The other driver didn't stop, but that doesn't mean it wasn't an accident."

Lottie looked at Henry, her shock notching up an extra level. "You didn't tell me about this."

"Because I didn't want to upset you." Henry threw a weighted glance at Max. "The police think another vehicle was involved. It could have been someone going too fast—someone who was drunk or hung over—who knows? We'll probably never find out what happened, and it doesn't change anything if we do find out."

"You're wrong." They were all looking at him now but Max stared directly at Henry as he said, "I *will* find out what happened. And it changes everything. Because I think they were murdered."

There were four competing outbursts, but Henry's rose above all of them, a laugh that was full of anger.

Lottie looked at him and said, "Max, you shouldn't say things like that. Why would anyone want to murder Maman and Papa?"

"They wouldn't." It was Henry who'd answered, his voice full of rage, his eyes locked on Max. "We don't live in the kind of world you live in, but please, feel free to share your theory."

"I will, in time. I think they were murdered, and I'll prove it, and then I'll deal with it."

"Good God."

Max felt his phone vibrate and took it out to check it—a number he didn't recognize. Normally he wouldn't have answered, and yet he did, almost in defiance of Henry. "Hello?"

"Mr. Emerson. It's Brad Kempson. I believe you wanted to talk with me."

"I did. Let me just go somewhere more private." He stood, looking at Alexandra and Lottie rather than at Henry. "I'm sorry, but I have to take this."

He vaguely heard Henry respond, but didn't even make out the words. And little did Henry know that it *was* the kind of world his family had lived in, and that his mother's former colleagues took her death seriously enough to return Max's call late on a Friday evening.

Chapter Seventeen

Max walked into his dad's study and closed the door behind him before putting the phone back to his ear.

"Sorry about that, Mr. Kempson . . ."

"Not at all, and please, it's Brad. It goes without saying that I'm so sorry for your loss."

"Thank you."

"I'd like to meet with you, if I could."

"Of course, I'd appreciate that."

"Good, so why don't we say eleven o'clock tomorrow morning in front of the dock for the paddle steamer at Vevey-La Tour?" Max smiled to himself, but as if picking up on it Kempson added, "I know, it all sounds very cloak-and-dagger. If you'd rather meet somewhere else . . ."

"Not at all, that's fine. How will I know you?"

"I'll find you. Look forward to it."

"See you tomorrow."

Once Max had ended the call, he sat on the edge of his dad's desk and looked down at his whisky, swirling it around the glass, thinking it meant something that Kempson was willing to meet him so soon—that it was more than just respect. He was also thinking he didn't want to go back into the drawing room.

He got up and walked around the desk, turning on the computer, sitting down as it booted up. He picked up the yellow pad and held it to the light, studying the imprint of what had been written on the sheet above—*Time to get back into oil?*

He smiled, and said, "No, Dad, wrong call." And he wished he could be here so they could sit over a couple of drinks and discuss the pros and cons, whether oil would go up again soon, whether it would ever go up again.

Almost immediately as the desktop appeared, he saw a PDF his dad had downloaded on that very subject and he sat and read it for an hour, sipping at his whisky, becoming interested enough in the end that he made a couple of notes himself.

When he returned to the drawing room, they'd all gone. Max strolled through to the kitchen and found Madame Bouchet and Thérèse sitting at the table, each with a small glass of port or sherry in front of them. They'd been talking, had stopped as the door opened, but relaxed again when they saw it was Max.

He smiled and sat down. Thérèse got up and came back with another small glass.

"Thank you." He raised his glass and they clinked theirs against his and they all drank. It was port.

Madame Bouchet said, "Monsieur Duret is coming tomorrow."

He nodded. This was what they'd been talking about. "He'll want both of you here for the reading of the will."

"Yes, he said so."

They still looked concerned, and he could understand why. They knew already that Henry and Lottie planned to sell the house, sooner rather than later, and as generous as his parents might have been in their will, the two women would have a less certain future than they might have imagined a week ago.

"How long have you lived here, Madame Bouchet?"

"Thirty-five years. I was here with the previous owners for four years."

Thérèse said, "And I came when you were five: nearly thirty years."

"I remember." He smiled, acknowledging their long, shared history, all the times he'd sat at this table with them, drinking milk and hot chocolate and lemonade, then later with wine and drinks, through all the minor ups and downs of his first two decades. "I don't know what will happen tomorrow, but whatever happens, you know I'll look after you." Madame Bouchet started to object. "Madame Bouchet, you're more like family to me than the people sleeping upstairs. I don't want either of you worrying—I'll take care of everything, and that's a promise."

She didn't object this time, just put her hand on top of his and nodded.

He left them shortly afterwards and went up to his room, but he'd only just closed the door when there was a knock on it.

"Come in."

The door opened and Henry stepped in.

"I waited until I heard you come up. Can I have a word?"

"Take a seat." Max gestured to the small armchair in the corner and Henry walked across to it and sat down, looking around the room with the air of someone who'd never been in there before. That seemed unlikely, but Max couldn't remember and it felt strange for Henry to be here, so much so that he wondered if his brother really hadn't ever visited his room before. Max pulled the chair from the desk and sat facing him.

"It's pointless me saying how angry I am with you."

"Are you talking about the last few years or specifically about tonight?"

"How could you talk like that in front of Charlotte? How could you talk like that at all?"

"They were murdered."

"They were not."

"Did you know Mom was in the CIA?"

Henry gave a patronizing smile in response and said, "She worked for the State Department in a minor role. She gave it up not long after you were born."

Max got up and crossed the room, went into his bag and came back with the letters. He handed him the one Duret had read. Henry opened it and started to read, and Max could see the tension in his face, his jaws clenched together as he saw the comments about Max and the will.

Then he got to the part about their mother being in the CIA and his mouth almost dropped open. Max could see his progression through the letter just from those shifting facial expressions. And sure enough, at the end, he shook his head a little, genuinely baffled by their unshakable love for their youngest child. Finally, he came back to the crucial fact within the letter.

"Maman was in the CIA. How could I not have known that?"

"It's why they sent you and Lottie to boarding school. It seems her job was quite dangerous, and probably played a part in the two miscarriages she had. If I was spoiled, and yes, Henry, I'm sure I was spoiled, it was because they thought they'd never be able to have another child."

"Why did they leave this letter to you? Why not to me?"

It hadn't occurred to Max, and yet it was typical that even now, Henry saw it as another sign of favoritism. He'd wanted Max cut from the estate, and had succeeded, but still railed against the leaving of a letter.

"Maybe for the same reason you want me out of this family, because they imagined I might have the contacts to look into it."

"Will you speak to this person from the embassy?"

"In time, if I think it's worthwhile."

"What were the letters they mention?"

Max held up the other three letters and handed them over as he took back the letter his mom and dad had left to him. Henry opened one and did a slight double-take as he looked at the single line of type. He turned the sheet of paper over to look at the back, then began to pull open the next envelope.

"They're all exactly the same, and they all arrived in the last month or so."

"So you think . . . someone from Maman's past?"

"In the light of the letter they left for me, that seems most likely. But you've missed quite a telling detail—look at the stamps, and the postmarks."

Henry looked at the first envelope, holding it up to the light to see the postmark, then said, "Oh, good God." He looked up at Max, his tone almost accusatory. "You're not suggesting I had anything to do with this?"

"I'm not really sure how well I know you, Henry, not anymore. But I'm pretty certain you wouldn't kill your own parents. And I'm absolutely certain you wouldn't be stupid enough to mail threatening letters from the city where you live. So, no, I'm not suggesting you had anything to do with it. I'm guessing it's someone Mom crossed a long time ago, someone who finally tracked her down."

Henry looked back down at the envelope before passing all three back to Max. "Are you going to the police with these?"

"No."

"Good." Henry looked surprisingly meek, but then the reason became clear. "It doesn't matter that it's nothing to do with me. With those postmarks, and the way word gets around . . . Alex and I both have legal careers to think about."

"Then it's lucky for you that I'm such a shady character. I don't need the police."

Henry nodded, apparently missing the humor in Max's comment, then stood and said, "I wouldn't even mention it to Nicolas. He might feel duty bound to look into it."

Max doubted it somehow, because Nicolas never struck him as the most diligent of people.

"I only mentioned it to you because I thought you might remember something, and you don't, but I guess that's because they tried to shield you from it."

Henry stood there looking awkward, perhaps feeling he'd been too friendly, or that those postmarks made him beholden to Max in some way. "Well, I should go. Will you come to the reading of the will?"

"I doubt it. What time is Duret coming?"

"Eleven."

Max shrugged. "I've got to go into town so I'll probably go then."

"Well. Good night."

"Sleep well," said Max and watched him leave, gently closing the door behind him as though fearful of being overheard.

Max continued to sit, looking down at the letters in his hands, different thoughts vying for his attention. For one, as stilted and awkward as it had been at times, that had probably been the most normal and uncombative conversation he'd had with his brother in about five years. Then there was the fact that Henry hadn't known the truth, that his parents had managed to protect the two older children entirely from the reality of their mom's profession.

He was thinking about the timing of Duret's visit too. It could have just been coincidence, but he wondered if Brad Kempson had chosen eleven o'clock for their meeting precisely because he knew Duret would be coming to see the others at that time.

And finally, that in turn made him wonder why it was him meeting Kempson, why he was the one who'd been left the letter. Perhaps it was as he'd said to Henry, that they knew Max would be in a position to do something about it, and that, ironically, his world was the closest to the one they'd once inhabited themselves.

It was the ultimate joke, that despite his partial estrangement he was the one who'd be best placed to find the truth, the one most likely to secure retribution. That was why they'd written to him, and it was the last duty he could perform for them as a son, to find the people responsible, and to punish them.

Chapter Eighteen

Max drove down with half an hour to spare the following morning and parked a little way along the lake from La Tour. The lakeside path was busy with people enjoying another fresh sunny morning. He strolled among them, settling into the same sedate pace as the crowd, looking for someone who might be Kempson, looking for other people who might be with Kempson.

One of the white paddle steamers was making its way from Marché and he reached the dock at La Tour just as the boat was maneuvering into position. He looked around, but still saw no one who seemed a likely fit.

"Mr. Emerson?"

He turned. The guy standing there didn't look much older than Max, a sporty look about him, curly brown hair, a tan, broad smile.

"Brad Kempson." He shook Max's hand. "I was watching you, just to make sure you were alone. I hope you don't mind."

Max smiled, thinking to himself that this was why he was in finance rather than intelligence, and why he employed people to do this kind of thing—Marco or Lorenzo would have spotted Kempson, he was sure of that.

"I don't mind at all. And thanks for agreeing to meet me. I have to be honest, I was expecting someone older."

Kempson shook his head, unsure of Max's reasoning.

"Oh, just because, I don't know, I assumed you worked with my mom, or . . ."

"I see. No. I met her, of course, but she'd officially retired long before I joined." Kempson pointed to where people were now boarding the paddle steamer. "Shall we? I bought us first-class tickets—the upper deck's usually quite empty."

Max nodded and followed him. Once on board, they climbed the steps and walked out onto the deck at the front. Kempson was right and they were the only people out there. They stood at the rail and said nothing as the boat left the dock.

He thought of that day many years before—"Look at the boats, Max!"—and he seemed to remember now that it had been on an upper deck like this, and that maybe his mom had been standing across the deck talking to a stranger. Had his dad been trying to distract him? Had it been a pre-planned meeting much like this one? It made him see, perhaps for the first time, that his mom had been a mystery to him, always there, a serene and comforting presence, yet a mystery all the same. And it was too late for it to be any other way, for her to answer all the questions he might have had.

With the boat heading along to Montreux, Kempson turned now and said, "It hardly needs saying but I'm sorry for your loss. It must have been a terrible shock."

"It was, and thank you. But the letter they left for me was even more of a shock. I had no idea."

"That she was in the CIA?" Max nodded, and Kempson didn't bother to point out the obvious: that it was a *clandestine* agency. "And I'm guessing she told you to contact me if anything happened to them?"

"She told me if they both died they were probably murdered."

That piqued Kempson's interest.

Max took out the letter he'd brought and handed it over to him. "There were three like this, all the same, all sent from Vienna in the weeks before they died."

Kempson took the letter and looked at it, pulling the note free inside, the sheet of paper fluttering in the breeze. "They were driven off the road, weren't they?"

"It seems that way."

"Do you mind if I keep this?"

"Not at all."

Kempson nodded, folding the sheet with some difficulty and slipping it back into the envelope before putting it in his pocket. "Mr. Emerson—or Max, if I may." Max nodded. "We've been asked not to assist you, not unless you show willing to help the Bureau with their investigations."

Max had to wonder how the FBI had known he was likely to ask for help, but more importantly, he sensed an equivocal note in Kempson's tone.

"But?"

"But we're aware of your situation. We're aware that you'll never help the FBI because if you did, it would be suicide—there are a handful of Russians and a few very powerful Italians who'd panic and seek to make sure your cooperating days were over. So even if you wanted to help the FBI you couldn't, and that leaves us conflicted, because Patricia Howard was a patriot and a hero, who put her life on the line on many occasions to protect the interests of the United States of America, and if there was even a suspicion that she was murdered because of the work she did, we wouldn't rest until we got to the truth."

"You'll have to forgive me, Brad, but there's a lot to take in here. It's wild enough to learn that my mom was in the CIA, but the kind of stuff you're talking about—heroism, putting her life on the line—it makes me wonder if I knew her at all. She just never seemed like that kind of person."

"That's so often the case. But you're right, there's a whole side to her you probably didn't know, and I'm sorry to say the nature of her work means you're never likely to know, not unless you live for a very long time."

Max said, "I understand."

"Good. But all that said, we did look into it when the news of her death broke, and we weren't overly convinced there was anything suspicious, but these letters could change that. The fact is, she was very active in the late '60s and the '70s—active in a way that could have made long-standing enemies."

"I noticed it meant something to you, the Vienna postmark?"

Kempson smiled. "Like I said, we're in a difficult position, which is why I'm meeting you privately. If I can help, if we can help each other, then I'll do my best, but I can't promise anything."

"I'm grateful you agreed to meet me at all. The Special Agent from the FBI acted like I was public enemy number one."

"I'm not sure why—it's not as if you've broken any laws."

There was a teasing, jesting quality about Kempson that Max liked.

The boat turned to head into the dock at Clarens and as the thought came to him Max said, "What I don't get is why someone would wait until now."

"Maybe they were in prison; maybe they only found out recently where she lived. Who knows?"

"But these enemies she made, they'd be old people themselves, and it's a long time to wait for revenge."

"I imagine it depends on how much you want that revenge. If the need's strong enough, thirty-five years is hardly any time at all. But you know, it might prove to be nothing more than a speeding driver knocking another car off a mountain road and failing to stop. I'll be in touch whatever happens, Max, but if I find out anything I can share, I will."

Max nodded, but then Kempson pointed and said, "I'll be jumping off here, but you should stay—it's a beautiful day. Take the round trip to Chillon. And I guess you don't want to be back at the house before they're finished with the will."

Max smiled and shook his hand, and he watched as Kempson left the boat and crossed over and climbed the steps, disappearing from view even before the boat had left again. He sat down then on one of the benches and thought of something Kempson had said and wondered if it had been intentional or a slip.

Either way, he took his phone and scrolled through for Klaus's number.

Klaus answered almost right away. "Boss, how's it going up there?"

"It's good, but I want you to do something for me, if you've got the time."

"Always got the time, boss."

"I want you to look if there were any big news stories or trials or arrests around 1981 in Vienna, particularly relating to spying or espionage, anything like that."

"Sure, I can do that." Klaus sounded intrigued. "Just '81, or around that time?"

"Try '81 first, then look a year or so either side. I'll be back Monday, but take your time. Let me have it whenever you're ready."

"Not a problem, boss."

"Great, thanks, and see you soon."

"Take care, boss."

Max got up again and walked to the railing, looking down over the deck at the front of the boat. It was crowded with people, a few young families among them, and he watched the parents with small children, feeling a mix of nostalgia and longing.

What a tight little unit a family seemed to be, and yet it was full of secrets and mysteries. Those children below probably didn't have much idea of who their parents really were, just as they'd become a mystery to their parents in turn once they became teenagers.

Max hadn't really known very much about his parents, nor had Henry and Lottie, and yet that ignorance had in itself been the result of Jim and Patricia Emerson's love for their children and determination to protect them. It seemed every decision they'd made had been dictated by that one desire, to protect their family.

And what had been the result? The group of them sitting around that dining table the night before. It filled him with a terrible sadness, because his mom and dad had tried so hard, and yet had left behind a pretty unappetizing collection of near-strangers, for whom a shared ancestry no longer seemed enough.

Chapter Nineteen

When Max got back to the house, he found only one car parked out front. Lottie was alone in the drawing room, looking at a book, although he could see she wasn't reading it, her mind elsewhere.

He stood in the open doorway for a moment, watching her, the swell of affection he'd always felt, remembering the way she'd sweep him up in her arms when he was little, struggling to hold him aloft.

She looked up and smiled, and he saw she'd been crying. She reached out a hand and he went and sat next to her, put his arm around her.

"They left so much money."

"They were successful. They had a good life, and they achieved more than we could dream of."

"I guess."

"Where is everyone?"

"Henry and Alexandra took Felix into town. Nicolas took his laptop into Papa's study—catching up with work." She looked up at him. "Henry's very cross with you."

"Oh." He'd thought there had been the slight beginnings of a thaw the night before, although he supposed it was too much to expect. Maybe Max had caught him off guard with the letters, but Henry's underlying complaint was still intact—that Max's line of business was immoral, a black mark against the Emerson family name. "Any idea why?"

"Just the usual, I think. He seemed to get worse after the will was read."

"I wasn't in it, though. Was I?" She shook her head, a look of regret, as if she were breaking bad news. "What about Madame Bouchet and Thérèse?"

"They did pretty well. They got a lump sum—a hundred thousand, I think—and provision put aside to keep paying them and to cover their pensions."

But they'd have to leave this place. Maybe it was what they'd want as they got older, or maybe they'd want to do something completely different, and yet he couldn't imagine them living in some little apartment. He wondered if they might like to come and live in Maggiore, but he knew they still had friends and family locally.

"I wish you hadn't said those horrible things last night." Max struggled to think back to the night before, trying to recall which horrible things in particular might have upset her. "About Maman and Papa being murdered."

"I see. Well, I said it because it's true, and we're all adults. You know from Nicolas' job, even from your work at the WHO, you know bad things happen in the world, and it doesn't help anyone to pretend they don't."

"I know. The way you said it, though; it was such a . . ." Lottie's sentence ran out of steam and she sat for a moment before speaking again. "You found out about her being in the CIA?"

"Henry told you?"

She nodded and said, "I think that was another reason for him being cross, like he needs more reasons—he can't understand why they told you and not him."

Max was about to respond, but reeled back through the last few things she'd said, seeing something in that sentence—*You found out about her being in the CIA?*

He moved away slightly and looked at her. "You knew! How long?"

"Years. Fifteen years, maybe more." She shrugged. "Funny you mention the WHO—it was one of my colleagues there whose father had worked with Maman."

"But you never said anything. Did you ever mention it to Mom?"

She shook her head. "I guessed she went to a lot of trouble to make sure we never found out, and I didn't want to make her uncomfortable. Besides, it was probably only office work, not the kind of thing that would get someone killed years later." She looked at him, a sad indulgent smile forming on her lips, and with an apparent leap in the subject, she said, "I worry about you, Max."

"You don't need to—my world isn't dangerous at all."

"I don't mean that. I mean, you're so cut off from us—okay, that wasn't entirely your choice, but you didn't help. You're single. From what I can tell, you don't even really have friends. I mean, are you still in touch with any of your friends from university?"

"You know that isn't fair. When me and Stef broke up, she insisted people choose . . ."

"And they chose her."

"They were more her friends than mine anyway. I kind of lost touch with my old friends in the two and a half years we were together."

"I still worry. You were so driven, even when you were little, always pushing for things, the next thing, always wanting to move on, never really satisfied with what you had. And maybe that's what's made you so successful, Max, but if you're not careful, you'll end up very lonely."

"Yes, well, there are worse things than loneliness, but thank you for your concern."

"You're annoyed."

"No, I'm not."

"*Yes, you are!*"

"Okay, maybe a little."

She reached out and squeezed his hand, laughing. He liked to see her laugh, even at his expense.

"I think she'll be coming to the funeral, by the way."

"Who?"

"Stef." She said it as though it should have been obvious. "She sent a card, just to the Emersons as a whole, saying how sorry she was to hear the news, and how she hoped to see us at the funeral."

It was ridiculous, but even now, even after all these years, he wasn't sure he could trust his face to mask the confusion of feelings, the odd mix of excitement and trepidation at the thought of seeing her again. And given the occasion, he wasn't sure any of those feelings would count as appropriate.

"When did the card arrive?"

"This morning. Ask Madame Bouchet to show you."

"No, I . . . I don't need to see it. I just . . ."

"Are you still in love with her?" She was curious, but not teasing now.

"No." But Stef was there, always, never far beneath the surface of his thoughts—he had to accept that. "Maybe I'm still in love with the idea of her."

"Because you're not happy."

Max looked at her questioningly.

"If you were happy with who you are now, you wouldn't be dwelling in the past like that. I thought you were dating a ballet dancer."

"She moved eighteen months ago. She got the chance to become a principal with the New York City Ballet, so . . ." He thought of Viola now with a pang of regret. She'd cried because he hadn't tried to stop her going, and he'd reassured himself he was doing it for her benefit because it was a once-in-a-career opportunity, which it was, but he was still a liar. "The thing is, I think what attracted me to her in the first place was that she reminded me of Stef in some way, not to look at, just . . ."

121

"Oh, sweet little Max! You really are messed up." She was teasing again but followed it with a frown. "Will you be okay?"

"Of course I'll be okay."

"I worry about you, that's all. And I want you be happy."

He smiled, but said no more because he didn't want to lie to her again, not about something so unimportant.

Chapter Twenty

Wherever they'd gone, Henry and his family stayed out for the whole day, so it ended up just being Max, Lottie and Nicolas having a much more relaxed dinner on their own.

As they sat at the table finishing the wine afterwards, Lottie said, "This has been lovely."

"Hasn't it?" Max smiled and added, "So it's clearly not me who's the problem."

She looked vexed, as though dealing with a quarrelsome child. "You know it's harder for Henry. He's the eldest, and . . . he's a corporate lawyer, for Heaven's sake. Maybe if you hadn't called it Emerson Holdings it might have made a difference, but even then, people would've made the link."

"The link with what?"

Lottie didn't answer, perhaps thinking he was being facetious.

"Anyway, I know lots of crooked corporate lawyers. If my business is likely to embarrass anyone, it's Nicolas."

Nicolas shrugged—the look of a man who knew enough about the real world to be on Max's side in this bizarrely petty family squabble.

"If you were asking me for inside information, yes, it could be a problem, but as things stand, not at all."

"So there you are. Whatever problem Henry has with me, it's not about his professional reputation."

Although, thinking of the conversation the night before and Henry's eagerness for him not to go to the police with the letters, Max reasoned that Henry obviously put a lot of store in such things.

With what at first seemed like a shift in subject, Lottie said, "You know the funeral won't be a requiem?"

"I thought it was decided."

"Maman included a note in the will. She just wants a normal funeral service. She says a lot of non-Catholics will likely attend and she doesn't want them feeling out of place."

He smiled, because his mom had seemed increasingly distant and mysterious to him in these last few days, and yet that was exactly what he'd have expected of her, to put other people first, as much as her religion had meant to her.

"You think that was why he was more angry with me after the will was read?"

Lottie didn't look sure, but Nicolas shook his head and said, "I don't think so. I think it's deeper than that. You know, it's like he thinks you're the prodigal son: selfish, doing everything wrong, but instead of coming back in rags, you're the big success."

Lottie didn't look convinced. "Maybe it's a little bit of jealousy, but honestly, I don't know what it is. I've tried to talk to him about it once or twice, and he goes on about the family's honor and reputation and how you consort with criminals and you're an accomplice in terrible crimes, but I always get the feeling that's just his reasoning, after the fact—that it's something deeper."

Max could have pointed out that she'd done a pretty good job of tacitly siding with Henry over the last three years, but he knew that wasn't fair, and Lottie and Henry had always had that closer bond. Maybe it was just natural for her to side with him. Max said only, "Well,

I guess it doesn't matter much in the end anyway. After this week, we won't be seeing that much of each other."

"I hope that's not true." Lottie looked at the wine in her glass, raising it to her lips but putting it back down again without drinking. "You know we're going tomorrow?"

"I might leave myself. I was planning to go back Monday, but it'll probably be more comfortable for everyone if I go tomorrow. I'll wait until you leave, though."

"Good. I want you to."

◆ ◆ ◆

Max kept his word and they all saw Nicolas and Lottie off after lunch on Sunday, but as he was turning to go back inside to pack his things together, Alexandra called after him. He turned back to face her, and with Henry and Felix standing behind her it made for a disturbingly formal family portrait.

Alexandra looked almost apologetic as she said, "I hope you don't mind. Only, we booked a table tonight for dinner, at the Hotel du Lac."

Did they really find his company so difficult?

"No, that's fine. I think I'll head off this afternoon anyway, so it's really not a problem."

It was hard to see any response in Henry and Alexandra, but Felix looked stung.

Alexandra offered a polite smile and said, "Of course, and we should have checked. Our mistake." She seemed to pick up on his own look of confusion then. "Well, naturally, we meant for you to come with us. We thought it might be . . . nice."

"I see. Okay. Then it's me who's misunderstood." Max was shocked at how grateful he felt, still a little bit the baby brother who wanted the approval of his older siblings, but they'd come a long way from

125

childhood, and at the same time he wondered what Henry's motive might be, or if it had even been Henry's decision. "Er, I'd love to come—sure."

"But . . . ?"

"I don't have any set plans, and no one's expecting me back until tomorrow anyway, so it's not a problem either way."

"Splendid. We'll arrange a taxi for seven thirty."

Alexandra looked relieved as much as pleased. Henry's face was still an unreadable blank. Felix smiled, his alabaster features reforming momentarily into those of the young boy Max remembered. He wasn't sure why it meant so much to his nephew that he should go with them, and could only conclude that he was set to be disillusioned, no matter what his expectations.

Max spent the rest of the afternoon in his dad's study, once more on the computer, studying financial reports and market reports from his various subscription services. It felt like work but really he was just killing time, and he had to admit that Lottie had been skirting around a truth the previous afternoon, and that without his pursuit of money and success, his life was pretty empty.

A little before seven he went up and took a shower and dressed, but then called in to the kitchen. Madame Bouchet and Thérèse were doing crosswords while something cooked in the oven, filling the room with an aroma that made Max want to change his mind about going out for dinner.

"Max! Sit." Madame Bouchet rose and walked across to one of the counters, bringing three glasses and a bottle of red wine back to the table. As she poured, she smiled at Thérèse and said, "We don't know what to do. We talked and talked, and still, we don't know what to do."

"What do you mean?"

"Your brother will sell the house."

"But we have so much money," said Thérèse. She gave an exaggerated shrug, still in shock at the generosity of the will.

"Would you stay here, if you could?"

"Of course!" Madame Bouchet laughed, surprised by her own conviction. It was as though the Emersons had only been temporary custodians, and Madame Bouchet was the true chatelaine of this house. "But it's to be sold. What will we do? We don't know."

The door flew open and Felix burst in, looking more energetic than Max had seen him in the last few days, almost like a real fourteen-year-old.

"Uncle Max, the taxi is here."

"Then let's go." He knocked back his wine in one go, feeling he might need it, then took the glass over to the sink and washed it.

They didn't speak on the short journey down into town. Max could easily imagine that Henry and Alexandra never spoke in front of a driver. And when they got into the restaurant they talked only formalities to begin with, choosing their wine and food, ordering some champagne to start.

With the aperitif poured, Henry raised his glass and said, "To Maman and Papa."

"Sure. To Mom and Dad."

They all raised their glasses and drank, and then Felix said, "Why do you call them by different names?"

Max thought the question was aimed at him, but it was aimed at the two of them as brothers, and it was Henry who answered.

"I can't really remember if we ever called them that. Charlotte and I had a French nanny when we were small. And when we went to boarding school everyone else called their parents Maman and Papa too. It was just natural." He looked at Max. "You probably don't remember, but when you were very small you used to call them Jim and Pat."

Max laughed. "Really? I don't remember that. I guess I heard them calling each other by their names." He turned to Felix. "I went to the international school here, and I had friends of all nationalities, but a couple of close friends who were American too. So I just always called them Mom and Dad. I knew Henry and Lottie called them Maman and Papa, but . . . When I was a teenager and they were grown-ups and still calling them that, I just thought it was artifice, you know—like they were being pretentious."

Henry chuckled to himself. "Whereas Uncle Max was the golden boy." Max smiled, grateful in some way for the normality of petty sibling rivalries. "I suppose there were good reasons for that, in retrospect, but when you're in your late teens, and all your achievements are well received but inevitably followed by some comment from Papa about what a whizz Max is with figures, or from Maman about how fearless Max is, and *so* popular . . ."

"It's true, though—I was an exceptional child."

"In what way?"

It was Felix, in earnest, but Alexandra smiled at him and said, "Max is joking, Felix."

"Oh."

He looked mortified, out of all proportion to such a simple misunderstanding, as if he'd been offered the chance of sitting with the grown-ups and had blown it, but then Henry said, "Perhaps, but you *were* an exceptional child, Max. You could have gone on to achieve great things in any field you set your mind to."

"I haven't done badly."

With the air of someone stepping in to steer them around a hazard, Alexandra said, "I'd forgotten how beautiful the view is from here."

Henry turned and so did Felix, and for a moment they all looked out at the darkened lake and the snow-capped mountains across the water and the lights twinkling on the far shore. Alexandra was right about its beauty, but it also made Max want to be home again, even though there wasn't much to be there for at the moment.

Despite Alexandra's attempts at distraction, he thought of what Henry had said, seeing for the first time how tough it must have been. And if their parents had doted on Max as much as he'd said, then maybe his brother and sister had every cause to resent him, although if Lottie had shared Henry's feelings it had never shown.

The waiters arrived with the first course and the conversation moved seamlessly on to the food and other topics.

Felix was allowed a little wine, and became marginally more relaxed and chatty as the meal went on. It was as they were eating their dessert that he looked up casually and said, "Is it true you deal with the Mafia?"

The three adults at the table froze momentarily before his mother replied. "Felix, I'm not sure that's a question Uncle Max would feel comfortable answering."

Once again, Felix looked chastened, and Max felt for him.

"I don't mind answering. Unless . . . ?"

He looked at Henry questioningly, asking if he objected to Felix hearing what he had to say. And the truth of it was that Henry was probably just as intrigued—for all his criticisms and outrage over the years, he'd never actually asked or been told the story of how Max had become the family's embarrassing secret.

"Feel free."

Felix smiled at Max, gratefully it seemed, or maybe just relieved.

"We were all left some money by a grandfather we never knew. Although maybe your dad knew him . . ."

"Yes, I met him a couple of times, but I don't really remember him."

"Anyway, the money was put in trust, and I got mine in my final year at university. I was already interested in finance by that stage, so I decided to use it to form my own financial business. Early on, I wasn't even sure what I wanted to specialize in. I was dabbling, speculating, but I did well. Then a couple of years in, the global financial crisis happens, and guess what?"

Felix stared back at him, enraptured, a spoonful of dessert suspended halfway between plate and mouth.

"I *kept* doing well. People were losing money all over the place, going out of business, but Emerson Holdings thrived. I'd like to say it was skill, but I think the biggest part of it at that stage was luck. By 2008, the company was hugely successful, dwarfing anything Dad had ever done. And I guess that brought me to the attention of different people. One day in June of that year—I was based in Milan by this stage—I got a visit from a lawyer, the lawyer for someone called Luciano Vicari, telling me his client had very lucrative business operations and wanted to invest some of the profits, or specifically, that they wanted Emerson to invest them on their behalf, with very generous terms for doing so."

Henry said, "Did you know he was?"

"I had to Google him. Even then, I probably didn't realize quite how powerful he was. On the one hand, I was nervous, but excited too—you know, I was in my mid-twenties, I'd seen all the Mafia movies and TV shows, so there was a bit of a thrill. But I didn't forget my professionalism. I checked the nature of the deal, then worked out changes to the terms that would make sure I was in the clear. I checked it with Dad, too. Even had Monsieur Duret look over it . . ."

"Papa knew?"

"Yeah, he knew who I was dealing with, and he expressed his concerns, but he couldn't find any legal or contractual reason for me not to be involved. So I started handling Vicari's money: middling amounts for the first few months, but then, big—very big—sums of money. It went well, returns were good, then other people started to approach us, quite a few Russians among them, but really, people from all over. Almost by default, it became our business, and we're very good at it. That's how it is."

He was conscious of Alexandra turning to look at him as she said, "But didn't you ever have any moral concerns about the people you were dealing with?"

"I can't lie, Alexandra, it never even occurred to me. I've had it pointed out since, that the money I'm handling is the fruits of despicable crimes, drugs, extortion, prostitution, including child prostitution, but these things are happening anyway. Money is money, and as far as I can see, it has no inherent moral value."

Henry looked bemused.

"Max, the same argument could be used by people who profited from the looting of Jewish-owned artworks during the Third Reich. The Jews were being rounded up anyway, so what harm is there in benefitting from the side-product."

"No, for it to be true equivalence, you have to imagine that it was the US and British governments buying those looted artworks from the dealers, in the full knowledge that the rightful owners had been rounded up and murdered." Henry frowned. Felix looked on, mesmerized. "You have to remember, we were still coming through a global financial crisis caused by the most immoral behavior imaginable, most of it rubber-stamped by governments. You have to remember too, that Emerson was already using tax havens by this point, the vast majority of them within US or UK jurisdiction."

Felix said, "But I thought tax havens were illegal?"

Max nodded at him, trying to make clear it wasn't a stupid question. "You'd think so to listen to the European Union or to the UK or US administrations, but how they talk and how they act are two different things."

"Uncle Max is simplifying. We'd like to close down tax havens, of course we would, but it would require global agreements. Western governments can't do it on their own."

"Henry, please, Western governments aren't even trying. They're complicit every step of the way, and if you want proof of that, here it is—I do something that you consider morally reprehensible, you almost had me exiled from the family, and yet with the exception of some student high spirits and a couple of speeding tickets, I've never broken the law, not once."

Max had never broken the law—it was the truth, but even as he said it, he knew it was a mangled and distorted truth.

Henry shook his head, knowing he had no answer. But it was equally clear that the logic of Max's argument did nothing to appease him. Henry held to a higher morality than that of governments and he could never come to terms with the fact that a member of his own family fell so spectacularly short—if only he'd known.

Felix said, "What's he like? The Mafia boss?"

There was a little bit of the youthful intrigue that Max had felt all those years ago, and he could still remember the low-level excitement of approaching Vicari's yacht. It seemed ridiculous in retrospect, particularly in light of the pact he'd entered into shortly afterwards. What was Vicari like? He was dangerous, and in one way or another he contaminated everyone he came into contact with, including Max.

"I've never met him."

Felix looked disappointed, and for a moment Max told himself he was lying for the boy's benefit, when in fact he was lying for his own, as he always did. "Part of my agreement was that I didn't want any direct dealings with him or his people, didn't want to know anything about his business, just a purely financial arrangement, always on our terms."

Henry was curious again. "And he accepted that?"

"Of course. Because we take his money and we make him a lot more. I've met some of our clients, but it's not the norm—we always try to keep one step removed."

Henry appeared to be engaged in some internal argument, but finally said, "I still can't accept it, and I find it hard to forgive how inconsiderate you were, how little thought you gave to the impact on the rest of the family. Even that weekend three years ago, Maman had talked to me about how worried she was by your business, and yet you sailed blithely on."

Was that the real reason his mom had been so short with Henry at the table that night, because she'd spoken to him privately and felt he was betraying that confidence by bringing the subject up? Nicolas had suggested the same to Max, that it had been tough on Lottie, tough on his parents.

"Henry, I'm not sure . . ."

"No, Alexandra, Henry's right. I make no apologies for my business—I just can't, because in the grand scheme, I don't think I'm doing anything wrong. My company's an amoral financial institution in an amoral global economy. But I do accept I could have handled things better, could have thought more about the way it might upset you and Lottie, Mom, and Dad. The thing is, Henry, I can't go back. None of us can."

Henry stared back at him, offering no response, his expression unreadable.

But Felix had been following the conversation avidly, and after a moment's silence, he said, "At least you're eating together."

Henry laughed and turned and ruffled his son's hair, and Max saw how emotional his brother was, how hurt he was at a level that seemed deeper than all of this. It filled him with an intangible sorrow, one that he couldn't attach to anything, because there was no way of knowing what had made Henry like that, and no way of fixing it, except perhaps for Max to disappear from his life completely and become the brother who was only ever talked about in the past tense.

Chapter Twenty-One

Max got home late the following morning and found Francesco studying the cards and notes attached to the flowers that filled the main hall. Francesco turned and saw him, breaking into a broad smile.

"Max, good to have you back." He came over and held him by the shoulders, kissing him on both cheeks. "Did you have a good trip? Difficult, but hopefully . . . ?"

Max thought of the dinner the night before, glad he'd stayed for it. He wasn't sure there'd ever be a way back for him and Henry, not helped by the fact that there hadn't ever been any particular closeness between them in the first place, but things had at least reached a level of cordiality.

"It had its tricky moments, but it was good to see them."

"Excellent. I'm pleased." Francesco held his arms out, gesturing to the flowers. "Isn't this incredible? A sign of your popularity that so many friends want to offer their support at a time like this."

Max nodded, taken aback that all these people even knew about the death of his parents.

Francesco took him by the elbow, moving him around the room like a dignitary. "These are from the household staff: so beautiful. These are from me and the rest of the team. These are from the ballet, the children's hospital, Monsignor Cavaletti's office. Over here from some of the local families—Manfredi, Borromeo, and of course, Buonarroti. Many more. So many."

"It's incredible." It also felt quite unreal. Most of them didn't really know him, and most of these flowers and condolences were a response to his generosity, not his person.

They walked toward the office together as Francesco said, "The German is around somewhere—he has some information you asked for. And the lady from the FBI called this morning, said she needed to speak to you, that there has been a development."

"She say what it was?" It felt like weeks since he'd spoken to Catherine Parker. He had a vague memory that she'd talked about searching for a way of working together without compromising his position, but then her colleague had been trying to arrange a meeting with Vicari, so he guessed they didn't care how they got Max to comply, as long as he did.

"She said she'll call back today."

Max nodded and they walked in and said hello to Rosalia.

With the greetings out of the way, she said, "The Buonarrotis would like to invite you to a small private lunch to meet Isabella, once the funeral is out of the way."

"That sounds nice." Max turned to Francesco. "Do you think the poor girl has any idea how desperate they are to marry her off?"

"I think she's a free spirit. I suspect they're just keen for her to meet someone suitable, stable." Francesco laughed. "And, of course, rich enough to pay for her lifestyle."

Max could just imagine the hapless Isabella Buonarroti—a highly-maintained party animal, flitting from one social engagement to another, always at risk of embarrassing her family. So they had at least one thing in common.

The phone rang and when Rosalia answered, she put the call on hold and said, "It's the lady from the FBI."

"Put her through." He went into his office.

Francesco followed behind, idly picking up a magazine and sitting on the sofa.

Max took the call. "Miss Parker, what can I do for you?"

"If you don't mind, Mr. Emerson, I'd like to pay you another visit. Things have changed quite dramatically since we last met, as I suggested to your consiglieri."

The word was designed to taunt him, but he said, "You watch too many movies, Miss Parker, but perhaps you could spell it out. How have things changed?"

"You told me you had no need of immunity, but that was before the abduction and possible murder of Saul Goldstein—a crime in which two of your employees might be implicated, and by association, you also."

Even as Max tried to absorb the disconnect of hearing that Goldstein had been murdered, and that the FBI might try to implicate him in it, he was conscious that Catherine Parker seemed to have used a lot of hedging in a very brief statement—*possible* murder, *might* be implicated.

"I have no idea what you're talking about, but given the seriousness of your allegations, how about tomorrow afternoon at two?"

"I'll be there. And Mr. Emerson, whatever our differences, I was sorry to hear about your parents."

He'd had a lot of condolences in the last week, but he was in no mood to hear hers.

"Thank you. Tomorrow at two." Max hung up, and Francesco put the magazine down.

"Problem?"

"Possibly. Is Lorenzo about?" Francesco nodded. "Could you tell him to come and see me right away, then Klaus in ten minutes."

"Of course."

As he stood, Max said, "The FBI are claiming we kidnapped Saul Goldstein. And possibly murdered him."

Francesco frowned, a rare look of anger crossing his features. "It's as I said, Max: governments play by their own rules."

He left and Max turned and looked out of the window, thinking of Saul Goldstein, his dreams of becoming a writer, his girlfriend in Tribeca. It was too bad, but whatever had happened to him, it was Max's problem too.

Catherine Parker had talked about a possible murder, so Max assumed Goldstein really was dead, the only question being one of how he'd ended up that way. An accident or an overdose? That was too unlikely somehow, as panicky and jittery as he'd seemed, but the alternatives were less appetizing.

If one of Max's clients had found out about Goldstein, they might have been tempted to shut him down, but there was no way they could have found out about him without a massive breakdown in Emerson's security, something that would surely have been picked up by Marco or Klaus.

And that left only the FBI—they were apparently happy to exploit his death, but could they have killed him themselves? He didn't even know if the FBI engaged in black-ops, and felt naïve for not knowing, but if they *had* killed Goldstein, it suggested a level of seriousness way above the vague threats Catherine Parker had made.

He heard the approach of steps and Lorenzo came into the office, Marco and Francesco behind him.

"You wanted to see me, boss?"

"Yeah. What did you do with Goldstein?"

"Like you said, took him to the airport, bought him a ticket, took him to the departure gate."

"Good. Is there any way of proving it? Because the FBI claims he's been murdered and we did it."

Marco nodded, businesslike. "I'll speak to a contact, see if we can get the CCTV of Lorenzo and Domenico leaving him at departures, then leaving the airport alone. It's too bad he never went back to the apartment, but at least we know there's no real evidence to implicate us."

Francesco could still barely conceal his anger. "They won't need real evidence. This is what they do."

Lorenzo turned to Max and said, "You think they're trying to set us up?"

"No, I don't think so. They're trying to create leverage, but that means the more evidence we've got, the better. What did we find out from Crazy Mouse?"

Lorenzo said, "Not much. No information on a cousin at *The Atlantic*. The hedge fund he mentioned, Padbrook: no links to us, but also, he said he got the tip from a guy called Joel—nobody called Joel working at Padbrook."

"What about on Goldstein himself?"

Marco's frown gave a clue even before Lorenzo answered. "That's where we're having real problems. Crazy Mouse and the German have both been coming up blank. It's like Goldstein's completely off the grid."

Max thought of the detail Klaus had given him, that there'd been no electronic devices in Goldstein's apartment in Luxembourg. They were also sure he hadn't been law enforcement, although if he was dead it hardly mattered anyway.

"Well, he's off the grid now. Get the footage from the airport if you can."

"Sure thing, boss."

As they left, he heard them speak in the outer office and a second later Klaus appeared in the doorway, holding a few printed sheets in his hand.

"Come in, Klaus."

"Thanks, boss. So, you asked me to look for treason or espionage trials in Vienna around 1980."

"You found something?"

"I think so." They sat down and he handed the sheets of paper to Max. "One of these is from an American paper, but mostly the sources were German, so I just listed the details. But it's all there— two high-ranking Austrian intelligence officers were arrested in late '79, and their trial took place in '81. They were found guilty of trying to hand over secrets to the East Germans. It was a big case, but it dealt with very sensitive information and a lot of the details were kept hidden, including the names of the two men. From what I found out, they were released in 2006, but there's no more public information."

"So we don't know who they are."

Klaus shook his head. "Maybe someone like Crazy Mouse could find more, but—"

"No, I don't want to involve him in this. But I do need to find out who these guys were." Klaus was studying him closely, curious. "It turns out my mother was in the CIA, and in the weeks before she died, she got some letters from Vienna, suggesting someone was looking for revenge."

"So you think she was involved in bringing them to justice? But then, these guys would be old men by now." Klaus shrugged, apparently answering his own question. "Leave it with me, boss. I have a friend in Vienna— he's not a contact I like to use very often, but he owes me a favor or two."

"I appreciate it, Klaus, thank you."

Klaus nodded, stood and left, and Max picked up the pieces of paper and looked at them again. The article from the US newspaper suggested a possible nuclear connection and said the CIA had "played a central role in uncovering the plot, working in conjunction with foreign intelligence services."

It was such an intentionally vague comment and it seemed extraordinary even now to imagine that those catchall words concealed the truth of his mom's other life, and perhaps the reality of her death, too. This was who she'd been, a woman who'd created headlines, who'd created enemies, and at the same time a woman who'd managed to conceal it all, even from her own children.

Chapter Twenty-Two

Tuesday was so warm and still that it felt like the beginning of the season rather than the end of it. Max took his lunch with Francesco, sitting out on the terrace. They'd just finished eating when Max heard the slow purring engines of a boat and turned to see the Guardia di Finanza patrol boat pulling up against the jetty.

"We have a visitor."

Francesco looked over his shoulder and said, "Ah, young Mercaldo. He's a good man. If ever he wanted to earn more money, we'd do well to employ him."

"I think he enjoys what he does, and I don't think money bothers him."

As ever, there was a little envy underpinning Max's words, wishing his life as simple and fulfilled as the imagined existence of Lieutenant Mercaldo. He came up the steps onto the terrace then, offering a relaxed salute and walking toward them with his casual swagger.

"Good to see you, Lieutenant. Come and join us."

With a pretense of being upset, he said, "You didn't save any for me?"

They shook hands and sat down again. Laura came out with a glass and Mercaldo accepted some white wine.

He raised the glass to his lips, but hesitated, remembering himself, and said, "My sympathies, Signor Emerson—I heard the news."

"Thank you." Max felt like he'd spend the rest of his life thanking people for their kind words. "Are they keeping you busy?"

"Not too bad, but busy enough." Mercaldo smiled, a little mischievous. "I probably shouldn't tell you, but I heard a rumor that the FBI have been poking their noses around, asking my superiors for any information they could share about you and your company."

Francesco was passive, but Max could see what he was thinking: that this was how it was going to be, that the FBI would keep digging until they found something.

"Any idea what your superiors told them?"

"Nobody likes other people poking their nose in, but they told them the truth—that yours is a respectable business, and that you are a very respectable man, Signor Emerson."

Max smiled, hoping it was Catherine Parker who'd received that reply personally.

She arrived just after Mercaldo left. In fact, Max could still see the pale-gray patrol boat making its way across the lake as Domenico showed Catherine Parker out onto the terrace.

He immediately thought she looked more friendly this time, which was ironic in the light of her reason for visiting.

"Thanks for agreeing to see me again, Mr. Emerson, particularly at a time like this."

At first, Max thought she was talking about Goldstein's murder, but then understood that she was talking about his parents. "You're welcome, Miss Parker." He looked at Domenico who was still standing near the doors onto the terrace. "Thanks, Domenico. Could you ask the kitchen to bring us a pot of coffee? I think we'll sit down on the lawns."

"Okay, boss."

Max gestured toward the steps, but then said, "I'm sorry, would you have preferred a drink, or just something colder?"

She smiled, and once again it seemed a genuine smile, enough for him to find the change in her slightly disconcerting, enough for him to wish he could get to know her in a normal way.

"Coffee's just fine, thank you." She headed down the steps and Max pointed to the table and chairs set near the lakeside in the shade of a chestnut tree. "It really is the most beautiful place."

"I'm very lucky." As she took her seat, Max said, "No lessons on the social cost of it all this time?"

She smiled again. "I wasn't particularly subtle, was I? It doesn't change how I feel, but I'd like us to be able to cooperate in a more amicable way, if at all possible."

"By accusing me of murder?"

The smile remained, but the first hint of steeliness showed behind it now.

"I didn't accuse you, but there are questions to be answered, as I think you know."

"By you, perhaps—not by us." Catherine Parker raised her eyebrows in response, a look exaggerated enough to be comical. "Saul Goldstein committed a criminal act against my company. He was offered the chance to come out here and explain himself rather than have us going to the police—an offer he was all too keen to accept. I'm sure you have photographic evidence of him being escorted to my company's private plane by Lorenzo and Domenico. After I finished interviewing him, he was taken to the airport, a ticket was bought for his return to Luxembourg, and he was taken to the departure gate."

"A ticket was bought for him, but he never boarded the plane."

"I'm sure that happens all the time."

"We have photographic evidence showing your men walking him out of the terminal."

"I bet you do."

"It's our contention that Goldstein escaped and made his way to the airport, bought a ticket back to Luxembourg and aimed to fly home, but your men intercepted him, murdered him, and disposed of the body."

"Do you have a body?"

"No, we don't, but nor do we have a living person." She paused, the briefest moment, but it felt dangerous, as if she might suddenly mention Hayden Manning, another person who'd crossed Max Emerson and disappeared without trace. But of course, that was only Max's paranoia. "We also have motive—we know what Goldstein was doing in your office: trying to expose your company for what it really is, and, as you made clear in our last meeting, that's an issue that's serious enough to get someone killed."

Max saw that he had one additional card to play. "I have no doubt you know what he was doing in our office, because it seems his main intent was the same as yours—Senator Colfax." Her expression gave nothing away, but he got the sense all the same that she wasn't surprised, that she'd known already about Goldstein's interest in Colfax.

She said, "I guess it would make a tempting story for any freelance journalist, but a dangerous one to investigate."

Laura came down the steps carrying a tray, and Max stopped to look in her direction as she headed across the lawn to them.

"Thank you, Laura." As Laura placed the tray and started to take the things off, he looked at Catherine Parker. "Do you take sugar, Miss Parker?"

"No, thank you."

"Cream?" She shook her head. "You can take the sugar and cream back with you, Laura, thank you."

Laura nodded with a smile and put the sugar and cream back on the tray before taking it away.

"So, where were we? You were accusing me of murder, I think."

Max was conscious of sounding like a supervillain, the exact opposite of what he was trying to do here.

"Not yet, not quite. We believe a US citizen has been abducted and quite possibly murdered, and there's compelling evidence to suggest that you and your employees are persons of interest with regard to that matter."

"Of course there is. On the other hand, the CCTV footage from the airport would show my men buying Saul Goldstein his ticket, then leaving him at the departure gate, but it seems, astonishingly, that a full two hours of the entire airport's footage has been eaten up by a glitch in the system."

Catherine Parker looked confused. "I don't know anything about that. Really. I didn't know."

She appeared put out enough that Max believed her, and he could see that she looked irked at a professional level, as though she suspected a colleague of trying to undermine her.

"Even so, it puts a question mark over your case. In addition to which, I know that the photographic evidence you have is faked, and I could spend a great deal of money to prove it. So if your only purpose in coming here is to threaten me, Miss Parker, you'll need something more substantial than the possible murder of Saul Goldstein."

"You talk as if it's a game. Well it isn't. Saul Goldstein was a twenty-six-year-old man with his life ahead of him, and whatever he was doing in your Luxembourg office, he didn't deserve to die for it." There was real contempt in her voice, perhaps for the first time in their two meetings. "You just don't care about him at all, do you?"

"I didn't care for what he was doing. Beyond that, he seemed decent enough, and if he's dead, I'm sorry to hear it. But whether or not his death bothers me, it actually has nothing to do with me, and you can't prove otherwise with a little doctored evidence."

Catherine Parker looked out at the lake, but there was nothing to captivate her on the water today and she turned back to face Max. "We don't have to prove you murdered him. We know he was taken from his apartment and he's now missing, presumed dead, and we know that the people who took him from his home did so on your orders. And yes, we do know he was interested in Colfax, a fact that will inevitably come out in the investigation into his disappearance, whether you want it to or not. So trust me, this is the moment for you to reconsider."

Once again, the parallels seemed uncomfortably close, and Max could only imagine how they'd come after him if they ever did get a handle on Manning. But for the time being Max had one big advantage: that he had nothing to do with Goldstein's disappearance. Catherine Parker had inadvertently shifted the focus from things Max had to lie about to the one thing about which he could confidently tell the truth.

He smiled as he said, "When you were here last you suggested you'd try to find a middle option, something that would allow me to help you bring down Senator Colfax whilst simultaneously protecting my position. What you've actually done is fabricate evidence in an attempt to blackmail me into doing something suicidal. And yet you also had the temerity to lecture me on morality. Is that the real reason I got no homilies this time? Because you've had to accept that you're no more morally superior than I am?"

She looked indignant. "We are not at all alike, Mr. Emerson. It may suit you to believe it, but there is no comparison."

"That's true. Because I'm honest about what I do. I take money from people who do some bad things, and I turn that money into gold, and to your frustration I do it all without breaking any laws. Why? Because Western governments built the machine, and they wring their hands and talk about how immoral it is, but all the while they keep oiling that machine and they go to great lengths to protect it from anyone who might break it."

"This isn't about what you do, it's about one man who . . ."

"*Senator Robert Colfax*, a disgrace to his office. I'll never hand him over, but I'll tell you this—the money trail you're so desperate to follow ends in a US jurisdiction, and so do the money trails for a lot of other powerful people, but the government turns a blind eye. Screw up your tax return and the IRS will come down on you like a B-52 strike, but *nobody* wants to prosecute the likes of Robert Colfax, not really. If they did, you'd be where the money is, not four thousand miles away, drinking coffee in the grounds of my beautiful house."

She'd been lifting her cup to her mouth, but almost in response to his comments she put it back down on the saucer. "Well, I can see I'm not getting anywhere."

"It seems I'm the one giving the homilies this time. I'm sorry, I didn't mean to harangue you."

She shook her head, dismissing it. "Don't be. It showed me one thing: that maybe you're principled after all, even if your principles are completely upside down." She sipped at the coffee now. "And for what it's worth, I can see the pointlessness of pursuing you over this—I know you'll never give him up—but I don't call the shots. And if you don't help, I can guarantee that my superiors will do everything within their power, *everything*, to pursue you over the Goldstein case."

"It isn't a case. There's nothing to pursue."

"Oh, come on, Mr. Emerson, you're smart enough to know that makes no difference." Catherine Parker stared at him, frustrated, almost pleading. In the end, she shook her head and sounded regretful when she spoke again. "They'll throw everything at you until you give them what they want. They won't give up. So, if you can think of any way to surrender Colfax without compromising your own position, any way at all, I'd give it some very serious consideration."

"I have, and I can't."

"Then I guess we're done."

"I guess we are."

Once again, Catherine Parker looked as if she wanted to say something else, but she remained silent and they both drank their coffee. And Max supposed that was how it was—what other kind of conversation could there ever be, between a federal agent and the owner of Emerson Holdings?

Chapter Twenty-Three

Max had planned to drive back to Vevey on Sunday afternoon, but while he was having breakfast he got a visit from the triumvirate of Francesco, Lorenzo, and Marco.

Lorenzo got straight to the point, saying, "Boss, Francesco told me, and I can understand why you don't like your family seeing you with bodyguards and armored limousines . . ."

"But?"

"But it's like Francesco said, the funeral's in the public domain, and you're a very rich man. It would be strange for you to go alone."

"Okay, what did you have in mind?"

Marco said, "We thought we'd keep it low-key. I'll drive you—that way it's just like I'm a chauffeur."

Max nodded his assent and that was how they set off that afternoon, with him sitting in the back of the limousine reading various articles on his tablet, like a regular businessman.

Not that he took much of it in. He spent a good part of the journey wondering how the others would react to him turning up like this. Maybe they'd just think Marco and the black limousine were what Max considered appropriate for a funeral.

Marco had obviously been thinking about it too, because as they got close to Vevey he said, "Is there anything I need to know, boss? Any way I need to be around your family?"

"No, as long as you don't kill any of them." Marco laughed, but at the same time Max realized he no longer cared too much about what his family thought. He didn't want to upset them, and he'd prefer it if they could come to terms with what he did for a living, but it was pointless trying to hide the reality of his life—or most of it, at least. "Truth is, Marco, they know what I do, and they probably imagine I'm surrounded by bodyguards the whole time, so it's no big deal."

"I look forward to meeting them. You know, I liked your parents a lot—they were good people."

They *had* been good people, and alone among his family had come to the house on Maggiore for a couple of extended visits. In a strange way, those were almost the only times he'd ever really appreciated the house for what it was, for its beauty and potential.

"Well, just to forewarn you, the others aren't quite like my parents."

Both the hire car and the jeep were parked out front when they got there, but the house seemed quiet. Thérèse came out into the hall and threw her arms up in the air before hugging Max. He introduced Marco, and she seemed immediately smitten.

She said, "He can stay in our guest room. We'll look after him. And it's better to keep the other rooms free for family, you know."

"Are we expecting family?"

Thérèse made a show of regret, saying, "Your sister is hopeful, but . . . it's such a long way."

"Where's everyone now?"

"They went for a walk with the little ones, and they're still out. Except Felix. He's playing the piano." Max looked along the hallway—the house was completely still. It was a shame in a way, because Max hadn't heard anyone play the old piano in a long time. "No, not in the music room. He's using a special piano he brought with him. He's in the drawing room."

"Okay, I'll pop in and see him once I've taken my bag up. You can take care of Marco."

Thérèse smiled. "Are you hungry?"

"He's always hungry," said Max, pointing at Marco.

Marco nodded and said, "The boss speaks the truth."

"Good. We'll feed you." Thérèse looked back at Max with a curious smile, perhaps finding it strange to hear their little boy being described as the boss. "I'll make something for you too, Max. Come into the kitchen when you're ready."

He nodded and took his bag up to his room. He hung up his black suit before heading back down to the drawing room. Felix was sitting on one of the sofas, wearing headphones and leaning over a keyboard on the coffee table in front of him. Next to him on the sofa was an open folder full of manuscript paper.

Max stayed in the doorway for a moment or two watching him. The boy played some notes, the keys producing no sound beyond his headphones, then wrote something on the top sheet of paper before going back to the keyboard, repeating the process. He was composing, and he'd told Max he did that but it was still a surprise to see him, looking every inch the artist rather than just some kid with a hobby.

Felix glanced toward the door and jumped up with a smile, pulling the headphones free. "Uncle Max, hello!" He looked on the verge of coming over to hug him, but changed his mind and held back. Even so, Max was baffled that his nephew seemed to like him so much.

He walked into the room and said, "Good to see you, Felix. I didn't mean to disturb you."

"Not at all. Please." Max came over and sat on the sofa opposite and Felix sat again too. Felix pointed at the keyboard. "It's better I do it like this, so I don't make too much noise."

"It's a shame," said Max. "I think it'd be nice to have music in this house again. Your dad played a little, I think."

Felix pulled a face, making clear what he thought of his dad's musical ability.

"My mom played, and so did Lottie."

"Oma was very good. Aunt Charlotte is . . . quite good. But the piano in the music room, I think it needs maintenance, and some tuning."

Max nodded, thinking he should have that done, then wondering what the point was. He imagined the piano and everything else being sold off by Henry, or cleared out by the new owners, then imagined Madame Bouchet and Thérèse packing up their possessions and heading up the drive one last time.

He couldn't allow it, and knew instantly what the solution would be. He even wondered now if he'd known from the start that he would buy the place himself. It was an extravagant thing to do for the sake of Madame Bouchet and Thérèse, but he couldn't stand the thought of them losing what they'd always known, and it would probably be a good investment anyway. He'd email Francesco about it while the thought was still fresh.

"It's a shame you've never been to my house, Felix. I have a beautiful 1920s Steinway, rosewood, and that never gets played, though I've had the guy come in twice a year to maintain it."

Felix smiled, intrigued and confused. "But you don't play?" Max shook his head. "So why did you buy a piano?"

"Oh, it came with the house. It's in the ballroom, which is pretty big, but to get it out would still take some doing. I think it's probably been there since the '20s."

Either that or Oblomov had bought it and had it installed at great expense—just one more part of the Russian former owner's culture Max was passing off as his own.

"Your house has a ballroom?"

"Yeah, it's a big house. But you can't think that's so odd—your mom's family are aristocrats."

Felix laughed. "But they don't have ballrooms. They all live in apartments. Once, when I was small, we saw a castle and Mama told me it was once my great-grandfather's, but no more."

Max wondered if that was the old boy who'd done time for fraud, but he couldn't remember the details of what Alexandra had told him.

"You know, my dad once told me that trying to keep family money from one generation to another is like trying to hold water in your hands—it all slips through your fingers in the end. Much better to instill in your children a passion. That's why it's good, what you're doing. Keep making your music."

Felix looked a little embarrassed by the mention of his music, and Max could easily believe that, being a teenager, he wished his life were like someone else's, maybe even like Max's.

"Do you have a passion, Uncle Max?"

In the distance, Max heard the front door open and a chorus of voices, including those of the two girls he'd only ever seen as babies.

"Not really. Only making money, but I'm really good at it."

Felix laughed, but then they heard footsteps and Henry was speaking even as he came through the drawing room door.

"Felix, do we have visit—?" He saw Max and stopped short. "Oh. Max. Hello. So I guess the black limousine is yours?"

"Yes, it is. My bodyguard's in the kitchen with Thérèse."

Even as Max said it, he realized he'd meant to describe Marco as his driver, and Henry pounced on the word.

"Your *bodyguard*?"

"My bodyguard." It was obvious Henry wanted some sort of explanation, and maybe after everything that had happened, it was better to be candid. "You know how it is: very wealthy people sometimes have the threat of kidnap, that kind of thing. This is one of those times."

"Someone's threatening to kidnap you?"

"No." Max laughed. "My security team's very cautious at the best of times. They don't like me driving alone. And a bereavement, a funeral—they're things that are in the public domain, so . . ."

Far from looking reassured, Henry looked gravely concerned, and then Max saw how his attempt at openness had misfired.

"So the same people could easily kidnap your nephew or nieces, all the better to extract a ransom from you."

"No."

"Why not? That's how kidnapping works, isn't it?"

Max could still hear the voices of the others out in the hall. He looked across and saw that Felix was following the conversation closely, his fascination with his uncle apparently undimmed.

Max stood and said, "Let's have a word in Dad's study."

He didn't give his brother chance to object, pushing past him and heading across to the study. A moment later, Henry came in behind him and closed the door.

"Henry, my team really are just being over-cautious. No one's trying to kidnap me. I don't think kidnap has even been that big a thing for quite a while now. Sure, it still happens, and not just in Italy, but . . ."

"There have been cases in Germany recently."

"True. And look, you should take natural precautions. Forget having me as an uncle, even your own wealth could make Felix a potential target." Henry looked skeptical. "Henry, the sale of this place alone would make you wealthy, but on top of everything you already have and the rest of the money from the estate . . . You can't wrap him in cotton wool, but it makes sense to think about security."

That obviously struck a chord, because rather than another combative response, Henry nodded to himself, giving the impression it was something he'd already been thinking about.

"I suppose we've been living in denial slightly, about just how comfortable we are. But we know so many wealthy people in Vienna—it gives one a feeling of normality." He looked up then, remembering they were talking about something far from the normality of middle-class Vienna. "I don't want details, but I need to know, Max—is there anything going on in your life right now that we should be concerned about?"

"Why do you ask?"

"For one thing, because you have a bodyguard. Felix likes you, so does . . . I just want to know."

If Max was ever going to have a relationship with his brother or the wider family, and he realized now that he did want that, then he knew it would be better to be honest with Henry as far as he could be. At least, there was nothing to be gained in the long term by concealing the truth.

"A few years ago, I invested a tranche of money, some of which was a fee a US senator had received for setting up some deals. I don't know the details, but I'll admit, I knew he wanted to keep it beyond reach of the authorities."

"So you laundered it?"

"No. I deal in laundered money—that doesn't make me a money launderer."

"You've got to be kidding me."

"Henry, I have news for you, we're all dealing in laundered money—I'm just closer to the source than you are." He thought of Colfax with his oily demeanor and the sound of his sexual laughter. "And yes, in this particular case, I was even closer than I'd have liked, but I still stayed the right side of the law, you have to believe that."

"So why are you telling me about it?"

"Because the FBI is trying to put pressure on me to hand over evidence against the Senator, something I can't do, because—well, I just can't."

Henry shook his head, almost like a nervous tic, locked in some internal dialogue. Finally he said, "Don't you see, that you reap as you sow? You got involved in this world and never stopped to think that you might get dragged in further than you wanted to be."

"You of all people should know life's never that simple. Would I rather this hadn't happened? Yes. But it's one of those things, and I'm lucky. I have a lot of people who can make sure nothing comes of it."

"The FBI has its own way of deciding what comes of a situation."

He sounded like Francesco, and Max found himself wondering if the two of them would get on.

"So put it this way: if it turns bad—if any of it ever turns bad—I'll put so much distance between me and the rest of you, you'll never know I was your brother."

Momentarily, Max remembered what Henry had said in the morgue in Morzine, "Now there are just the two of us," but he chased the thought away.

For a few seconds it seemed Henry wouldn't respond at all, but eventually he said, "I just can't accept it. I'm sorry, Max. I want to, but I can't."

He turned and walked out. Max looked around the study and eventually he smiled, because Henry had walked out, had balked yet again at accepting Max's world, but he'd at least said he was sorry about not accepting it—and that in itself felt like an improvement on where they'd been little more than a week earlier.

Chapter Twenty-Four

Max didn't see his nieces. Lottie took them up to change them after the long afternoon walk, then bathed them and put them to bed. He didn't even see his sister.

A little before dinner, Marco was waiting for him as he came down the stairs, and said, "Boss, do you mind if I eat with Thérèse and Madame Bouchet?"

"I expect I'll be safe during dinner."

"I'm not so sure about that—most people are killed by someone they know." Marco smiled. "I just thought that, the first night, it's more relaxing for you if it's just family."

"I appreciate that, and sure, eat wherever you're most comfortable."

"Thanks, boss."

The cellar door opened and Henry and Felix emerged carrying bottles of wine.

"Henry, this is Marco, joint head of security for Emerson."

"Hello. I'd shake your hand, but as you can see . . ."

"Hello, Signor Emerson, pleased to meet you, and I'm sorry for your loss."

"Thank you."

"And this is Felix, my nephew."

"Ciao, Felix."

"Hello."

Marco nodded and said, "You know where I am, boss."

He walked off back to the kitchen, and Max turned to Henry. "Is there anything I can do?"

"I don't think so. I meant to bring the wine up earlier, but we can decant it. Alexandra's in the drawing room if you want to say hello."

Max found her in there, poring over what looked like a hefty legal document. Sitting on the sofa, engrossed, she looked so much like Felix—it was as if nothing of the Emersons had found its way into the boy's genetic makeup. Even her smile was similar when she looked up and saw him there.

"Max. Good to see you. I was helping Charlotte with the children."

He went over and kissed her on the cheek. "Did it make you broody?"

"Goodness, no. They're delightful girls, but I wouldn't want to be going through that again. And Felix is so special."

"He is—really special." Max had no right to say anything else, not when he hardly knew the kid, and yet he felt the need to fight his corner all the same. "But I guess he's at that age where he'd probably just like to be normal too. Don't you think?"

Alexandra's smile fell away, and he was ready to apologize for being insensitive, but she nodded sadly in agreement. "I do worry about that. I do. He doesn't make friends very easily. He's so focused, and in some ways so adult."

Max had an alarming moment of revelation, wondering if Felix looked up to him because he seemed confident and easygoing and fun, when in truth Max had become the kind of person Felix wished he wasn't—no real friends, too focused. And yet Max had been the opposite of that at his age.

"What were you like as a teenager, Alex?"

"A rebel!" She chuckled. "I was so unruly. But, I still managed to get my education."

Max would have liked to have known her then. "Maybe I could take Felix to Ibiza next summer—hit the clubs, the beach scene."

"That's a terrible idea!" Alexandra raised an eyebrow. "Do *you* go to Ibiza?"

"No. I was kidding."

She shook her head with a smile.

Then Max said, "I'm sure he'll be okay. What's normal anyway?"

"Exactly. But he likes you. It's strange—I think you know Henry has said some harsh things about you these last three years, but it only seems to make Felix more fascinated."

That was the alternative, of course, that Felix liked him only because he'd been told not to like him.

"So maybe he's a normal teenager after all."

"Maybe." Alexandra slipped her document into a briefcase beside her and said, "Do you think we can go in to dinner? I'm so hungry after all that fresh air."

"We can try."

She stood and they walked through to the dining room where they found Felix decanting wine under Henry's guidance. Nicolas came in from the kitchen then, carrying two bottles of champagne, and a moment later Lottie came in with the glasses on a tray.

"Hello, Max. Sorry I haven't seen you yet." She walked over and managed to kiss him on the cheek while holding the tray to one side. "Can't wait for you to see the girls again, but right now, I'm ready for a drink."

"Me too."

The champagne was poured and they gravitated to their places and the meal progressed. Thérèse and Madame Bouchet both seemed in high spirits, and he could imagine Marco charming and entertaining them, even though they were both old enough to be his mother.

Once they were all eating, Lottie said, "Oh, Max, I forgot to tell you. Stef will be arriving tomorrow. She's flying in from London—that's where she's living at the moment."

"She's flying from London just for the funeral?"

"Well, she did come here quite a lot when you were a couple, and you know, she was so fond of Maman and Papa. I think she'll be going to Zurich for the rest of the week. She's staying in the Hotel du Lac."

"How do you even know all this?"

"She messaged me on Facebook."

"You're friends on Facebook? Hold on, you're *on Facebook*?"

"Of course! I'm not friends with Stef on there, but she messaged me. It was nice to hear from her. I always liked Stef." Lottie turned to Nicolas. "She was Max's girlfriend at university."

Nicolas nodded, looking uncertain as to what his response should be.

Max said, "She could have stayed here instead of paying for a hotel."

"I did think about offering, but then, we wanted to keep the rooms free in case of family . . ."

Henry looked askance and said, "None of them are coming, are they?"

"No, not as it happens. I'm sure they'd have liked to, but . . ." She looked disappointed, but shrugged and turned to Max again. "I also thought she might find it a bit awkward staying here, after all these years."

He nodded, but at the same time wondered why Stef was coming at all. She'd liked his parents, but she'd probably spent no more than a few months in their presence across the two and a half years of their relationship, and that had been more than a decade ago.

Whatever the reason, he couldn't deny being curious about seeing Stef again—a low-level anticipation that had been lurking in the background since Lottie had first mentioned that she'd be at the funeral. Idly, he even wondered if that was the real reason she was coming, because she was curious too, wanting to see him again.

Max was brought back to the present by Nicolas saying, "Oh, it's outside my area, but I asked a friend to keep a close watch on the investigation into the crash. I can't promise anything, but if there should be any developments, we might hear quicker than we would through the usual channels."

Henry looked at him with an expression that was hard to fathom—perhaps discomfort at the turn the conversation had taken, perhaps irritation. "It's kind of you to do it, Nicolas, although I'm sure if there were anything significant we'd have heard by now."

"Yes, perhaps, and I believe there is no sign of the truck. I also heard that the cyclist later said he wasn't sure it was a recovery truck—that it might have been a courier, like a FedEx."

Alexandra said, "How on earth could he confuse the two?"

"Exactly. This is why they think the cyclist might not be so reliable."

"But the car was still hit from behind, no matter how unreliable the witness." They all looked at Max and he felt a terrible sense of déjà vu, but he couldn't stop himself. "I told you last week, they were murdered."

Henry said, "You also said you'd find out who did it."

"And I will. In fact, I already think I'm quite close, though I'm not ready to share with the group just yet."

Nicolas looked at Henry, perhaps waiting for another response from him, but when none came he said, "Max, from a professional point of view, I have to say that you really should share anything you have with the police, and in fact, you should really just allow the police to do their job."

Henry looked up the table at Max with a faint smile, acknowledging that he understood how unlikely it was for Max to go to the police at all, let alone share his information with them. But it was a smile still tinged with bitterness and regret, that they should have someone in the family who operated like that.

"I think what Uncle Max is doing is very noble." Felix looked instantly alarmed, perhaps surprised, that he'd spoken aloud. "I mean . . . Well . . ."

Alexandra smiled at him and said, "It's okay. You can say what you think."

"I just think, if someone killed Oma and Opa, then those people should be found. They should be punished."

Henry nodded, but with the look of someone who thought they were discussing the day's news, not the death of close relatives. "It's natural to feel that way, Felix, and yes, I think you're right that what Max is doing is noble." He glanced at Max, then back at his son. "But surely that's why we have a legal system. It may not always be perfect, and the penalties handed out may never be enough to satisfy the victims of crime, but is that not how a civilized society works?"

Max was conscious of Alexandra looking at him, and he met her gaze and exchanged a sorry smile, a postscript to their conversation about Felix's lack of normality. It was hard to imagine how the boy could ever be normal when his father engaged with him at this level.

"I know you're right, Papa, but it's still the way I feel."

Max said, "You know what, screw civilized society. I think everyone around the table now knows that Mom was in the CIA."

It was immediately clear from Felix's expression that he alone hadn't known.

"She served her country, at great personal cost, and she was enjoying a happy retirement. So you can take your laws and you can shove them, because I'm going to find the people who did it, and I'm going to make them pay."

From the little he'd learned about his mom these last weeks, it was the least she'd have expected of him. If he was her son, he would show some of the grit and courage she'd apparently shown in her professional life, and avenge their deaths.

Nicolas shook his head. "Max, I can't be hearing this."

"Then don't hear it. You all cast me out for three years, but if I see this through and you cast me out forever, it'll be a price worth paying."

To his surprise, Henry said, "No one is being cast out." He smiled at his son before looking back at Max. "I have grave misgivings about the way you earn a living, and I make no apologies for my stance three years ago, but we're all family, and we have an obligation to Maman and Papa to pull together, to be a family, as much as we're able."

Lottie said eagerly, "Henry's right, we need to stick together."

Max nodded and raised his glass by way of response, and they all drank. Felix looked moved and relieved, and Max felt for him, because as much as he too hoped they could put their differences aside, he suspected it would be a struggle once the people who united them were in the ground.

Chapter Twenty-Five

The next morning, Max finally met the twins, Alice and Clara—one mousy, the other dark, both cute in a way that resembled neither parent. He thought they might be shy around him, but in the spirit of three-year-olds, they actually paid him no attention at all.

By contrast, they immediately gravitated toward Marco, pulling him by the hand, clambering over him when he sat, jabbering away to him. And in turn, Marco fussed over them and pulled faces and made coins appear magically from behind their ears.

Halfway through the morning, Lottie and Nicolas took the girls out. Henry and Alexandra were out on and off too, arranging things for the next day. Madame Bouchet was dealing with the caterers. Felix spent the morning in his room, composing.

Max called in on him at one point, but the boy had his back to the door, headphones on, a repeat of the process he'd seen the day before. Felix was so absorbed he had no idea anyone else was in the room, so Max left him, once again feeling a slight pang of envy—even if he was a bit of a freak right now, at least he had purpose.

From his own room, Max looked out and saw Marco walking about the lawn, talking on his phone, his face betraying the seriousness of the call. Then Max got a message on his own phone and looked at it.

It was from Klaus, containing an address in Vienna—no phone number, but a name, Fritz Harrer, which seemed to offer up the promise of a door into a world he hadn't even known about until a week earlier. Fritz Harrer had been in the Austrian Army Intelligence Office in the '70s and '80s. More than that, he'd handled the case that led to the treason trial, and according to Klaus's contact, he'd be happy to see Max any time he was in Vienna.

Max sent a message back to Klaus. "Can we trust him?"

He'd meant Harrer, but Klaus obviously thought he meant his contact, because the answer came back a few minutes later. "Absolutely. He's a reliable source—only reason I don't like to use him is he's my cousin."

Max nodded to himself, happy that he wasn't the only one who had family issues, but before he could reply, another message came through from Klaus. "And according to him, Harrer wouldn't have agreed to meet without checking you out first. He's meeting with you because of whose son you are."

There it was again, the suggestion that Max's mom had been the kind of person in her career to demand respect and loyalty. And with every such revelation, the woman he'd known seemed to become vaguer, slipping more and more out of focus.

He thanked Klaus, then headed downstairs, through the drawing room and out into the gardens. It was the first time Max had been outside today, and although the sky was clear again, there was a hollowness in the air that immediately made him nostalgic, memories that lay just beyond reach.

Marco finished his call just after Max came out, and walked toward him. "You wanted me, boss?"

"Yeah. Problems?"

"Kind of. The police took Domenico in for questioning about Goldstein's disappearance. I'm not sure why they didn't take Lorenzo too. Anyway, they were okay about it, and Francesco had him out within an hour. They even told Domenico they don't think Goldstein is really missing, that they're just following protocol."

"But?"

"They told him they'd been put under pressure to look into it."

"By the FBI?"

Marco shook his head. "Sure, I guess they're behind it. But the request came from Interpol."

"Okay."

"I'm sorry, boss."

Max nodded. It was a big organization and Nicolas was just one small cog in the machine, but it still raised the question of whether he'd ever been asked about Max's business, if he'd ever supplied information. He wouldn't have had much to share, but the thought of him having that intent was disappointing in a way Max couldn't quite define.

"Nicolas probably doesn't know anything about it. But the FBI undoubtedly knows I've got a brother-in-law at Interpol—I could imagine Catherine Parker doing this to rattle me."

"You're right, boss, and we've got everything covered. *And* we didn't kill Goldstein."

"Lucky for us. Okay. I just had a message from Klaus, information I asked for, so I'll be going to Vienna for a few days, straight from here, maybe on Thursday."

"You want us to drive or fly?"

"I'll take the train." Marco looked ready to object. "Relax, Marco. The funeral's public domain, but Vienna isn't. I'll take the train, you drive home, and you can send the plane up for me when I'm finished."

Marco nodded, but said, "If you don't mind me asking, boss, is it something to do with the death of your parents?" Max raised his eyebrows. "The German told me something like this might come up, and that you might go alone. So I brought a gun, and a shoulder holster, just in case—I'd be happier if you took it with you."

"I seriously don't think I'll be in any danger, but okay, I'll take it if it makes you feel better."

"Good. I hope you don't think I acted out of turn, boss. We were just—"

"Being cautious. That's what I pay you for. And entertaining my nieces." They started to walk back to the drawing room. "Tonight, I might want to go down into town, maybe after dinner. I can drive myself if you want."

"I can drive you, boss. Your old girlfriend?"

"Who told you?"

"Madame Bouchet. They liked her, thought you made a good couple, and they wish you hadn't broken up."

Max shook his head. If he'd been as invested in the relationship as everyone else had, maybe they'd still be together.

He shouldn't have suggested going after dinner, because he couldn't concentrate during the meal. He kept looking at Nicolas, trying to read that sleepy and nonchalant expression of his, wondering whether he had more interest in Max's business activities than he'd ever suggested.

Then, as the meal went on, his mind started darting forward constantly, thinking of the imminent meeting with Stef, a nervous energy pulsing through him—thoughts that wouldn't quite settle. At any other time, he was sure the others would have noticed, but with the funeral the next day they all seemed preoccupied, all except perhaps Felix.

As they prepared to move through into the drawing room afterwards, Max said, "I won't join you this evening. I don't want the funeral to be the first time I see Stef after all these years, so I thought I'd go down and catch up, break the ice."

Lottie smiled and brushed his cheek with her hand, a sympathetic gesture that made him want to tell her she'd misunderstood, that Stef didn't mean anything to him anymore. But he just smiled back and went through into the kitchen to find Marco.

Chapter Twenty-Six

When they parked up at the hotel, Marco said, "I'll wait in the car, but I'll be here."

"Thanks."

Max went to the reception and asked for Stef, waiting while the concierge called her room. The phone seemed to ring for a long time and he began to think she might be out or having dinner, or that she might not be here alone. Eventually there was an answer, though, and the concierge spoke to her in German and then put the phone down.

"She'll be here shortly."

"Thank you."

"You're welcome. You were here last week, for dinner."

Max was impressed, saying, "That's a great memory for faces."

She smiled. "Not really. You're Max Emerson." He looked at her name badge—Sara. She was pretty, with green eyes, but not familiar. "You won't remember me, but you were at school with my brother, Pierre Bonneton."

"Pierre? I remember you now—but you were a little girl!" She laughed. "I remember we'd be up at your house at Jongny, and you and your friend were always on the trampoline, always laughing at us boys. It used to drive Pierre crazy." Sara laughed again, her eyes full of life. "How is Pierre?"

"He's well. He owns an extreme sports business near Interlaken. You know he was always into that kind of thing."

"Sure."

"And you?"

"Oh, I'm in finance. I own an investment company."

"Wow." She was being polite—Max was under no illusion about how exciting most people found finance. "And do you still live in Switzerland?"

"No. Lake Maggiore, but on the Italian side."

"So you should really get in touch with Pierre. He's on Facebook— you should message him."

"I'll do that." For a moment, Max imagined being part of that other world, in which people messaged old school friends and caught up over a few drinks, but he knew it would never happen, that he'd traveled too far. The phone started to ring on her desk. "I'll let you get that, but good to see you, Sara."

"You too."

She answered the phone and Max turned just as the elevator doors opened at the other end of the lobby and Stef stepped out. He'd traveled too far, from most of them at least—but not from her. He raised his hand and walked toward her, and he was thinking that twelve years seemed like a long time but perhaps it wasn't because she hadn't changed at all.

She was dressed casually, wearing jeans and a striped top, and he was glad he'd seen her first like that and not in the formal black of a funeral. She was mousy, he supposed, a girl-next-door type with a faint band of freckles across her nose and cheeks; not glamorous, not striking.

When he'd first shown an interest in Stef, a friend had asked him why, dismissing her as nothing special, and Max should have been angry but had been amused instead because he could see it and his friend could not. In Max's eyes, she'd been the most beautiful girl he'd ever met, and he was reminded of that feeling all over again now.

As she reached him, she smiled and put her arms around him, hugging him, and again, she still felt so familiar that he had to remind himself that this was just a hug, that it signified nothing more—it was a reminder of intimacy past, not an intimacy in itself.

She stepped back a little then and he said, "It's good to see you, Stef. You haven't changed at all."

"Nor have you."

"Really? I feel older."

She gestured through to the bar and they walked in together and sat down.

"You could have stayed at the house, you know."

"I'm not sure that would have been such a good idea. But I was so sorry to hear about your parents' accident." The barman came over and Stef looked at Max and said, "Since living in London, I've developed a taste for an occasional single malt."

"I could handle a Talisker."

The barman looked at Stef. "Two Taliskers?" She nodded and he left.

"So what do you do in London?"

"I'm a literary agent—translation rights. I started in Zurich and moved to London five years ago."

"That sounds good. I don't get around to doing much reading nowadays, but . . ."

"Only financial pages and company reports?" She was teasing, but he nodded, acknowledging she had a point. "Lottie told me you're very successful with your company. I'm pleased for you."

Stef's phone started to ring. She took it out, looked at it, and turned it off. And for the first time, he noticed the ring.

"You're married?"

She looked down at her hand, as if to remind herself. "Two years."

She offered no additional details, no name, no occupation or nationality, no tale of how they'd met, and Max didn't ask and didn't want to know.

"Children?"

"No."

There seemed to be some amount of qualification within that one small word, the way she sounded doubtful saying it, and Max wondered if they'd been trying or if one of them didn't want children. He was curious this time, but resisted the urge to ask.

The barman came over and placed the two drinks on the table. Max waited for him to leave again, then picked up his glass.

"To old times?"

"Why not." Stef raised her glass and they drank. "I have thought about you. Often."

"Me too."

She smiled. "I doubt that! I'm sure you've been living a grand life. Although Lottie did tell me you're single."

"Wow, I'm beginning to think Lottie should have come and had a drink with you." Max put his glass back on the table. "Actually, I thought about you just the other night. I live on a lakeshore . . ."

"I know—Maggiore. Lottie—"

"Told you. Of course she did. I was out late and there was a party along the shore. It just reminded me of that night at your parents' place when there was a party nearby. You remember, we thought about crashing it?"

"Is that how you remember it?"

"Isn't that how it was?"

"Not quite, I don't think. We heard the party, and we joked about crashing it, but I was just joking and I could see you weren't. You really wanted to crash it, and I couldn't understand why. We had the place to ourselves that weekend, and we'd had such a lovely evening. I couldn't understand why you'd want to crash a party with people we didn't know.

But I think now it's the way you were. You always wanted something more than you had, always wanted something new."

Max was sure she was wrong, but there was a niggling doubt in his memory of that night now, and so he accepted her version and said only, "It's the human condition, I guess."

"It's the condition of some humans—that's not the same thing." Stef smiled, drawing a line under it, and finished her drink in one gulp. "Let's get out of here and go for a walk along the lake."

"Sure. It's chilly, though—you'll need a sweater."

"I'll go get one."

She stood and left the bar. Max looked down at his whisky and wondered how wise this was. It had taken him a long time to fall out of love with her. He could still remember waking up one morning—in Casper, Wyoming, of all places—and realizing that for the first time he had not thought of her upon waking. That had been three or four years after, and even now, nearly ten years on, he knew it wouldn't take much.

He finished his drink, put some notes on the table and walked out through the back door of the hotel. He waved to Marco, who got out of the car as Max descended the steps.

"Ready, boss?"

"No, we're taking a walk along the lake. Just wanted to let you know."

"Good. I got you covered, boss."

Max nodded and walked back in, reaching the lobby at the same time as Stef came back out of the elevator, wearing a red sweater now.

She smiled and they walked out together, down through the garden to the lakeside. There were plenty of people walking about under the lights, wrapped against the chill.

Almost instantly she linked her arm into his and they walked in silence for a while before she said, "I'm not with my husband anymore."

Max looked at her, confused.

"It wasn't a big wedding. It was . . . crazy. I met him almost right away in London. Three years later . . . I guess things hadn't been going that well for a little while, and on a whim we got married, maybe thinking it would help. But it didn't."

"I'm sorry."

Someone laughed somewhere behind them and she glanced back, but then said, "Oh my God. You'll think I'm crazy, but a big guy in a suit, he followed us out of the hotel, and I think he's still following us."

"Black suit, short dark hair?"

"That's him."

"It's Marco. He's my security."

Stef stopped walking, pulled herself free and looked at him, but couldn't resist another backward glance before saying, "Security? You have a bodyguard?"

So Lottie hadn't told her everything, after all.

"I have a security team."

"Why? I know people who own financial firms, hedge funds—I don't know anyone else who has bodyguards."

"Trust me, if anyone owns a company as big as Emerson, they will have bodyguards, even if you don't see them." That wasn't entirely true, but this was hardly the time to explain that Emerson handled money for unsavory people in any number of different countries. "It just goes with the territory, like being a politician or, I don't know . . ."

"A celebrity?"

Stef was teasing again, which pleased him, and he smiled in response. "As you can see, I'm besieged by fans wherever I go."

She linked her arm back into his and they started walking again.

"It just seems weird. And I mean, I knew you were successful, but I never thought of it like that."

"It's normal for me now. I don't really think about it."

They walked on for a few paces before she said, "Do you keep in touch with anyone from university?"

"I don't, as it happens. Most of our friends were your friends, and you must remember you issued an ultimatum." Max felt her arm tensing slightly. "Truth is, I wasn't good at keeping in touch anyway."

"It was wrong of me to do that. I just didn't want to be meeting you all the time."

"I'm not sure why—it was you who broke up with me. Without much of an explanation, as I recall."

She shook her head. "Let's not talk about it. It's such a beautiful evening. And I've missed this place."

"Yeah." He left the word hanging for a moment before adding, "I have to be straight with you, Stef. I know you always liked my mom and dad, and if you lived in Montreux or Lausanne, I could understand you coming to the funeral, but . . ."

Max thought she might object, but she didn't, and after a few seconds she said, "I did like them, a lot, and when I heard the news it made me think of how kind they were. You know, they kept sending me Christmas cards for years after we broke up."

"Really?" He hadn't known that, but thinking about it, it was just about the only revelation of the last few weeks that didn't surprise him.

"Hearing the news, it made me think about times here, our time together, and yes, if I'm truthful, a part of coming was curiosity, to see you again." She looked over her shoulder, conscious now of Marco's presence. "You probably think it's stupid. I just thought, maybe if I saw you again, in a strange way it might help me understand what went wrong with Sam."

"Sam's your husband?" She nodded. "I'm not sure how seeing me again would help."

"Nor am I, except . . . I think I liked him at first because he reminded me of you."

Max felt an odd warmth course through him, and he wanted to tell her that his one significant relationship of the last decade had been founded and had foundered on the same hopeless ground. It made him feel sorry for Viola all over again, because she'd deserved more.

"I'm flattered, of course, but as much as I hate to remind you again, you broke up with me, so it doesn't make the most sense."

Stef stopped walking and turned, looking out at the lake, light-strewn in the dark. "I know it doesn't. I'm thirty-four, I've just come out of a five-year relationship that didn't work, and I'm sad and I don't know what's next, so I'm thinking about the past. Is that really so stupid?"

Max shook his head, and reached up and put his hand on her cheek, the warmth of her skin sending a jolt of adrenaline through him.

She smiled sadly at him, and he wanted to kiss her, could feel his blood stirring, but then she frowned and the moment was lost as she said, "Doesn't it bother you that you're being watched?"

At first, he didn't know what she was talking about, but then he understood. He let his hand fall away. "He's not watching me. He's watching the world around me. I guess I'm used to it."

"I guess so. Look, I'm sorry. Ignore the things I said. I'm just feeling nostalgic being back here. And it's been nice to see you again, Max—thank you for coming down tonight."

He couldn't quite understand how the shift had taken place. A moment ago, it had seemed they were on the verge of something, a rekindling, and it had felt to him that the attraction was still there, still mutual. Yet now there was a businesslike edge to her tone, somehow making clear that the night was over.

"Sure, you must be tired. Let's go back."

They started walking back to the hotel but she didn't link her arm in his now and she looked at the people walking ahead of them and sounded cheated as she said, "Oh, he's gone."

"No, he hasn't." Max couldn't see him either, but he knew Marco would be there, probably somewhere in the shadows beyond the trees that lined the promenade.

Sure enough, as they reached the steps up to the hotel garden, Marco emerged again, and Stef looked at him and smiled.

"Hello."

"Good evening, Signorina."

Max and Stef walked up the steps and through the garden and the lobby, and Max stopped then and said, "I'll see you tomorrow, then."

"Of course. And thank you again for coming." She kissed him on the cheek but it was perfunctory, with no hint of what had seemed momentarily possible out there on the lakeside.

Max wasn't even sure what he'd hoped for anyway. He'd spent a lot of the last twelve years wondering what it would be like to see her again, and now it had happened and it had seemed too easy and too normal and too strange all at once. He watched her stepping into the elevator and she turned and looked back at him, raising her hand in a wave before the doors closed.

"Ready, boss?"

He turned to Marco and nodded. Then he looked across at the concierge's desk, but it was empty, the past falling away from him on all fronts.

Chapter Twenty-Seven

Max sat in the front as they drove back out of town and up the hill. At first they drove in silence, but finally Marco spoke.

"You liked her a lot, didn't you, boss?"

"Was it that obvious?"

"And now?"

"I'm not sure. Yeah, I still find her attractive. You probably don't think she's that beautiful, but for me there's something about her. The moment I first met her . . ."

"You're wrong, boss, she *is* beautiful. Any man who says different isn't a real man." Max laughed, remembering his friend at university who'd been so dismissive of Stef's charms. Marco clearly thought Max was laughing at him, but he ran with it. "I speak as an Italian—it's in our blood to know these things."

They both laughed now, but then Max said, "Well, I'm glad you could see it. She meant a lot to me, and I never really understood how we didn't end up together."

Marco repeated his earlier question. "And now?"

"And now I'm not so sure. She's married, but separated. And I think it's maybe partly why she came here, but I'm not sure. You know, you can't go back."

"Very true words." He waited a beat. "Does she know about your business?"

Max understood what he was getting at, the reality that Max's life had changed a great deal in the years since they'd been a couple. Even if there was still some spark there, for all they'd had in common, it would never be a matter of picking up where they'd left off. Perhaps it didn't show, but they were desperately different people now.

"She knows I'm in finance. If you mean, does she know I look after the Mafia's money and the FBI wants to indict me for kidnap and murder, then no, she doesn't." Max looked across at him. "Why? You think I should have told her?"

Marco laughed again, shaking his head, his eyes fixed on the road ahead.

When they got back to the house, Marco said, "Will you be needing me again tonight?"

"No, thanks, Marco. Good night."

"Good night, boss."

Max walked through the hall. It was just eleven but the house was quiet. Then he noticed there was still a light on in the drawing room and he went in and found Henry sitting there, a drink in his hand, looking reflective, perhaps even sad.

He looked up at Max and smiled a little. "Join me for a drink?"

Max nodded and poured himself a whisky, then went over and sat opposite his brother. He thought Henry might ask how his evening had been, but it seemed he'd waited up for a reason and he got straight to it.

"I've been meaning to ask you since dinner last night, but there's never really been the opportunity." He meant they'd never been alone together. "You said you were getting close to finding out about Maman and Papa, the accident."

"So. The time has come, said the Walrus, to talk of many things . . ." But it was immediately clear Henry didn't get the reference, and Max wanted to ask if they'd never read that to him as a child, but held back because he didn't want to offer up yet another reminder that the two of them had not shared the same childhood. "Mom was involved in a case that exposed two Austrian intelligence officers who'd been handing over information to the East Germans. Their identities were kept secret, but the Austrian guy who worked with Mom on the case has agreed to speak to me. I'll be heading to Vienna later this week."

Henry looked ready to speak, but no words came and he seemed to be struggling to formulate a response.

"Don't worry, you don't have to see me. You won't even know I've been there."

"It isn't that. I meant what I said at dinner. You'd be welcome to stay with us, of course."

He didn't sound certain about that, and Max still wasn't convinced that the thaw would last in its present form. Quite simply, Henry disapproved of the way Max lived, disapproved of it at an essential moral level.

"Thanks, but it'll be easier if I stay in a hotel, and I really won't be hanging around."

"Then we can at least meet."

"Sure," said Max, resisting the urge to point out that it was only a few days away, and that they were meeting right now.

"So you think it's connected to the letters?"

"It would seem likely, don't you think?"

"Circumstantially, perhaps. But it's a human failing that we draw patterns where none exist. I'm not a criminal lawyer, but isn't that the defense attorney's job, to unpick those patterns, to expose the difference between the circumstantial and the absolute?"

"I have no idea what you're talking about."

Henry smiled. "Maman received threatening letters from Vienna, and then she's killed in an accident when her car is driven off the road. Your mind makes a pattern, linking the two together, but there's no proof that the two are linked. You hear of a case that she worked on in Vienna, so your mind makes another pattern, but again, it might not be a real pattern, only one in your own mind. Why did you say that you knew it wasn't me? Do you remember, you said you didn't know me well enough to know if I would send the letters . . ."

"But you're not stupid enough to send them from Vienna."

"Exactly! So unpick the pattern. If you planned to kill a woman for revenge, you don't want to be caught—so why would you send threatening letters for several weeks beforehand, and why would you send them from your home city?"

"Well, now that you put it like that." Max sipped at his drink and Henry followed suit.

"There may be something in it, and maybe you'll discover something in Vienna, but it seems too neat for my liking."

He was right, of course, and Max saw now what he should have seen all along: that the trip to Vienna was unlikely to yield answers. It had all fallen together too easily. And maybe it was curiosity as much as anything else that was driving him forward—yes, he wanted to find out who'd been responsible for their deaths, but he was also eager for even the briefest glimpse into his mom's secret world.

Henry almost seemed to be thinking similar thoughts, because he said now, "I've written a small eulogy for tomorrow, but in the light of what we've learned this last week, I'm not sure that I'm all that qualified. I really don't know how well I knew either of them."

"I suppose that's normal—parents and children only ever know one part of each other's lives."

Henry nodded blankly, as if he hadn't really heard. "The ambassador's coming from Bern. She'll give a small speech, too."

"That's good, that they're showing respect."

"And at least it means you won't be the only one with a security detail."

Max laughed, because that was about as close as Henry ever got to cracking a joke, and he felt sorry for him this evening. He was the eldest, had adopted the mantle now of head of the family, and yet he looked lost and forlorn—a sadness far beyond the loss they'd all suffered, a sadness that was his alone.

Chapter Twenty-Eight

The morning of the funeral saw a change in the weather, the clear skies of the previous days giving way to low gray clouds that clung to the hillsides like mist. Madame Bouchet was convinced there would be rain and seemed pleased by that, believing it appropriate weather for a funeral.

They set off just before eleven. Madame Bouchet and Thérèse went in Thérèse's car because they wanted to get back as quickly as possible, to make sure the caterers weren't causing problems. So Max was alone in his car with Marco driving, at the back of their small procession to the church.

It was only as they got there that Max understood for the first time just how popular and respected his parents had been. He looked at the mass of parked cars, and the people still making their way inside, hardly recognizing most of them.

Marco got out and opened the door for him, and as Max stepped out he said, "It's a beautiful place, boss."

Max nodded and pointed over the roofs of the houses. "Usually you can see the lake there and the mountains, but not with this mist."

"It's still beautiful." Marco looked up at the trees from which leaves were gently falling here and there.

The coffins were removed from the two waiting hearses, the first time Max had seen them, and as they were taken into the church he tagged on at the back of the family group. It was only as he got to the doors of the church itself that he realized two of the people he'd presumed undertakers were actually part of the ambassador's security detail.

He looked out for Stef as he walked up the aisle but couldn't see her in the sea of funereal black. The coffins were placed at the front and the family filled the first pew. Lottie's girls were being loud and jolly, pointing things out that seemed new or interesting to them, and flutters of relieved laughter came in response to their exclamations.

Max stepped into the second row, which had also been left empty. Henry turned, saw him there, and said, "We can make room."

Max wasn't sure how, because, between the seven of them, they were more than filling the pew.

Nicolas turned now, frowning. "Max, please take my place. You should all be together."

Nicolas, always so easy, always so relaxed, and Max had no reason to think it wasn't genuine, but he couldn't shake the idea that his brother-in-law might be helping the FBI, that his commitment to the law would always win over his frayed ties to Max.

"I'm okay here. You stay with Lottie and the girls."

He could see Henry still looking concerned, the symbolism of it weighing more on his mind than it did on Max's—there was the Emerson family, sitting all together, and there was the youngest child, Max, sitting alone in a pew behind them.

Eventually Henry faced forward again and Max looked across the aisle where an elegant black lady was nodding as a man in a suit whispered into her ear. He guessed she was the ambassador, but it was only as the man finished talking that he glanced over his shoulder and smiled at Max—it was Brad Kempson.

Max nodded back but was distracted then as someone appeared beside him. He saw the black of her clothes, then looked up and saw it was Stef.

"Sorry I'm late. Of all times, there was a problem with my hire car. I had to get a taxi."

He stood and stepped out of the pew to let her in. Lottie turned, her eyes already full with tears, and smiled when she saw Stef and the two hugged awkwardly and Stef made some whispered comments about the girls. Henry didn't turn this time.

As she sat down she reached out and held Max's hand, and he wasn't sure if it was for her comfort or his, but he was grateful for it all the same.

"You can come in my car up to the house. Assuming you'd like to come."

"Of course, thank you. I mean, if I'm welcome."

"Why wouldn't you be?"

He looked past her as Marco appeared at the other end of the pew and sat. Stef turned too and he guessed she must have smiled at Marco because he nodded respectfully back at her.

The service was short, which pleased Max. He suspected it pleased a lot of the other mourners too, because a fair number of them didn't seem to know the responses—his mom had certainly been right to insist on not having a requiem. There was a choir, and Max even noticed that they alone seemed to sing the hymns. It was apparently an alien environment for a lot of the congregation.

Henry gave his eulogy, stoic, looking old and somber, the bare details of their lives, nothing of their essence. He could have been talking about almost any elderly couple in the world, and a stranger wouldn't have been left with much impression of who was being buried there that day.

Then Father Anselm said, "And now I'd like to invite the US Ambassador to Switzerland, Mrs. Arlene Bernard, to say a few words."

He nodded and the ambassador rose from her place and stepped up to the lectern. She looked over at Henry and Lottie, smiling sympathetically at them, and Max wondered if she thought they were the only children.

"I only met Jim Emerson on a few occasions, but he struck me always as a warm, witty and intelligent man, and a wonderful husband and father. But you'll forgive me today if I restrict my comments primarily to the commemoration of Patricia Emerson. For nearly two decades, she gave dedicated service to the US government, unheralded, and only modestly rewarded, although she did meet Jim in the course of her work, and I'm still enough of a romantic to think of a husband as some sort of reward." Polite, almost dutiful laughter rippled across the church, although Max heard someone whispering in French a few rows behind, asking what she'd said. "Much of the work Pat did is still classified, so it hardly needs saying that I can't go into details here. Some of you, of course, know a little about it anyway, and you'll know that she was a woman of tremendous courage, and integrity, and humility. She was fiercely intelligent but wore that intelligence lightly. She was brave and loyal and, above all, a true patriot. I never worked with her, and only came to know her in the last six years, but knowing what I know about the valuable work she did, work that saved countless lives, it gives me great pride to stand here today and honor an unsung American hero." She paused, the silence so weighted that Max was convinced she intended to continue, but after long seconds, she said only, "Thank you."

She stepped down and, somewhere behind, nervously, someone started to applaud, then someone else, and then across the church. Stef pulled her hand free and joined in, and Max noticed the girls and Lottie and Nicolas joining in too. Henry and his family refrained, and so did Max, and he smiled, thinking perhaps they weren't so different after all, that they'd both grown up, eleven years apart, believing a church was no place for applause.

At the end of the service, as a soloist sang the *Ave Maria* and the congregation followed the coffins into the adjoining cemetery, it became clear that the ambassador wouldn't be staying for the interment. She shook Henry's hand and offered him condolences, then kissed Lottie and did the same, remarking on how cute her little girls were.

She was about to walk on when Brad Kempson pointed and said, "And this is Max, Jim and Patricia's youngest son."

"Oh? Delighted to meet you, Max." It was obvious the ambassador was surprised, that her briefing hadn't been quite as thorough as it might have been. "You have your mother's eyes."

He didn't, but it was sweet of her, he thought.

"Thank you for coming, Mrs. Bernard. It means a lot."

"I wouldn't have missed it."

And with that she was swept off toward her waiting car, and the rest of them filed into the cemetery and toward the prepared plot. The rain did not come, disappointing Madame Bouchet, but nor did the misty low-level cloud look like clearing, so the burial took place as if cocooned in that autumnal air.

Stef stayed by Max's side, and he looked once and saw that there were tears tracked across her cheeks, and he knew that, whatever her complex reasons for coming here, she'd thought a lot of his parents. It made him sad too, imagining what might have been and how much a part of their world she'd have been these last twelve years if they hadn't broken up. But that had not been his choice.

As soon as the burial service was complete, Thérèse and Madame Bouchet set off quickly to get back and keep an eye on the caterers. The other mourners relaxed visibly now, and Henry and Lottie were eagerly telling them to come up to the house—the genial hosts.

Max still stood by the graveside, even as people drifted toward the gate, and Stef stood with him. She slipped her hand back into his and squeezed it, and he smiled in acknowledgment.

He looked down at the coffins, handfuls of earth scattered upon them, his own hand still gritty and dusty from that final act of farewell. And he was overwhelmed again by the mystery of their absence, by the fact that they were there and not there, that they'd always be present, but only ever in memory now, and incomplete memories at that.

He felt a tear break free, but almost immediately Stef reached up and brushed it away, her fingers cool and soft against his cheek. Anyone else might have offered him some comforting platitude, but she knew him well enough to say nothing.

When Max finally lifted his gaze again, they were almost alone, the last of the mourners making their way through the gate to the cars beyond. Marco stood a few feet away on the other side of the grave, solemn and contemplative. And a little way distant, Brad Kempson was standing, his intent clear.

Max took a deep breath and said, "Marco, would you take Stef to the car and wait for me there? I just have to speak to somebody."

"Sure thing, boss." He smiled at Stef. "Signorina?"

She let go of Max's hand, but glancing across at Kempson, said, "Who is he?"

"Just someone from the embassy."

She nodded, looking unconcerned, and then walked away with Marco.

Max headed across to Kempson and they shook hands.

"Good to see you again, Max. It was a nice service—simple, understated, the way they'd have wanted it." He looked toward the gate. "Sorry about Arlene not knowing who you were. That was my fault, really. Truth is, she didn't even really know your mom, and certainly doesn't know what she did, but she's a good woman."

"It was a nice eulogy. If anything, I felt a bit sorry for Dad—his achievements kind of got lost somewhere."

"Well, call me sentimental, but I think both of their achievements were there for all to see, sitting in the front two rows."

Max smiled. "That *is* pretty sentimental. But thank you."

"You're welcome. I won't be coming up to the house, but there are a few things I wanted to cover with you."

"Of course."

"I heard you had another visit from the FBI."

"I did. So you know about Saul Goldstein. It's their latest attempt to get me to roll over on Colfax, trying to pin the kidnap and murder of a freelance journalist on me."

Kempson frowned slightly and said, "Goldstein isn't a journalist, he's an activist hacker." Max recalled what Klaus had said about the apartment containing no tech, and it seemed to make sense now. At least it meant he hadn't been working for a competitor, or for the Bureau itself. "He's part of some outfit who call themselves the Hackstars. They're just a bunch of rich kids who smoked too much weed and dropped out of college. Goldstein carries himself like some kind of folk hero, but he's a trust-fund kid who still lives with his parents on the Upper East Side."

"Really? He doesn't live in Tribeca?"

"He probably couldn't find Tribeca on a map. Why, is that what he told you?"

Max nodded, thinking back to how he'd believed in this imagined life of Saul Goldstein, how he'd even envied it, and it had all been fake, probably even the girlfriend.

"Do you have any idea why they were trying to access our systems?"

"Well, you're the bad guys anyway, so causing you problems would be an added bonus to them, but the person they're really after is Senator Robert Colfax."

"I don't get it. I thought Colfax was a nobody. I'd never heard of him."

"Nor had the Hackstars, I expect. Between you and me, the FBI has been feeding them leads for a long time. And it wouldn't surprise me at all if it was the Hackstars who made the link between Colfax and your company."

So the two were linked after all, which was reassuring in some respects, and more so because Goldstein and his friends had made the link between Colfax and Emerson, but not to Hayden Manning.

"So Goldstein *was* FBI—he just didn't know it."

Kempson nodded, acknowledging the ingenuity of the FBI's methods.

"Do you know what happened to him?"

"If you didn't kill him, he's almost certainly still alive. He probably got spooked and disappeared himself. These are paranoid people. They think they're some elite corps locked in a deadly battle. Which they're not, of course. He'll show up sooner or later."

"Sooner would be better, for my benefit."

At first it looked like Kempson didn't understand, but then it hit home and he smiled. "I'm not infallible, but I think I can say with almost one hundred percent certainty that the FBI won't pursue you on this one—they'd face too big a risk of exposing their own activities. No, you may be on their radar for the future, and you might want to think about that, but Goldstein won't be a problem. I have a feeling even the Colfax situation will sort itself out in time." He pointed to the gate. Apart from the workers waiting to fill the grave, they were the only people left in the cemetery. "Shall we walk?"

Max nodded and they set off at a sedate pace.

Max said, "You wanted to talk about something else?"

"A couple of things. For one, the threatening letter you gave me— we've looked into it, but we've drawn a blank. It seems unlikely it's related to the accident."

Was Kempson trying to deceive him, persuade him to back off, or did he genuinely not know?

"So you don't think it's linked to the two Austrian intelligence officers who Mom helped expose?"

Kempson didn't respond at first, but there was grudging humor in his voice when he said, "I knew I'd made a mistake as soon as I said it—thirty-five years—I knew you'd do a search. And look, it's just possible the letters are connected with that case. It also seems the letter your parents left for you was written after the threats started arriving, so it gives the impression of a causal link where there is none. I'm not saying they weren't murdered, but I'm saying it's looking more unlikely, and it's highly unlikely it was linked to Vienna."

He was the second person to spell it out like that, and Kempson's argument sounded even more persuasive than Henry's.

"Okay, you may be right, but just so you know, I'm going to Vienna from here. Fritz Harrer's agreed to speak to me."

"Wow." Kempson walked another couple of paces. "In fact, wow on so many levels. Firstly, that Harrer agreed to speak to you. Second that you even found out about him. Third that you, er, you don't waste time."

"I have a good team working for me."

"So it seems."

"You don't object to me going?"

"I can't stop you, and it won't do any harm. I just don't think it'll do any good. I meant what I said, Max: if someone killed Patricia Emerson, we'll be relentless in tracking them down. I just think the letters are a false lead."

They were almost at the gate and Max could see Stef laughing at something Marco was telling her as they stood by the car.

"You said there were a *couple* more things you wanted to discuss."

"Yes." Kempson stopped walking and looked off into the gray middle distance for a moment. "Yes. In the light of our conversation, the other's less important. I'm certain we'll meet again, Max, so maybe we'll discuss it then."

"Okay. Well, thanks again for coming."

They shook hands, and Kempson said, "You know, before I met you, I assumed you were very much your father's son. And I didn't know

189

Patricia that well, but now that I've met you, you really do remind me of her. Take care, Max."

He walked away and Max turned and looked one last time toward the grave of his parents. In truth, he didn't feel he measured up to either of them—their lives had been so full and so rich, and his amounted to nothing more than the accumulation of wealth. His grave was out there somewhere too, he felt that keenly now, and it seemed to him there would be nothing of importance to write on his stone when the time came, no real eulogy to give, and most likely no one to give it.

Chapter Twenty-Nine

When he rejoined the other two he found them discussing London. But as Max approached, Marco broke off and opened the car door. Stef climbed in and Max got in after her.

"Thanks, Marco."

"You're welcome, boss. It was a beautiful service."

"I guess it was."

They set off and Stef said, "It'll be strange to see your house again." She smiled. "I remember the first time I visited, I was so shocked—I don't think I'd ever known anyone live in a house like that, like a mansion. You never acted rich back then, but when I saw the house, I knew you were."

"Your parents live in a house on Lake Zurich."

"But not a big house."

"I repeat, it's *on* Lake Zurich. By most definitions, your family's pretty rich too."

"I know. We've been very lucky. I was still amazed, the first time I saw your house." She looked out of the window briefly, then back to him. "Will it be sold?"

"Why, were you thinking of putting in an offer?"

She laughed. "I wish. I was just curious."

"You'd love my place on the lake."

Marco nodded and looked in the rearview and said, "It's true, Signorina, the most beautiful house—a little piece of heaven."

"There you go, and Marco does not lie."

She nodded. "Well, maybe I'll visit one day."

"I'd like that."

But he wasn't convinced that she really meant anything by it. She was a single woman on the wrong side of a short and miserable marriage, revisiting her past in the hope of finding a way forward. Even if she wanted to rekindle what they'd had, and he wasn't sure that was the case, she was almost certainly doing it for the wrong reasons.

They reached the house and immediately became separated, Max pulled away by people who remembered him as a boy and wanted to talk to him again now, all the usual polite but tedious questions about what he was up to, followed by Max's rehearsed and even more tedious answers.

As he circulated, constantly searching for a way out of the maze of people, constantly searching for Stef again, he saw Henry and Lottie, similarly locked into the same cycle of condolence and polite conversation. Within an hour, he felt he was suffocating and took the opportunity to step out through the French doors, and onto the lawn.

Max felt instantly revived by the cool air, by the clinging mistiness brushing his skin, by the peace. He'd done his duty, but he wouldn't go back in there, not until they'd all gone.

He'd been outside for ten minutes when he heard the door open. He turned with a feeling of dread, but saw Stef come out and close it again behind her.

"I thought I'd find you out here. I'll be leaving soon, so . . ."

He smiled. She relaxed him. Just seeing her made him feel better. "I've really missed you, you know."

Stef smiled sadly. "I've missed you. It's a shame you can't break up with someone and stay friends."

"That's not how I've missed you. Well, not the only way."

"No. Me neither." Some laughter reached them from the drawing room—an exaggerated and hearty guffaw that made both of them laugh too. But she looked back at the French doors, perhaps fearful of being disturbed. "Shall we walk?"

Max nodded, knowing what she meant, only that they should move out of sight.

They followed the lawns around a stand of shrubbery, and he said, "On that subject, and now that it's a long way distant, why *did* you break up with me?"

"It still bothers you?"

"Of course it does. Why would it not?"

She seemed to accept that and frowned, visibly putting her thoughts in order before speaking.

"I remember, a few months before we left university, it was your birthday and you found out how much you'd inherit from your grandfather's trust. I don't remember the exact amount, but it was a lot, half a million dollars or something like that."

He nodded. Five hundred and thirty-six thousand and fifty-two cents.

"You know, like you said earlier, we both had privileged upbringings, and most people in our position would have looked at that money as a great security blanket, something to fall back on as we launched our careers. But you became obsessed, about how you might turn that half a million into *serious money*. You were so driven, so focused on investment vehicles and hedge funds and all kinds of things I didn't even understand. And that was when I realized that there'd be no future for us, or at least not the future I'd imagined."

"You imagined a future for us?" She nodded, and he felt a pang of grief for that additional layer of loss.

"That was when I knew I had to break up with you. It took a while, because I was still in love with you, or wanted to be. We'd talked about traveling in South America that year, but you were already busy setting up your company—so busy I could barely get your attention. So I broke up with you, and I went to South America on my own."

He nodded at the familiarity of it all. He remembered so vividly the excitement of those early days, the burning passion, and he understood that she hadn't left him, that he'd found a new love and that it had consumed him. He even wondered now if it had consumed him from the inside, if his own remarkable success was the very thing that had left him feeling so empty for so much of the time, so rudderless. Wasn't that the real reason his thoughts returned to her so often, because she represented a time before he'd lost his substance and replaced it with cash?

"Thanks for telling me."

"I didn't want to hurt you, Max. And at the time, I think it hurt me more—I was so unhappy in South America. Whereas you just seemed to take it all in your stride."

"Because you're right—I was obsessed with Emerson Holdings." Max laughed, struck by the narcissism of it, given the company name. "If I'm honest, it was maybe a week or two later that it really hit me, and then I just got angry and threw myself into the company even harder. I think I had an idea that I'd prove you wrong, whereas I guess I was actually just proving you right."

Stef stared at him, a few moments slipping past, but finally she said, "You asked me if I'd imagined a future for us. I think part of the reason I came here was to see if I could still imagine one."

"And?"

"I don't know." She looked ready to say something else, to explain herself, but the effort defeated her and she shook her head. "I don't know." She looked at her watch. "I have to go."

"Do you need Marco to . . ."

"No, there's a taxi waiting." She stepped closer and kissed him, her lips lingering on his for just a moment, long enough that he closed his eyes and breathed deep, the years falling away. And it was a wrench when she pulled away again. "Don't come with me to the car. I just . . . Bye, Max."

He looked back at her, thinking there was something he was meant to say, but whatever it was, he couldn't find the words. She'd decided it wouldn't work again, he was certain of that, and at some deeply buried level he thought he knew it, too. They were both lonely in their own ways, both sad, but they were no longer the solution to each other's problems.

So he said nothing and watched her walk away, taking his past with him, it seemed. He kept looking across the lawn long after she'd disappeared, trying to pinpoint the hollowness he felt, and then a little while later the preternaturally pale figure of Felix appeared and waved to him.

"Hello, Uncle Max. Aunt Charlotte was wondering where you'd got to."

"Well, you found me." He looked around at the trees. "Did you ever see my tree house?"

Felix nodded, but said, "I was never allowed in it, though. Papa thought it was dangerous."

"It probably was. But I'm still here. Let's take a look."

Max didn't wait for a reply but walked through the trees, the route hardwired into his brain even after all these years. When he reached the tree, almost in full leaf, as it would be for a few weeks yet, he thought for a moment that it had gone. But it was still there, lodged up within the trunk: the wooden platform, the little house itself. Only the ladder had long gone, but Max had hardly ever used it anyway.

Felix stood next to him and looked up.

"I guess you're too old for this kind of thing now anyway."

"I think so." But there was a look of curiosity in the boy's eyes, a suggestion of the childhood he hadn't had.

"Why don't you get up, take a look for me, and see if it's still sound?"

Felix looked alarmed. "But there's no ladder, and Papa always said . . ."

"That was when you were a little kid. I'll give you a leg up to that branch there and you can pull yourself up."

"Really?"

"Of course." Max moved to the trunk and linked his hands into a stirrup, and with a mixture of uncertainty and excitement, Felix placed his foot in Max's hands. "Okay, ready? I'm lifting you."

He heaved Felix up, surprised by how light he was, and the boy laughed and then his weight disappeared as he pulled himself clear. Max looked up as Felix clambered gingerly around the branches and stepped onto the old platform.

"It feels very old. I think it could fall apart very easily."

But he looked down at Max, what probably seemed like a vertiginous drop, a reckless freedom, and he grinned, looking happier than Max even remembered him being as a child. Seeing that smile made Max happy too—a real happiness, one that he also realized had been missing from his own life for far too long.

Chapter Thirty

They saw Nicolas and Lottie off late the next morning, with Lottie in tears as they drove away, perhaps because she was leaving the house behind as much as anything else. What Henry had said was true: it had never been a proper childhood home to the two of them in the way it had been to Max, and yet Lottie's attachment was palpable.

Max and the others walked back to the drawing room and then Max said, "When are you leaving?"

"Not until Sunday. It transpires there are still lots of people to see, banks and that kind of thing, so I want to get as much done as I can in the next few days."

"Oh. So I won't see you in Vienna."

"You won't still be there?"

"No, I'm staying a couple of days at most."

It was apparent that Alexandra and Felix hadn't known about his visit, but Felix took them all by surprise when he said, "Can we visit Uncle Max's house in Italy?"

An awkward pause followed. Despite the easing of relations and the talk of no one being cast out, there was no doubting that Henry and Alexandra were still uncomfortable with the idea of becoming too much a part of Max's life.

Alexandra looked at her son and offered a slight smile. "Felix, Uncle Max hasn't even invited us, and of course we're all so busy."

"That's true, we're all busy, but you're always welcome if ever the opportunity arises, maybe in the spring when the weather's good but the crowds aren't so bad."

Henry said, "Yes, who knows, it might work out."

Max knew what that really meant, that there wasn't much chance of it happening any time soon, as though they feared Felix might be contaminated by so close an exposure to Max's unscrupulous world.

But Felix hadn't noticed the subtext and sounded hopeful as he said, "I'd like to play the Steinway, if I could."

"I'd like that."

They fell into a brief silence, all smiling to varying degrees, all probably interpreting the conversation in different ways. It was too soon for Henry, Max knew that, but they still seemed closer right now than they had been in three years, and maybe even in their whole lives.

◆ ◆ ◆

Max left early the next morning before they were up and about. Marco drove him to Lausanne for an early train to Zurich, sounding like a concerned parent as he checked repeatedly that Max was happy with the gun, that the shoulder holster was comfortable, that Max knew to get in touch if there were any problems.

It was a reminder of the many times he'd made this trip in the past. And as the second train skirted along the shores of Lake Zurich, he was hit with another wave of nostalgia and longing and regret—not just for the distant past but even for the day of the funeral, certain he'd handled things wrong with Stef, that a different outcome had yet been possible.

It was early evening when the train arrived in Vienna, but he was in no mood to delay, so he dropped his bag at the hotel and then had the same taxi drive him directly to the address Klaus had given him.

It was a respectable old apartment building in a quiet neighborhood and the taxi driver said, "You want me to wait again?"

"I'll find my own way back, thanks."

Max paid him and got out, approaching the door and pressing the buzzer for Harrer's apartment. Harrer answered a short while later, sounding cautious, almost as if he didn't want to admit to being in at all.

"Herr Harrer, it's Max Emerson. I'm Patricia Emerson's son. You might have known her as . . ."

The door buzzed open and he stepped forward quickly into the lobby and headed up the stairs. The door to the apartment had been left slightly ajar, and when he knocked, a voice called out, "Come in, Mr. Emerson."

Max stepped in, closed the door behind him, and walked through the apartment to a sitting room. He assumed Harrer was himself an old man, and from the outside of the building he'd expected something dated, locked in an earlier decade, but the place was minimalist in feel with white walls and modern prints.

Harrer was standing waiting for him: elderly but trim and fit-looking, with short gray hair and a lean weather-worn face. He was wearing chinos and a polo shirt, but also a pair of incongruous purple Nikes.

"You're lucky to catch me. I was just about to go out, but it can wait. Pleased to meet you, Mr. Emerson. Please . . ." He gestured toward an armchair and Max sat. "Can I get you a drink?"

"No, thank you, and thanks for agreeing to see me."

Harrer waved his hand and sat down. "I didn't keep in touch with your mother. You know how it is with work, and she left . . ." He smiled, seeing the connection. "To concentrate on you! But she was the most wonderful woman, completely fearless when it came to her own safety. I still consider it the best part of my career, working with her."

"You know she died recently?"

He nodded, but didn't look inclined to reply.

Harrer had already said what he thought of her, but Max was greedy for more, knowing how rare an opportunity it was to be with someone who'd known her professionally back then.

"What was she like?"

"She was your mother." Harrer smiled, only half-teasing. "You ask because you can't believe the woman you remember also belonged in this world. But I'm sure she was exactly the woman you remember. It's just that she was also tough and resourceful and determined. More than anything, I remember there was always a sense of calm, no matter how bad the situation—at her very core was this calm."

Yes, that was the woman Max remembered too.

"It's possible her death wasn't an accident. She received some letters from Vienna, threatening, or at least implying, a desire for revenge. I know the two men you exposed were released in 2006 but I don't have their names. I was wondering if you could help."

Harrer nodded again, but it was a few seconds before he spoke. "I think it's unlikely, personally, but I'll help in any way I can. Of course, you do understand their names were kept secret for a reason."

"I do, but I only want to talk to them, to find out what they know."

"I don't think you only want to talk to them at all." The old man smiled. "Did she have a good life, your mother? I remember she always talked so proudly of her Jim and of her children—the other children, I mean, the older ones."

"Yes, I think she did." With some shame, Max wondered if the only real worry in his mom's later years had been his own business activities.

"I'm pleased for her. I'm divorced myself, but it's worked well, and my children have been good to me." Harrer smiled, lost in some thought or other, and for a moment Max wondered if he'd forgotten what they were talking about. But then the smile fell away. "The men you ask about wouldn't be responsible for this, but maybe people working on their behalf. And if that's true, maybe they look for me too."

"I can't lie to you, Herr Harrer. I want to find the people who did this and I want them dead. From what I've heard, it's what my mom would have done for someone close—I feel I owe it to her, to both of them."

"Perhaps." Harrer nodded. "And I think it would be the right thing for you to know a little more." He paused, but seemed to have come to a decision. "Willi Lang and Joachim Bauer. It was a real betrayal. Both were colleagues, but Bauer was also my friend—it's such a blow to learn that you don't really know somebody at all. Lang died a year after he left prison: cancer of the pancreas. Bauer is in a private nursing home—I can give you the address. He's no older than me so it's sad for him to end up in such a place, but that's where you'll find him."

"Thank you."

"I've thought many times that I might visit him, but I can never bring myself to do it." Harrer looked ready to say something else, but hesitated and frowned a little. "Perhaps it's for the best."

"And you think he'll remember my mom? I mean, you think it's possible he could still hold a grudge all these years on?"

"You have to find the answer for yourself. But I'll tell you this, Joachim was charming, and may be still. Don't be deceived. This is a man who murdered two of his colleagues, and who came very close to murdering your mother."

"How?"

"That's too much detail, even after all these years. What I can say is that she took the most vicious beating from that man, but she still brought him in, and he spent longer in the hospital than she did."

Max found it hard to imagine his mom grappling and fighting with anyone, let alone a man, and hearing it filled him with a strange mixture of emotions—pride and sorrow, and a simple wonder that she could have been this other woman. Then the pieces fell together in his mind, the snippets he'd learned about her these last weeks.

"That was when she lost the baby."

Harrer looked pained. Max thought he might be about to deny or ignore it, but he seemed to have slipped back fully into his own past for a moment, bringing the raw memories back with him.

"It should have been me there that night, but I didn't know she was pregnant. *She* didn't even know, and it was very early, but the damage—afterwards, they thought she would never have more children. It's why it meant so very much to her when you came along. A gift from God, she said. And I never knew anyone who deserved it more."

Max smiled, because he couldn't speak, couldn't find words. It wasn't just his mother, but all of this, the torrent of information, the fullness of all these mysterious lives.

His mom and dad's world had centered around him as a child, perhaps because they saw him as that gift—a chance to be parents, to be a family, without all the additional fears and stresses her career had brought with it. It was natural, he supposed, for a child to be egotistical, to assume his parents' lives had always been like that, but it was shocking that the egotism was only falling away now, when it was all far too late.

Chapter Thirty-One

The nursing home was in a leafy suburb on the edge of Vienna, so the next morning Max hired a car and drove out to it. It was a nice place but with a scent about it that immediately made him want to escape. It made him grateful in a way, too, that of all the possible futures his parents had lost, this was also one of them.

He approached the reception desk and the plump, blonde woman sitting there smiled up at him.

"Hello. I'm sorry, I haven't arranged an appointment, but I'm here to see Joachim Bauer."

"It's not a problem—you don't need an appointment. Are you family?"

"Not quite. An old family friend."

"I'll just call someone. If you can sign in here, please."

He thought about using a fake name, but wasn't sure it would serve much purpose—he wasn't about to do anything wrong. So he signed in as the receptionist spoke to someone on the telephone.

The receptionist had ended the call and gone back to her computer by the time he finished. He moved into the middle of the lobby, where a tall, dark-haired nurse came out and smiled at him.

"You're here to visit Herr Bauer?"

"Yes. My name's Max Emerson."

"And you're a family friend?" Was there a suggestion of doubt in her voice, of suspicion?

"That's correct. Actually, he knew my mother. She spoke of him often, but she died recently and I thought, while I was in Vienna . . ."

"It's kind of you, and he always likes to see people—he has so few visitors—but you do know Herr Bauer is suffering from Alzheimer's?"

"I didn't." The disappointment must have been visible on his face, easy for the nurse to misinterpret because she could never have known how much Max had wanted to meet someone fierce and vengeful, someone with easy answers—someone he could hate.

She nodded sympathetically. "Please, this way."

They started walking, and Max said, "You said he has few visitors, but what about the family?"

He was guessing, but it earned a look of derision from the nurse. "The family? He has no family. The daughter and the grandchildren have been not one time. It's shameful. If it were not for Doctor Meineke, he'd have no visitors at all."

Max made a show of recognizing the name. "Doctor Meineke, that sounds familiar—I think he was one of my mom's friends too."

"Then you should visit him also, while you're here—he doesn't live so far away. You know, Doctor Meineke pays the fees for Herr Bauer."

"Then I'd definitely like to see him. I don't have an address, though, so I'll have to wait until I get back and look at my mom's address book. Maybe on my next visit."

The nurse smiled, and Max could see already that she'd help him. If he'd asked outright for the address she'd have refused, but he'd cast himself instead as someone who merely wanted to meet up with his mother's old friends, which in a way was true.

She opened a door into a sunny room, albeit with that same tainted antiseptic smell. A man was sitting in a chair, staring through the window onto a garden, although with no indication that he was actually seeing anything. He was wearing an alpine-knit jumper, his gray hair sparse and slightly unkempt, his eyes a dazzling pale blue.

Harrer had said Bauer was about the same age as him, but the man sitting in the chair looked dramatically older. He'd been handsome in his time but he looked decrepit now, parchment skin draped over a once striking bone structure.

Max guessed Harrer had known about the Alzheimer's, and maybe that was why he'd thought it would do Max good to see the reality. But Max wondered how Harrer himself would respond to the sight if he were ever able to bring himself to visit, and what it would do to his own memories and emotions.

Bauer made no response when the nurse spoke to him, but as she moved across the room he shouted something—more in frustration than anger, it seemed. She only smiled, but Max knew already that there was no reason for him to be here, that this man had certainly played no part in sending those letters or engineering an accident.

"I'm sorry, perhaps I should come back another time."

The nurse was about to reply, but Bauer turned sharply to look at him, smiling in surprise and delight. "Ah, American! Come, sit, sit. American, yes, come, sit."

The nurse pulled a chair over in front of Bauer and invited Max to sit in it, and even as he crossed the room Bauer held out a hand. Max took it in his and shook, the skin like waxed paper but the grip surprisingly strong.

"Yes, yes, please, sit."

"Thank you, Herr Bauer." He sat on the hard, upright chair facing him and the nurse moved to the side of the room. "My name is Max Emerson, Herr Bauer. My mother was Patricia Emerson."

Bauer laughed, once again looking delighted, an almost manic quality about him, suspended awkwardly between laughter and tears.

"She's tough! Really tough! Oh yes, Patricia—the American, the American." He nodded, thinking of something that seemed clear and present in his mind. "I didn't want to hurt her. It was difficult. Didn't want to hurt her. But she was . . . Oh yes, tough. Didn't want to hurt. Didn't want to."

Max was conscious of the nurse standing there, wondering if she might be changing her view about the kind of visitor he was.

"She understood that, Herr Bauer. It was just the job. She understood."

Bauer mocked a punch at his own face, laughing. "She's tough, tough. I was in the hospital. Oh yes, the hospital, it was . . ." He stopped, putting his finger to his lip, looking deep in thought. "It snowed. The snow was falling, and that was how—snow everywhere and the footprints were there: American footprints. It was how I knew, because the snow . . ." He gave a small laugh, so small it hardly escaped from his own private recollection. "The snow was falling. Yes. Yes." Another smaller laugh, little more than a fleeting hum, and his eyes lowered and closed.

He was asleep. And Max didn't know how he was meant to respond to this man. Before he'd even been born, Joachim Bauer had betrayed his country and beaten his mother into miscarrying, and she'd hurt him too, in some way that Harrer hadn't specified but enough to put him in the hospital.

But Bauer was a frail and elderly man, whose life had been one of prison and isolation, abandoned even by his own family. How could Max feel anything but pity for the man in front of him now? And, for all his thoughts of revenge, if his mom had been here with him, he was pretty sure she'd have felt the same way.

He looked at the nurse and she smiled and said quietly, "He was so happy to see you. It exhausts him, seeing people, but I've not seen him so happy in such a long time."

Max stood. "I'm glad." And he was surprised by the realization that he meant it.

"You'll visit again, I hope."

"Next time I'm in Vienna, if I can."

They left the room, the nurse closing the door gently behind them, and as they walked along the corridor she said, "It was jumbled, I know, but did any of it make sense to you? He talked about hurting your mother."

"I think he was confusing two things. I think their work together was quite dangerous. But when he was arrested, I remember my mom saying he was obsessed with the thought that he'd hurt everyone."

"Ah, I see." She'd bought the story, and Max guessed Bauer's ramblings could have been interpreted any number of ways. "So you know about his problems?"

"Yes, she did tell me about it." He thought of Bauer, falling away into a snow-filled sleep. "But it was a long time ago, and he paid a heavy price for it."

"I wish his own daughter would understand this." They'd reached the reception and she pointed at the desk. "Please, if you could sign out."

Max entered the departure time on the sheet, but when he looked up, the nurse was behind the desk, chatting to the receptionist as she wrote on a pad.

Casually, he said, "Well, thank you for your help."

"A moment, please."

Max stood, looking nonplussed, and then the nurse handed him a piece of paper. "Doctor Meineke's address and number. I'm sure he'd like to see you, if you have the time."

"Thank you, I'd like that. Bye."

He left and made for his car, glancing down at the address of Doctor Meineke, who paid all of Bauer's no doubt considerable fees. There was no question that Joachim Bauer had played no part in anything for some years, but somebody had mailed those letters, and Meineke seemed as likely as anyone.

Chapter Thirty-Two

Meineke's house was a little further out of the city, a substantial bunga-low that looked as though it had been built in the '50s or '60s, set in a large private plot, with shrubs and trees protecting it from the prying eyes of neighbors or people driving past on the quiet street.

Max parked on the drive, and could hear a small dog yapping even as he approached the door. He rang the bell, the dog cranking up a gear in response, becoming more manic, and then a woman's voice offered reassurance and opened the door.

Max guessed she was around sixty, with the look of someone who'd been something of a hippy in her youth but who'd settled into a quietly moneyed retirement.

"Frau Meineke?"

"Yes?"

"I'm here to see Doctor Meineke. I've just been to visit a mutual friend, Joachim Bauer."

A male voice called out from within the house and the woman looked apologetic, closing the door on Max as she called back. He heard her mention Bauer's name again, but the reply sounded impatient and unyielding.

She opened the door again and said, "I'm sorry, but my husband doesn't speak to journalists or to . . ."

"I'm not a journalist. Please, tell your husband that my name is Max Emerson, and I'm the son of Patricia Emerson."

It was obvious the name meant something to her. She stared at him, a mixture of fear and suppressed panic, and then, after a few seconds, a defeated voice called out, telling her to let him in.

"Please."

"Thank you." He stepped inside, and the dog yapped again but it was shut in another room. The house appeared up to date until she showed him into a study that was still lodged in the 1970s. It was cluttered too, the bookshelves spilling over and the walls lined with what appeared to be Asian and African artifacts—masks and tribal artworks.

It took Max a second to see the man standing on the other side of the room, wearing a loose-fitting shirt that looked African or Caribbean in origin, his gray hair in a ponytail, and small glasses on a round, pale face.

Frau Meineke closed the door as she left, and the man said, "I won't offer you anything, as I'm sure you can understand."

"Doctor Meineke?"

"Yes." Max glanced around the room again and Meineke gave a self-satisfied smile. "Not all doctors are medical, Herr Emerson. I'm a doctor of anthropology."

"I presumed as much. I was actually wondering what possible link could exist between you and Joachim Bauer."

"Then, please, take a seat." Meineke gestured to the other side of the room. There was a small sofa with a throw over it, once vividly patterned but faded now, and a high-backed reclining chair that also looked as though it had seen better days. Max sat on the sofa and Meineke took the chair, creating the impression of a conference between a tutor and student. As Meineke settled, he said, "I make no apologies to you or anyone else. I'm a member of the Communist Party and I'm fortunate enough to be in the position to help another member who's fallen on hard times, not least because of the treatment he received at the hands of his own country."

"What do you know about Patricia Emerson?"

"I don't know anything."

"Then why did you let me in?"

Meineke frowned and cleared his throat, stalling for time. "I know the name. That's not the same as knowing anything. Joachim talked about her, naturally."

"You know she's dead?"

Meineke looked startled, a response so reflexive that it couldn't have been faked, and Max's heart sank slightly in the light of that response.

"So you didn't know she was murdered, but the letters will lead back to you. The CIA sent them to Langley, so I'm sure it'll only be days before they make the link."

"What are you talking about? I don't know anything about letters and I don't know anything about the death of Patricia Emerson. And unless the CIA fabricates the evidence, something we all know they're capable of doing, there's nothing to link me to any of it."

Max knew he was lying, knew it instinctively. There had been a slight reaction to the mention of the letters, the smallest tell, but visible all the same. Meineke knew about it, and even if he hadn't been involved in the murder, he'd been a part of it.

Max could feel his anger building, and at the same time he became acutely conscious of the gun resting against his body. Joachim Bauer had been helpless, pitiable, but Meineke was far from either of those things, and Max was determined that one way or another he'd make him talk.

"Do you know who I am, Doctor Meineke?"

"You're her son, you announced it already." His tone was combative, an edge of contempt to it.

"But do you know who I am, what I do? Because I don't work for governments."

Meineke started to laugh, and maybe Max had overplayed the role of the bad guy, but he jumped up now, pulling the gun free and pressing the muzzle against Meineke's head. The chair tilted back at the same time, putting him in a prone position, looking in danger of tipping him right out onto the floor.

He squealed something in German, unintelligible, then said, "What are you doing? Please, you don't understand, I don't . . ."

"Tell me about the letters, or I'll pull the trigger and then I'll kill your wife."

"What! What are you saying? It wasn't even me! It wasn't me!" In his panicky repetition, Meineke reminded Max a little of Bauer's dementia-fueled rambling. "Please, I don't know what it's about. I just followed the instructions. I thought I was meant to send them."

"Why?" Max pressed the gun harder, and right now he hated this man so much he wished he could push the barrel right through his skull. Meineke had sent the letters, and even if he'd had nothing to do with his parents' murder, he'd sought to upset them, had added enough concern and worry to their final days that they'd been driven to write their own letter to Max.

"It was sent to me. I thought—I thought . . ." There was a moment of clarity and desperate hope in his face. "I can show—I can show what came."

"Then show me." Max stepped back, the muzzle leaving a welt on Meineke's forehead, but he kept the gun pointed at him. Meineke got up slowly, like a man who'd taken a beating, and Max noticed a small wet patch on his cargo pants where he'd briefly lost control of himself, and with his own anger falling away again he felt embarrassed and slightly ashamed that he'd put another human being in that position.

Meineke went to a drawer in his desk and retrieved a brown envelope. He held it out, his hand shaking visibly, and Max took it.

"This was sent to me. It contained the note you see there, and the letters, six letters. No, seven. I knew about the case, I knew . . ." He stopped, perhaps remembering Max's connection to this. "I thought it was from a comrade in Berlin—you see the postmark—and I should have known, because it made no sense. But I did it, for Joachim and Willi. I sent the first letter, and then two more, one each week, but I didn't understand what the end goal was, so I spoke to my comrade in Berlin and found it wasn't from them. So I stopped. Only then I opened the remaining letters, saw the note inside, always the same."

"You sent them without even knowing what was in them?"

"I thought it was from a comrade . . ."

Max looked at the envelope and used one hand to open it and look at the piece of paper inside, a brief printed note in German, telling him to send one a week. There were five other envelopes ready to send, so Meineke had been wrong—there had been eight in total. Two were addressed to Patricia Howard, the other three to Patricia Emerson. All had been neatly opened, and Max could imagine Meineke's mounting fear as he'd seen what he'd been sending. Apart from the German stamp and postmark on the main envelope, there was nothing to give away exactly who or where it had come from.

"I had no idea she was killed. I wouldn't have had anything to do with it. My whole life has been about peaceful means."

"You call sending threatening letters to an elderly woman peaceful?"

Meineke shook his head, in denial of the whole situation as much as in answer to the question.

And Max felt his own energy ebbing away—someone had set Meineke up, that seemed obvious to him now, and there was no clear way back from here to finding the killer. If there had even been a killer.

"You understand that if I took this to the authorities, you could be extradited to the US?"

Meineke looked at him but didn't reply.

"I don't want to do that. I don't think it would serve any purpose, but I need you to tell me if you have any idea at all who might have sent this letter and why."

Meineke shook his head. "If I knew I'd tell you, because it appears they wanted to blame me for their own actions, and I was stupid not to question it more. I just thought it was some small retribution." He fell silent.

Max put his gun back into its holster.

"My mom was doing her job. She didn't deserve any retribution."

Meineke didn't answer and Max walked past him and out of the house with the dog once more yapping from behind a closed door. He still had the envelope in his hand, and he knew it was no use to him, no more than the others had been, but he folded it and put it into his pocket.

He got in the car and drove away but quickly knew he'd have to stop again. He was trembling, a weakness in his muscles, as though his blood-sugar levels had plummeted. He persevered for a while, but pulled over then and turned off the engine, releasing his seatbelt.

His breathing was patchy too and he concentrated on slowing it down, getting it back to normal. It wasn't even the shock that he'd pulled a gun on someone, held it against a man's head, but that he knew how easily he could have pulled the trigger, how easily he could have let his anger and hatred get the better of him. It had been a moment of insanity and he knew now that he had to let this go.

As he became calm again, Max noticed a young couple standing at a tram stop a little way along the street. They looked like students and he guessed they could have just been friends, but their body language suggested otherwise—nothing overt but a subtle and understated intimacy.

He felt the familiar envy creeping in, wishing his life were more simple, wishing he could go back and appreciate the things he'd had, wishing he could appreciate the things he had now. But he caught himself in time and smiled, laughing at his own expense—he had been that young man once, and no life was ever as simple or enviable as it seemed from the outside. And with that thought, he started the car and drove on into the city.

Chapter Thirty-Three

Max dropped the car off and walked the short distance to the hotel, letting his thoughts clear. He wasn't sure what he'd really expected to get out of this trip. Both Henry and Brad Kempson had been right, and in retrospect it had been fanciful to think that he could follow a Vienna postmark and the truth would be laid out before him. Even if his parents had been killed because of something in his mom's past, it was beyond him to expose it, just as it was beyond him to find the part of them that he had not known.

He arranged the plane for the next day, ending the call as he walked into the hotel lobby and crossed to the elevators. But just as he pressed the button, someone called his name behind him. He turned and saw Brad Kempson standing there.

"I was waiting for you. Care for a drink?"

Max nodded, not surprised, and Kempson pointed toward the bar.

They sat down and Max ordered a gin and tonic, Kempson a gimlet on the rocks. Max took the folded letter out of his pocket and put it on the table.

"Meineke sent the letters, but someone else set him up to do it: Berlin postmark."

Kempson picked up the envelope and stared at it, his brow creasing. It was clear he knew who Meineke was, that he knew more about most of it than Max did.

"How weird. So either a coincidence—which happens more than you'd guess—or someone murdered your folks, but tried to point the finger at a group of washed-up old communists here in Austria."

"Which do you think it is?"

"Coincidence." There was no hesitation. "It just doesn't make sense. Someone gets run off the road, it's a hit and run. Add in the letters, you're flagging up that it's a murder. This . . ." He refolded the letter and put it in his own pocket. "This is probably the work of some other crackpot conspiracy geek like Goldstein. There are too many of them about, more than you could imagine, and they create one hell of a mess for the rest of us."

"It kind of makes their death seem worse in some way, you know, if it really was just a speeding truck driver."

"I know what you mean." They sat in silence for a while before Kempson spoke again. "I like the way you went after this, Max. The thing about my line of work, something your mom would have understood all too well, is you very rarely get neat conclusions, and you almost never get closure. It's a long game, often longer than any individual career."

"Yeah. And probably not helped by amateurs like me getting involved."

"It's funny you should mention that . . ." Kempson stopped because the waiter was approaching and he watched in silence as the drinks were placed, waiting for him to leave again. "The other day, I said there was something else I wanted to talk to you about. It might not come to very much, but at the very least it could keep the FBI off your back."

"Go on."

"It goes without saying that you've been on our radar for some considerable time. You deal with some very interesting people, people with whom we'd occasionally like to have channels of communication."

Max smiled, seeing where this was headed, and he was flattered too, because his dad had apparently once been recruited in a similar way and had met his future wife in the process. But that had been a different era. "Part of the way I run my business is that I hardly ever meet the end user. I deal with their lawyers. With the exception of a few of the Russians and a couple of people elsewhere, I don't have much direct contact."

For some reason, Max had imagined the contact they wanted was with Vicari, but that didn't seem to be the case, and Kempson looked unfazed.

"That wouldn't be a problem, not a problem at all. And I need to stress, this wouldn't be compromising your position in any way. If anything, it could enhance your reputation for being secure, because if you're assisting us we'd make sure that no other part of the administration caused you headaches. Incidentally, it's the Russians we're particularly interested in."

"I see." Max thought about some of his Russian clients, sensing a few of them would revel in the opening of this kind of channel, and maybe one in particular. "You understand I'd never give you information on any of these people. I wouldn't even give you a client list to work from."

"We wouldn't want you to. We don't want to utilize your information, we want to utilize your position of trust, to relay various proposals and exchanges of information, sometimes to make introductions. If I were to say, for example, that I might want to utilize your position of trust with Mikhail Leonov."

"Now there's a surprise."

But Max's interest was piqued, because he'd spent the last few days thinking that his life was empty and had come nowhere close to living up to the lives of his parents, yet this had the allure of offering some small element of the purpose they'd had themselves.

Even so he said, "What do I gain?"

"Nothing. You get the FBI to leave you alone, although I think you have them pretty well fenced in anyway, you get to help your country, you get to follow in the footsteps of your mom and dad, and in an unsung way I guess you get respectability. I'll admit, it doesn't add up to much, particularly to someone in your position, but that's what you'd get out of it."

"Okay."

"Okay what? You'll do it?"

Kempson sounded surprised, and Max wasn't sure why. Yes, he was attracted because it was his mom's world, but at a more hard-headed level he was doing it for all the reasons he'd refused to help the FBI, because this was good business, in many different ways.

"It's what my mom would have wanted me to do. So I'll do it, or I'll give it a go, see how it fits."

"Excellent." Kempson still seemed surprised, perhaps because of how intransigent Max had been with the FBI. "I don't want to rush you, but I know Leonov has a house on Maggiore, not far from yours."

"Yeah, but he's not there that often."

"Our information is that he'll be there in two weeks, staying for a month."

Max smiled. "You planned all this out."

"Of course. But I didn't know you'd say yes."

"Okay. He always gets in touch when he's coming. It's possible he's already told Francesco. So I'll invite him over, and if he's interested I'll sit you down in a room together."

"Sounds great, and I meant what I said, we'll respond in kind."

"I hope so. Give me a couple of days and then I'll let you have Francesco's details and you can sort things out with him."

"We already have his details, but thanks, and I'll wait for you to give the go-ahead." Kempson smiled and raised his glass. "Let's drink to it, then, and to your mom and dad."

They drank, but even now Max's thoughts found their way back to the letter with the Berlin postmark, trying to think of explanations and solutions. He needed to forget about it, because it was true what Kempson had said, that he was unlikely to find any closure there, even if he found answers.

Maybe the disappointment showed because as Kempson put his drink down he said, "I guess none of this has tied up as neatly as you'd have liked."

Max shook his head, admitting he had a point. "It's not just that. Something like this has a way of making you look back at your life, all the things you could've done differently, that kind of thing."

Kempson seemed to give it a lot of thought before speaking again.

"You know, Max, this world isn't perfect and sometimes you have to make the wrong decision, be ruthless when you'd prefer not to be, let things go when you really want to pursue them. Your mom understood that." Max assumed he was talking about the accident, but then Kempson said, "Maybe I'm barking up the wrong tree, but did your company have any involvement with something called the Greenwood development in Colorado seven or eight years back?"

Max felt a hollowness in his stomach and knew now that he'd been waiting seven years for someone to say those words.

"We have no investments in Colorado."

Kempson smiled, seeing the feint for what it was. "I knew it. The consensus is that Hayden Manning was killed by the Las Vegas Mafia, and maybe he was, but Greenwood doesn't seem like their kind of project to me. It does seem like Luciano Vicari's kind of project, and he has very close ties with the guys in Vegas, so . . . Of course, this is all just guesswork."

"How do you even know about any of this?"

"It's outside my remit to care, you're quite right. Hayden Manning was on our radar because he in turn had very close ties to a Mexican drug cartel. So, yeah, whatever your involvement, you can rest easy.

Manning was no tree-hugger, and the world's no worse off without him."

"It all sounds interesting, Brad, but I actually have no idea what you're talking about. I'm just a money man."

He smiled again. "If you were just a money man, we wouldn't be having this conversation."

Max smiled too, saying no more about it, and they both drank.

He wondered afterward why Kempson had raised the matter of Hayden Manning at all. It had felt like the granting of some sort of absolution, letting Max know that his ruthlessness hadn't robbed the world of a decent family man, that it had actually removed someone who worked with a Mexican drug cartel, someone just as crooked as Robert Colfax.

It was only much later that he saw the truth, that Kempson had probably intended to use his guesswork about Manning to put subtle pressure on Max to act as a middleman. That was why he'd been so surprised when Max had agreed readily, and why he'd then volunteered his theory about Colorado.

It gave some insight into just how ruthless the smiling and easygoing Brad Kempson really was. And, ironically, it left Max more confident than ever that the two of them would get along just fine.

Chapter Thirty-Four

The flight back was bumpy, particularly on the final descent into Milan. Max understood why when he stepped down from the plane with the sky clear but the wind billowing across the airport.

Marco and Roberto were there, standing next to the car, but there was another car waiting on the tarmac, and as Max approached, the door opened and Catherine Parker stepped out. Her hair immediately caught in the breeze, reminding him of that first day he'd seen her standing on the terrace, the day he'd also found out his parents were dead.

The two men greeted him and Roberto took his bag. Max paid no attention to Catherine Parker but she approached now.

"Mr. Emerson, I hope you don't mind me meeting you off the plane."

He turned and looked at her. She was undeniably attractive, and there was something about her he found intriguing, but he felt less well disposed to her than he had even on their previous meetings.

"Presumably it's important."

"Nothing we do is frivolous, Mr. Emerson. Why don't you ride with me and we'll talk on the drive to your house?"

Roberto was standing ready by the door of Max's car.

"Thanks, Roberto." He nodded his assent and Roberto opened the door, then Max turned back to Catherine Parker. "If you want to talk, you can ride with me. Your car can follow on."

He climbed in without waiting. Marco got in the front and a few moments later Catherine Parker got in and sat opposite Max.

As they pulled away, Max said, "What do you want?"

She looked surprised. "You seem to have lost your charm, Mr. Emerson."

"You had one of my men questioned by the police." She looked ready to object. "Please, Miss Parker, we both know it wasn't done at Interpol's bidding. The simple fact is, you have no evidence against me so you're trying to fabricate it. And if you think you might be detecting some hostility, you're absolutely right."

"We're not fabricating anything. Saul Goldstein is missing and . . ."

"Saul Goldstein disappeared, that doesn't mean he's missing, and I don't need to tell you that, because I suspect you know more about Goldstein than I do."

"What are you implying?" Max didn't answer, just stared back at her until eventually she smiled and said, "You're not the only one with sources, and I suspect mine are slightly more accurate than yours. Seven years ago you met with Luciano Vicari and Senator Robert Colfax on a yacht off the coast of Capri. In the months afterwards, Colfax arranged the deals for which he received the payments we're talking about. We'll keep searching, but even those two facts alone could be enough to get you indicted."

"I doubt it, even if they were facts, which they're not."

But although he didn't think it showed, she'd rattled him, because the first time they'd met she hadn't been sure if he'd ever met Vicari, and now she was reporting pretty accurately the one meeting they'd actually had. Max's brain reeled through the various possible sources, but he couldn't shake the idea that someone close might be handing over information.

She ignored him anyway and said, "I guess you felt like a real big-shot, meeting a top Mafia boss on his luxury yacht, being introduced to a leading US senator, getting to act like a power broker when you were, what, twenty-six?"

"Goading isn't your forte, Miss Parker, and besides, to taunt me you'd need to be talking about something that actually happened, and the meeting on the yacht sounds great, but it never took place. Now, is that all you have, or did you go to the trouble of meeting me off my plane after my parents' funeral for something more substantive?"

"You don't get it, do you, Mr. Emerson? This is how it will be from now on. All I'm trying to offer you is a way out. You think I'm an . . ." Her phone started to ring and as she reached for it she said, "I'm so sorry."

It reminded him of his own phone ringing during their first meeting. "Not a problem. If it's important, feel free to answer."

Catherine Parker looked at the screen and it was clear from her face that it *was* important. "I will, if you don't mind. Please excuse me." She answered and held the phone to her ear. "Sir, it's not exactly . . . Oh." She fell silent and seemed to listen for a long while before speaking again. "Okay, I understand. Thank you, Sir."

She ended the call, her face grim, even showing a trace of anger. Once she'd put the phone away, she looked at Max and shook her head slightly.

"Bad news?"

It took her a moment or two to answer. "Well, good for you. It seems you have friends in high places. The side of the investigation centering on you has been suspended."

Max noticed Marco turn slightly in surprise, and he was surprised himself, guessing that Brad Kempson was the person who'd pulled strings, and that he hadn't taken much time in doing it.

"Well, I'm sure you feel you've wasted your time, Miss Parker, but if it's any consolation, you'd have been wasting even more of it if you'd pursued this." She didn't respond. "Roberto, is Miss Parker's car behind us?"

"Yes, boss."

"Then could you pull over as soon as it's convenient."

"Of course, boss."

She offered the slightest nod of acknowledgment, and finally said, "You seem like a nice person, Mr. Emerson, and I mean that. Maybe that's why I find it so hard that you're happy to make money out of something so morally reprehensible. And it's true, governments have been complicit, but that will end, and life will become increasingly difficult for people like you."

"I doubt it. As the laws change, we'll change. If you put some of my clients out of business, we'll find new ones. I'm successful because I'm good at what I do, not because I'm a criminal."

"Maybe you're not a criminal, but you're not exactly Warren Buffett either."

He smiled. "Is that the best you have?"

"Looks that way. For now."

The car pulled to the side of the road and Marco got out and opened the door for her.

"Bye, Mr. Emerson."

"Take care, Miss Parker."

She got out and Marco closed the door again, and as Max sat there he supposed he should have been feeling triumphant. The FBI had been dealt with, and it seemed his willingness to help Brad Kempson had probably strengthened his position for the foreseeable future.

If only it hadn't been for the mention of the yacht. Somebody had told her about it, about Vicari and Colfax, and it was hard to feel triumphant when there was a real possibility that someone close might actually be working against him.

Chapter Thirty-Five

He was in his office when Klaus found him.

"You wanted to see me, boss?"

"Yes, come in, Klaus. Thanks for everything in Vienna, by the way."

"It was useful?"

"Very. Did Marco mention why I wanted to see you?"

"He said you thought there might have been a security breach."

Max nodded. "It could be nothing, but the FBI agent talked about something she shouldn't have known about. There are other places it could have come from, but . . ." Vicari wasn't one of them, and it was hard to believe even Colfax would have been stupid enough to talk about that meeting off Capri. "I was just thinking it might be cautious to, I don't know . . ."

Klaus nodded. Max had feared he might seem as though he doubted the loyalty of people who'd worked tirelessly for him, but if anything Klaus had the expression of someone who considered this completely normal. "Don't worry, boss, I'll look into the technical side, we'll do some sweeps, check everything out."

"Thanks. I'm sure it's nothing, but just to be safe."

"Can I be candid, boss?" Max nodded. "You're a good person to work for and you have a good team. I'd stake my life on the people here, but as Emerson gets bigger and more people come on board, it's a good idea to have a system of scrutiny in place, just for your own peace of mind. You know, maybe once a year you could get Crazy Mouse to do a search on all the people who work for you. Other connections too, relatives . . . Like, relatives who work for Interpol." Klaus looked apologetic at having brought it up. "I'm sure there's no connection, but unless you know for certain, you'll always have that doubt."

"You're right, I should do that. I know I can trust everyone here, but you're right."

Klaus nodded. "So I'll look into my side of things. But Crazy Mouse is something you need to do. And include my name in the list, boss—include everyone."

Max realized that Klaus wasn't talking about a plan of action for some hypothetical time in the future—it was something he thought should be done now.

"Okay, I'll get in touch with him. Thanks, Klaus."

"You're welcome, boss. I'll get back to you on my side of things, but you know where to find me."

He left and Max sat for a while staring at his computer screen. It was Saturday, so Rosalia wasn't in and the office was completely silent, a peacefulness that somehow seemed in contrast with what still felt like an act of disloyalty, of undue mistrust. But then Klaus hadn't seen it that way, merely as a standard procedure.

Eventually he opened a new email to Crazy Mouse and typed, "I want you to check out some names for me as a matter of urgency, looking for anything at all that I should be concerned about. Can you do it? Deal only with me."

Within minutes, the reply came back, "You pay the piper."

Max smiled to himself—this was why he usually had other people deal with him. But the smile fell away as he pulled up the two lists of employees and attached them to the response. Then he created another document and added six more names, together with the details he had for them.

Four of them were his own relatives, and they were there only because of Nicolas—he could hardly hold it against him if it turned out Nicolas had been helping the FBI, but he'd at least know not to trust him in future. The other two were more recent acquaintances, and he doubted even Crazy Mouse would dig up much on Catherine Parker and Brad Kempson, but he was intrigued to see the results all the same.

He sent it and then tried to put it out of his mind, going back to work, catching up on all the financial news he felt he'd missed. And it was only when Francesco came in a couple of hours later that Max shut down the computer.

They greeted each other, Max poured them both a drink, and they sat down as Francesco said, "How was the trip, and the funeral?"

"It all went well enough." Max felt guilty because, if he couldn't trust Francesco, he wasn't sure he could trust anyone. Nonetheless, he thought it better to wait until he'd heard back from Crazy Mouse before he shared too much about the potential working relationship with Kempson. "Actually, some things arose that could be interesting— a business opportunity of sorts—but it can wait until next week."

"I wonder, does this have something to do with the friends in high places who got the FBI to back off?" Max smiled. "Yes, of course Marco told me. It sounds intriguing, but it can wait until after the weekend. Likewise, there are things I need to update you with, Nevada and Mumbai, but it can all wait. Get settled back in first."

"And the Oblomov deal?"

"Nothing to discuss—I've put that in motion already." Max nodded. "Oh, and Rosalia left a note somewhere. Your lunch with the Buonarrotis is scheduled for Monday, unless you want to cancel."

Lunch with the Buonarrotis was exactly what Max felt like he needed, even if Matteo and Lucia did seem increasingly desperate for him to meet their daughter.

"After everything that's happened, I can think of worse things to do on Monday."

"I'm glad. It will do you good." Francesco looked at his drink, then back at Max. "By the way, the German took my cell phone off me. Any idea why?"

Max laughed, seeing that Klaus's approach to security was slightly more thorough than his own. And now that he was sitting with him, he also knew that Francesco could never be the leak: it was as the man himself had said—they were like family.

"Catherine Parker asked me about a meeting with Vicari and Colfax, a meeting off the coast of Capri seven years ago."

"Have you ever spoken about it?"

"No. You?'

Francesco nodded, looking distracted. "Just the other day. I spoke to Don Vicari himself, voicing my concerns about Senator Colfax, and he brought it up, the way you would mention a nice day spent together. So I think the German should maybe sweep my office too."

"I'm sure he'll do that anyway, but look, it could have been Colfax or, who knows, maybe Vicari's security isn't as good as he thinks it is. Either way, I'm pretty sure the FBI won't be troubling us again."

"I hope not." Francesco looked ready to say something else, but whatever it was, he let it go. He didn't seem completely relaxed and nor was Max. Too much had happened these last weeks, and above anything, Max just wanted to get back to his own stunted idea of normality.

Chapter Thirty-Six

The lunch at the Buonarrotis was a small affair for ten people, but Isabella wasn't one of them. With a mixture of embarrassment and feigned bemusement, her parents explained that Isabella had rushed off to Milan because a friend of hers was going through a boyfriend crisis. It left Max feeling he'd had another fortunate escape.

The meal was relaxed and informal, and reminded him somehow of the meals he'd had with his own family over the last two weeks, albeit without the simmering tensions that had been there to begin with. It made him wish for a more permanent rapprochement, although he didn't hold out much hope of that happening.

Paolo took him back across the lake afterwards, the mid-afternoon sun sparkling on the surface of the water and blurring the shoreline. He could just see Leonov's house and remembered that he needed to talk to Francesco about setting up a meeting for Brad Kempson.

But as they neared the jetty, Francesco and Klaus came walking down to meet them.

As Paolo tied off, Max stepped up onto the jetty and said, "What's wrong?"

Francesco looked sheepish. "I have a terrible confession to make."

Klaus shook his head with a smile. "Francesco, I told you, it could've happened to anybody." He looked at Max. "I found a very sophisticated piece of bugging software on Francesco's cell phone."

"Could it have been hackers?"

He was thinking of Goldstein and the Hackstars, but Klaus said, "I'd say it was government, so with the things we know, I guess the FBI has been listening in on Francesco." Francesco shook his head, disappointed in himself. "Everything else is clean, including the offices and cars."

Max took his own phone out and handed it to Klaus.

"You'd better check this too."

They started to walk back inside, and Max was relieved, because it offered an explanation for how the FBI had come up with the information about the yacht—Vicari had mentioned it to Francesco on the phone. No one was betraying him, and the trust he had in his team wasn't misplaced.

Francesco brightened up too, and said, "How was the lunch?"

"Good. But she wasn't there."

"Oh. Well, maybe it's for the best."

Max smiled, thinking Francesco was probably right, thinking a lot of things had turned out for the best in the last few days. And then he got back to his desk and as soon as he turned on his computer, the first thing he saw was an email sitting in his inbox from Crazy Mouse.

This was much quicker than he'd anticipated, so maybe it wasn't a report or maybe he hadn't found anything. Besides, he knew now where the leak had come from. And yet Max was nervous even about opening it, and when he did he felt his stomach sinking with the message inside.

"So, I found something. Actually, lots of things, but also something disturbing. You want the raw data or you want I make a report?"

Max stared at it, his hand tapping rhythmically on the desk, no response coming readily to him. He finally hit reply and his hands hovered over the keyboard. It was a simple decision, raw data or full report, and still he hesitated.

In the end, he wrote simply, "Don't send anything. I'll get back to you."

He stared at the screen, seeing nothing. Crazy Mouse had found something "disturbing," a very particular word to use. What could he mean by it? Just as Max had convinced himself again that he could trust his team without question, what did it mean to have found something disturbing?

He could find the answer right away by asking for the data, but he knew instantly that he wanted to hear this face to face, to be able to question it, challenge it. The hacker wouldn't like that, but if the fate of one of the people who worked for Emerson rested on this intelligence, Max had to give it every due diligence. He'd drive to Turin, and he'd drive there tonight.

He shut the computer off and as he walked through the outer office he said, "Rosalia, would you call the kitchen for me and let them know I won't be eating tonight. Maybe just a sandwich in my room around six."

She looked concerned. "Are you unwell?"

"No, it's not that. I had a pretty big lunch with the Buonarrotis."

She didn't look impressed, but shrugged and said, "I'll let them know."

"Thanks."

As he strolled into the hall Klaus intercepted him, holding out Max's cell phone.

"That was quick."

"Because there isn't much on it. Between you and me, boss, Francesco downloads apps, he opens links. His own curiosity gets the better of him. I've told him he must not do it anymore."

"I'm sure he'll pay no attention. Thanks, Klaus."

"Sure. Is everything okay, boss? You look kind of distracted."

He could tell Klaus. After all, it had been Klaus's idea to send the names to Crazy Mouse in the first place, so he was surely the one person he could trust unequivocally. And yet Max didn't want to tell him, because a part of him didn't want to acknowledge there might be a problem.

"I'm fine, Klaus. A heavy lunch, that's all, and the need for a siesta."

He left him and went up to his room, but instead of lying down, the first thing he did, without even thinking about why he was doing it, was to take his bag out of the closet and check that the gun was still inside it.

Chapter Thirty-Seven

It was just before seven when Max headed through the house to the garage. Before he got there, Domenico appeared and said, "Boss?"

The concern was evident. Was word getting around that he didn't seem himself?

"There's something I have to take care of, Domenico. But I'm okay."

Domenico shook his head, still not liking this at all, and Max could tell that at the very least he wanted to talk it over with Lorenzo or Marco. "I can drive you anywhere, boss, even if it's private. You know you can trust me."

"It's not that kind of private." Max laughed at the implication, not least because there was nothing in his life right now that required that kind of privacy. "But it's something I have to do alone. I'll probably be back before morning. If I'm delayed, I'll let you know."

"If you're sure, boss."

"I am."

Domenico appeared to accept there was no changing his mind and said, "Okay, take care."

"Thanks. I'll see you soon."

◆　◆　◆

It was just after nine by the time Max arrived in Turin and a fine, almost misty drizzle was falling on the city. The building was in the Centro Storico and he had to park the car a few streets away and walk. As grand as the building was, he saw a few young people heading into it, laden with books, and he guessed it was mainly students who lived there.

There was no elevator so he made his way up to the top floor, up wide stone steps, his ascent echoing through the center of the building, then found the apartment and pressed the buzzer. There was no reply, and for the first time he wondered why he hadn't thought to check, why he'd wanted to come here in person in the first place.

Yes, he wanted to see the evidence, or the presentation of the evidence for himself, but was that enough of an excuse on its own for driving out here? The reality was that he knew it was something damning, and he didn't just want to see something like that on a screen, cold and unyielding. Whatever it was, he wanted to be able to question it.

He could hear music coming from a nearby apartment, young voices laughing and talking. For all he knew, Crazy Mouse was in there with them, and if all else failed Max could always go and ask if they knew where he was.

He looked at the door again and was just about to press the buzzer for a second time when it opened. The man standing there facing him with a puzzled expression was old, although it was hard to tell how old—sixties, seventies—bald, bar for gray hair around the sides and a full gray beard.

Max looked at the number on the door, double-checking, and the man said, "Yes? Can I help you?"

"Er, I'm not sure. I think possibly I'm looking for your son, or . . . grandson?" Max had always imagined Crazy Mouse being in his twenties, maybe even early twenties, but with a sense of alarm he wondered now if he was much younger even than that. "I'm here to see Crazy Mouse."

"Crazy Mouse?" The man laughed, presumably at the name, but then looked curious. "Who are you?"

"My name's Max Emerson. Crazy Mouse does work for me."

The old guy did a double take and said, "Well! It shouldn't be a surprise, but I imagined you older."

"You're Crazy Mouse?"

"The young don't have all the tricks." He laughed again. "You shouldn't have come here. I don't like to see people, but for you, I'll make an exception. Come in, Mr. Emerson."

"Thanks." Max stepped into a hallway lined with bookshelves, and followed Crazy Mouse into what he guessed was meant to be the main living room but was set out like a large study.

Again, there were bookshelves, but also desks along the walls with computers on them, and another desk in the middle of the room with two more computers. Along the wall behind him was a long workbench covered with pieces of electrical equipment in various states of assembly.

"Please, sit down. Would you like water?"

"Thank you."

He left him and Max looked around and pulled a wheeled office chair free from one of the desks and sat. Crazy Mouse came back a few moments later and threw a bottle of water to him. Max caught it. It was chilled, and he was suddenly curious to see what the kitchen looked like.

"I'm sorry, I don't know your name."

"You do. At least, you know the only name you need."

Crazy Mouse walked over and sat behind the central desk, and Max scooted a little across the floor so that he could still see him beyond the computer screen.

"So, you didn't want me to email it to you because you don't think you can trust everyone?"

"No, it wasn't that, it was . . ." Crazy Mouse looked expectant. "If you've found something bad, I wanted to hear it in person. But I can trust them, I know that."

"No, you don't. You never know that. You can think it, feel it, but you can never know. Please, drink."

Max dutifully broke the seal on the lid and took a sip as Crazy Mouse busied himself at the computer.

"Okay, so there was a lot. Maybe I do it in reverse order of how much I found."

"Sure, whatever works for you."

"Brad Kempson. Apart from his official position, which is bogus—because, of course, he's CIA—I didn't find a single damn thing about him. You have to hand it to these guys, they know about hiding in plain sight. Catherine Parker was a little easier. Special Agent with the FBI. She got engaged six months ago, she's been in Italy for six weeks, and Skypes her fiancé nearly every night, late—she probably doesn't get much sleep. She's applied for a job with a consultancy in Washington and her bosses don't know about it yet. Nothing else suspicious. Now, on to the people who work for you. Domenico is gay."

Max smiled. "Everyone knows. It's not an issue."

"That's good. It's how it should be." Crazy Mouse nodded to himself, and Max guessed that whatever his own employment history, he was old enough to remember times when someone's sexuality might have been an issue. "Rosalia. Her son's business was having problems. It's doing better now; they're over the worst. But when it was bad, Rosalia borrowed twenty-five thousand euros to help him out. She's meeting the repayments, but it's still something to point out."

Max nodded, in shock that she hadn't come to him, or that he hadn't known. He thought of the people who worked for him as friends, and they were pretty much the closest friends he had, but it seemed he hadn't been looking out for them the way he should have done.

"But other than that, there's nothing at all that's noteworthy. That's very unusual, even for a small workforce like yours."

Max felt an incredible amount of relief and it took him a moment to understand that something was missing. "But I thought you said you'd found something disturbing."

"I haven't finished. I searched a little more on you first. I know you didn't ask me to, but I needed to be sure what your concern was. I know your parents died, that maybe it was suspicious, so I looked at this. Also, I looked at the FBI investigation, Goldstein, everything, just to be thorough. Your brother, Henry, I found nothing. The interesting person here was your brother-in-law, Nicolas Valfort. He works for Interpol."

"I know. And I know Interpol was working with the FBI against me."

Crazy Mouse frowned, as if Max were missing the point. "I have no idea if he was part of that collaboration, but I do know he has gambling debts."

"What? Nicolas?" It didn't square with the nonchalant and easygoing person he knew.

"Yes, and not just small gambling debts—over a million euros, to some pretty bad people. But it gets worse."

"Go on."

"He set up a new email account, and I wouldn't have known, except he made the mistake of using it to email someone else in his regular address book. You'd think he'd be smart, once he saw the mistake, and stop using that account, open another new one. But he wasn't smart, so I could see. A few weeks ago he paid ten thousand euros in cash—I know this only because of the email exchanges—to a former petty criminal who owned a garage in Albertville."

The recovery truck. Max didn't want to think it. *The recovery truck.*

"This was the week before your parents died, and apparently it was only the first half of the payment, but Valfort never paid the rest. The criminal was a drunk, fell asleep with a cigarette, or so they think, the place went up, and he went up with it."

Max was struggling to clarify his thoughts, simple as they were, but could only keep going back to that same thing, that the cyclist had been right, it had been a recovery truck. The rest of it—the fact that Nicolas, who'd always seemed such a benign and laid back and almost insignificant character, had built up insane debts and reached the point where killing his own wife's parents had become a viable solution—it was too much to take in.

What kind of tempest had to have been going on beneath that placid surface for him to reach that point? But then, for all Max knew, maybe there had been no tempest at all. The one thing he knew for sure was that he didn't know Nicolas, not really, and that maybe the same person who'd built up those debts could also have cold-bloodedly planned the murder of people so close to him, members of his own family.

"It's difficult to hear these things, no? I see worse, on a regular basis—it's the nature of my job—but it's still tough. You want a real drink?"

Max shook his head. "Thanks all the same, but I have to drive to Lyon."

"Tonight?"

"Tonight." He stood up, then sat again. "What about my sister?"

Crazy Mouse smiled ruefully, acknowledging that Max had asked the right question. "I thought the same. You never know what conversations go on in private, unless . . ." He left the sentence unfinished. "There's no evidence to suggest a connection with her, none at all. More than that, I'm pretty sure she doesn't even know about the debts."

Max nodded, relieved.

"What do you plan to do, Max?"

"Kill him." He said the words without any force or conviction, because it felt like such an undeniable truth, that Nicolas had to die for what he'd done to people who'd loved him like a son, and because he'd mourned them and been a part of their family in its grief. "I have to."

"I've given it much thought, and I think I'd feel the same way. It doesn't mean it's right."

"No."

"Or wise. People in your position, when things like this need to be done . . ." Once again, he left the sentence unfinished.

Max stood and looked around the room before facing him again. "I have to go, but thank you."

"You're sure you don't want that drink?"

He nodded again, and made his way out and down the stairs, away from the sounds of the low-key party, back out into the damp mistiness of the city.

Chapter Thirty-Eight

Max sat in the car for twenty minutes, trying to think but unable to get past the jumble of words and images and impulses spilling over each other in his mind. He kept seeing Nicolas, standing nonchalantly by Lottie's side, pouring champagne, with the girls by the graveside; kept hearing Crazy Mouse's words about the gambling debts and the garage owner and the ten thousand euros.

Ten thousand euros. This might have been an act of desperation, but it had been cold-blooded, calculated, even down to killing the person he'd hired to commit the murder. Max was conscious of the gun nestled against his body. He started the engine and drove, seeing no other way.

He stopped only once, sending a message to Domenico and booking a hotel, all the while feeling slightly separated from his own body, as though he were there looking down at himself drinking coffee in the strip-lit glare, his actions no less mysterious than those of the few other weary travelers sitting at nearby tables.

It was the early hours by the time Max arrived at the hotel in Lyon, and he fell onto his bed and slept fully clothed for an hour, then woke and undressed but struggled to sleep again, finding only a fitful rest through the early morning. He woke, showered and ordered some food.

And for the first time the foolishness of being here struck home. He didn't have a plan, except for some vague notion of meeting Nicolas somewhere, making him confess, shooting him. He'd be caught, of course, too easily, and would spend many years in prison, betraying everybody and everything all over again.

Crazy Mouse had suggested the proper course, and he'd been right, but still, even if Max couldn't have the pleasure of killing him, he'd have the satisfaction of confronting him, of letting him know what lay ahead for him.

Max called his brother-in-law's cell, and even that simple act reminded him that it had been Nicolas who'd broken the bad news to him, knowing full well that he'd brought about the deaths himself. The call went to voicemail and so for only the second time in all the years Max had known Nicolas, he put a call through to his office.

His secretary answered and said, "I'm sorry, Mr. Emerson, he's traveling at the moment and can't be reached. You could leave a message on his cell, or call back tomorrow."

"Thanks. It's just that I'm in town—I should have checked."

Max ended the call and sat staring into the void, one minute passing into another, asking himself the same question again and again: What was he doing here?

He checked out of the hotel and drove over to his sister's apartment. And his heart and his resolve crumbled a little more when Lottie opened the door because her eyes were red-rimmed, but she brightened immediately at the sight of him.

"Max! What are you doing here? Why didn't you tell me?"

He hugged her and said, "Just a flying visit. I tried to call Nicolas but he's out of the office."

Even as he spoke, Nicolas appeared in the hallway behind her, wearing a shirt and tie but no jacket. He smiled, and Max tensed in response but fought it, not wanting Lottie to notice. He hadn't wanted to see him here, not with her.

"I just flew back in this morning. Good to see you, Max."

"Likewise." Lottie stepped back to let him in and they walked through to the sitting room. He took in the silence for the first time. "Where are the girls?"

"Kindergarten. A shame you missed them, but let's have coffee."

Nicolas nodded and said, "I'll make it. You two sit down." He smiled at Max, and it seemed extraordinary now that he could be so convincingly relaxed. There was no reason for Nicolas to be any different, because he didn't know anything had changed, and yet Max was still surprised.

Nicolas left them alone, and as they sat down Max said, "Why have you been crying?"

"Oh, it's silly." And the tears did seem forgotten as Lottie stared at him, almost bursting with affection. It was a look he remembered well, from every time she returned from school or university and saw him again. "I'm so glad you called in. I've missed you, you know."

"I know."

"So has Henry."

"I'm not quite so sure about that."

"He has. I know him better than you do. He's always been very . . . buttoned up, but he feels things so strongly."

Max thought of him identifying the bodies of their parents, but instantly on the back of it remembered what the policeman had told him about his brother's comments, and he chased the thought away. They were beyond that now, even if not by much.

He heard the gentle percussion of Nicolas in the kitchen, reminding him that this was no ordinary visit. But looking at his sister's puffy eyes it was impossible to forget that there were always consequences, that it was never just one person who paid the price. Was it better for her to be the widow of a murderer or married to one?

"Why have you been crying?"

Lottie shook her head, embarrassed again. "Henry called just before you got here. The house has sold already, and I know it's silly, it wasn't our house any more, but despite what Henry says, it *was* our childhood home, ours as well as yours, and poor Madame Bouchet . . ." She was getting emotional again, but broke off. "Why are you smiling? You're laughing at me!"

"I'm not laughing at you. I'm happy." It was true, and for that moment, he'd almost forgotten what he was doing here. "Lottie, I bought the house."

"No, you didn't—it's a Russian who's bought it."

"It's a company with a Russian name—Oblomov—but that's me. I bought the house."

She laughed too now, incredulous. "*You* bought it, just like that? Of course you did. Twenty-five million francs?"

Max realized it was a question and said, "If that's what the asking price was—I don't know the exact details."

"No, why would you? It's just twenty-five million francs." Lottie laughed again. "Does Henry know it's you?"

"No, not yet. Naturally, I'll tell him in due course." Despite the partial thaw of the last two weeks, he'd still feared Henry might veto the sale if he'd known Max was behind it. "I'm keeping it as it is, and Madame Bouchet and Thérèse will stay there as long as they want. So you can visit whenever you like. It'll still be the family home, for the whole family."

Nicolas came in, carrying a tray. He was already smiling and she looked up at him, her eyes glistening.

"Did you hear? Max bought the house! It means the girls can grow up knowing it."

He nodded, placing the tray on the coffee table and saying, "But you won't live there, Max?"

"No. I thought we could all use it, but I did it mainly for Madame Bouchet and Thérèse."

"It's a beautiful gesture."

"He was always kind-hearted, even as a little boy. He always shared." Lottie sat forward to pour the coffee but looked at Max with a quizzical stare. "Isn't that funny. I can't remember how you take it."

"Black, no sugar."

"Of course. Henry used to take three sugars when he was young." A thought struck her. "Maybe we could all spend Christmas there!"

It was Nicolas who answered. "But remember, we promised Henry we'd spend Christmas with him this year."

"Well, I'm sure Henry wouldn't mind changing plans."

Max said, "I already have plans around Christmas, so maybe that's one to think about for another year. Besides I think, so soon, it might bring back the wrong kind of memories."

He turned to look at Nicolas as he said it, but there was no real reaction, just a casual nod of agreement.

Lottie yielded, saying, "Maybe you're right, but next summer, definitely."

"Definitely." She jumped up and hugged Max, and then hugged Nicolas and they both laughed at her exuberance as she sat back down again, and Nicolas' laugh looked genuine, as far as Max could tell.

They talked for twenty minutes as they drank their coffee, but whatever the subject, Lottie inevitably brought it back to the house in Vevey, a low-level excitement bubbling back to the surface time and again. Finally, she checked her watch and stood.

"Max, I have to go and get my cell phone. I left it at my friend's place and she's going away for two days, so . . . You'll stay until I get back? It's just around the corner."

There it was, the opportunity to do what he'd come here for, to confront Nicolas on his own.

"I'll stay. I can catch up with Nicolas."

Another casual nod, nothing to suggest his nonchalance was an act.

"Good. But wait there. I want to show you something first." Lottie walked out of the room and came back a few moments later clutching a picture frame. "I think this is my favorite picture of all of us." She turned it round and handed it to him.

He smiled at the sight of it. It was full summer and they were all outside, sitting at the big table, the gardens stretching behind them. They'd been eating, and food and drinks were visible on the table, but for the photo they'd all turned their chairs and were facing the camera.

There was Henry, dressed conservatively, looking slightly formal even in an open-collared shirt, like someone from an earlier period. There was Lottie, beaming with happiness. There was Alexandra, holding the young and laughing Felix in her arms, both of them so pale and blonde as to look like a fault in the printing process.

And there was Max, young and slim and brimming with a relaxed confidence, an easy smile, home from university for the summer. He stared at himself for a moment, wondering if this was where he'd wanted to end up just a decade or so later.

But his gaze moved to the center of the picture, to his mom and dad on the other side of the table, smiling and content in the midst of their sun-dappled family. For the first time as he looked at it, Max saw that his easy smile was his mom's easy smile, and he felt tears pricking his eyes.

Lottie didn't notice and said, "I don't know who took it. I wasn't with Nicolas then so it wasn't him, but . . ."

"Stef." Max glanced up at her. "Stef took it."

"Of course she did." She shook her head. "How could I have forgotten? I can get a copy of it, if you'd like."

"I would. I'd like that very much."

She became tearful again but was laughing too, hugging him, holding onto him.

"Oh Max, I'm so happy—not just the house, but us too, and Henry, after all that's happened. I'm just so happy."

"That's all I want."

Nicolas stood and walked out to the door with her, and Max took the opportunity to look down at the picture again, once more drawn to the center.

His mother's smile, her lively eyes. She'd always laughed easily. He'd never once heard her raise her voice, although she'd been able to express the fiercest disapproval with a single raised eyebrow. She'd enjoyed playing Mozart arias but never sang. She'd loved horses but didn't care for riding, had loved the snow but not skiing.

And she'd kept secrets. Yes, the woman smiling benignly out of that picture, and the man beside her, had kept so many secrets, all with the sole aim of protecting the family around them. And Max knew how easily he might shatter everything they'd tried to protect, for all the wrong reasons.

Nicolas came back into the room and fell into the armchair opposite Max, saying, "I put some champagne in to chill. Charlotte was so upset when Henry called about the house, so I thought, it's something to celebrate, no?"

Max nodded, but didn't look up. He continued to look at the picture, and finally he understood what he had to do, finally saw that what he'd planned to do even an hour before was the exact opposite of what they'd have wanted and what they'd strived for.

He'd thought so strongly that the way to emulate his mother was to avenge their deaths, to be as tough and ruthless as he imagined she had been. And yet he saw it now, so lucid and so sudden a realization, this picture telling him all he needed to know about how to honor their memory properly. A family was so easily broken—but it wouldn't be him, not this time.

"It's a great picture, no?"

Max looked up now and stared at him, and stared for so long that Nicolas smiled awkwardly and said, "Are you okay?" Max didn't respond, and after a few more seconds Nicolas raised his eyebrows, bemused.

"Max, you're freaking me out slightly." Still, Max didn't answer, but kept eye contact and now Nicolas laughed awkwardly. "Okay . . ."

"I know it was you, Nicolas."

He shook his head, perplexed. "What? What are you talking about?"

"I know it was you. I know about the gambling debts and I know about the garage in Albertville and the ten thousand euros. Did you honestly think I wouldn't find out? Did it never occur to you what I'd do when I did find out?"

Nicolas raised a hand and stroked his chin nervously, looking about the room, seemingly anywhere but at Max. "You're mistaken. Or someone gave you bad information . . ."

Max reached under his jacket and took out his gun. Nicolas stared at it, wide-eyed—the first sign of panic or agitation Max had ever witnessed in him. "Max, please! Think of Lottie!"

"Think of *Lottie*? Did you? When you were arranging to have threatening letters sent to her parents? When you were planning their murders? Did you think of Lottie then?"

"Max, you're mistaken." Max looked down at the gun and knocked the safety off. "Max, please, I'm begging you."

"Don't! Don't beg, or I will pull the trigger." He stared at him and Nicolas looked unsure of himself, his body tensing as though he was getting ready to spring out of the chair. "I'm not going to kill you, Nicolas, and I won't have you killed either, tempting as it is, but I'm too tired to sit here and let you lie to me."

Nicolas nodded, and Max could see that he was shaking, struggling to keep the last vestiges of composure. "What . . ." He ran the same hand through his hair. "What . . . er . . ."

"What am I planning to do?"

Nicolas nodded again, barely holding it together.

"Nothing."

Nicolas produced a strange sound, halfway between a gasp and a sob, and went through the same tics of stroking his chin, then the hand through his hair.

"As long as Lottie needs you, nothing. But let me tell you, Nicolas, if anything ever happens to her, if anything ever happens to me, whether it's your fault or not, you'll suffer more than you could ever believe."

"I wouldn't let anything happen to her. I love her, I . . ." Confusion washed over him. "I don't understand. Why are you doing this?"

"I told you, because she needs you. And because it's what Mom and Dad would have wanted. How could you, Nicolas? They loved you like a son. They'd have given you the million dollars themselves, no questions asked. How could you!"

Nicolas shook his head, breathing hard, trying to control it until something unseen snapped and gave way. His features contorted and he started to sob uncontrollably, bringing his hands up to cover his face. Max watched him, feeling nothing, not sure what he was meant to be feeling. And when Nicolas finally brought himself under control, he looked ashamed and broken. He looked up at Max after a little while.

"Will you tell her?"

Max put the safety back on and slipped the gun into its holster. "Why would I do that? You did a pretty good job of acting the part these last few weeks, maybe these last few years, and that's what you'll keep doing. Go and wash your face, and when Lottie comes in, you pour that champagne and act your normal genial self, and that's how it'll be every time we meet from now on. No one else will ever know. Just you, and me. You understand?"

Nicolas nodded, gratefully compliant. He pulled himself up from the chair, seemed to stagger a little, and left the room with his head bowed.

Max sat for a while, the sound of running water just reaching him from the bathroom. He stood then and put the picture on a shelf on the other side of the room, out of reach of the girls, but remained looking at it for another few minutes, lost in memory, until he heard the front door open and close.

"I'm back!"

At the same time, he heard the pop of a champagne cork in the kitchen. He hadn't even heard Nicolas leave the bathroom. He turned and Lottie came in and smiled, a smile that seemed to encapsulate everything they'd been through, all their shared history.

Max nodded in response and then she turned at the clink of glasses as Nicolas came in, saying, "It's probably not cool enough, but we have to drink a toast, no?" He carried the bottle and glasses over to the coffee table and looked up at Max. There was no sign of the tears, no sign that anything was wrong at all. "I guess you're driving, Max, but a small glass?"

He almost admired Nicolas, the way he'd seamlessly returned to that easygoing persona, but he knew now that it was a front, that it probably always had been, and there was nothing to admire there at all.

"Sure, why not."

He looked at Lottie and smiled, because he knew he could do this. This was how it would be. He was his mother's son, and he would smile that same smile for the camera, and carry secrets the same way she had, and no one but he and Nicolas would ever need know the truth.

Chapter Thirty-Nine

The following Friday he was sitting on the terrace after lunch, enjoying the sun, which already lacked the full warmth of high summer but was no less welcome for that.

Francesco came out and joined him, saying as he sat down, "You left me a list this morning."

Max nodded—bonuses for all the staff. "I've just been thinking it's good for the rewards to be shared—it's been an intense few weeks, and we have a loyal team."

"True, but everyone who works for Emerson is quite generously rewarded already. And these are big bonuses—I mean, fifty thousand for Rosalia?" Max nodded, smiling, but didn't answer. "It's a nice gesture, of course."

"We're all set for Leonov next week?"

"Yes, I spoke to him this morning. He's enthusiastic about meeting your friend, thinks it could be useful to him in the current climate. So it's advantageous for us too, I think."

"I think you're right. I guess things have turned out okay in the end."

He thought of Goldstein, one of the few loose threads that hadn't been tied off, and it was funny that he still imagined him in Tribeca with his bohemian girlfriend, even though he knew it had never been true.

"I never had any doubt—in business you make your own luck, and we make plenty."

Francesco pointed then and Max looked out as the Guardia di Finanza boat cruised past on the lake. Mercaldo was up top and saluted to Max and Francesco. They waved back and the boat carried on along the shore.

"No visit today."

"Just as well, I'm going to church."

Francesco did a double take. "You found religion again?"

"Not quite. San Michele—I told Monsignor Cavaletti I'd go over and see how they're getting on restoring the fresco."

"Ah yes, it's good that you have a hobby. And this is better than ballet, much better."

"It's hardly a hobby—it's not like I'm restoring it myself. And I'm still supporting the ballet."

Francesco looked unimpressed.

Max drove out to San Michele a little while later. It was a quiet place, almost deserted at this time of year, and the church was just a small parish church typical of the area, giving little indication that there was anything special inside.

He pushed open the door and walked in, but it was empty. The pews had been moved to the back to make room for a metal platform on wheels. There were lights set up, for illuminating the key section of wall. And there were work tables and various pieces of equipment here and there on the floor. But there were no restorers.

251

Max looked at his watch, guessing maybe they were still at lunch. He preferred that in a way, and walked up the church now to look at the fresco that covered one wall. Even in the shade, he could see part of it had been restored and how beautiful it would look in the end: the progression of the Magi toward Bethlehem, through a vast and detailed biblical landscape.

He turned on one of the lights, providing a little more illumination, a little more detail. There was something incredible, not just about the beauty of it or the greater beauty that would be restored with this process, but the fact that it had been on this wall for nearly six hundred years, and for a large part of that time had been taken for granted, with no one knowing that it was by Gozzoli.

The church door opened and he turned and saw a woman come in, wearing what he guessed were art restorer's overalls. She was dark-haired and had such a natural, understated beauty that for a moment or two he just stared at her.

Finally he spoke. "Hello."

"Hello." Her tone was questioning, and as she approached, his appreciation of her beauty was tempered slightly by the fact that she didn't seem very happy to find him there.

"I was just admiring the fresco."

She glanced over, but at the light he'd switched on rather than at the wall itself, her expression becoming even less accommodating. "Yes, it's beautiful. But you shouldn't be here. The church is closed to the public."

"I know. Monsignor Cavaletti gave me permission."

The mention of the name seemed to cause her some frustration, making Max wonder if there'd been a revolving door of people sent by Cavaletti, and her tone was fierce as she said, "Monsignor Cavaletti isn't in charge here. I am, and I've heard nothing about visitors, let alone agreed to them. I'm glad of your interest, really I am, but this is a very important work and too easily damaged by people coming in here who don't know what they're doing."

Max smiled, because she was angry and passionate and deadly serious, but he found her even more attractive for it, and wondered why he couldn't meet more women like this. "As it happens, I know exactly how important it is. That's why I'm funding its restoration."

That did the trick. She was visibly shocked. "*You're* Max Emerson?"

"I am."

"So! I thought you'd be much older."

People seemed to be saying that a lot lately. "I feel older than I look."

She smiled, appraising him, then said, "Maybe I wouldn't have skipped out on lunch if I'd known. I'm Isabella Buonarroti."

She reached out and shook his hand, and now he was the one smiling.

"Then we're both surprised. I imagined you . . . I don't know, very different."

"Don't tell me—blonde, all designer clothes, like some superficial socialite." He hoped his face didn't betray him, because that was pretty much exactly as he'd imagined her, and he was grateful that she didn't seem to want a response. "Trust me, that would make my parents so happy. They despair because I don't care about those things. I care about things like this." She pointed at the fresco, but then turned back to Max. "Was the lunch terrible?"

"Not at all. I like your parents."

"Yeah, I guess they're okay. Can I call you Max?"

"Of course."

"Good, so let's turn on some more of these lights so that you can really see what you're paying for."

He helped her turn on the other lights and then they stood before it and for a full minute neither of them spoke.

Finally, she said, "I always wonder about the gifts."

"Excuse me?"

She turned and looked at him with a smile before facing forward again.

"People always look—they see this new little family, they see the Magi, the three wise men, and in their minds the story ends with them giving tribute. But the gifts they brought would have been so valuable in that time, and surely it would have made the family quite rich in comparison to their neighbors. So, I wonder, did it change them, and what happened to those gifts, to that wealth? Why, thirty years later, is Jesus still working as a lowly carpenter? That's what I think about— what happened to the gifts?"

He nodded, and looked at the figures of the three Magi, still unrestored, covered by the soot of history. What happened to the gifts? They were always lost in the end, he supposed, just as the fortune he'd spent the last twelve years amassing would ebb away sooner or later.

"Would you like to come to dinner one night?"

She stared at him for a few seconds, not with alarm, perhaps just trying to read him, then said, "You know we're unlikely to be the match my parents so desperately hope we'll be."

"I know that."

"And you know I have no interest whatsoever in the world of finance."

"Why would you?" It was clear she wanted more than that. "You know what, it would just be nice to have a friend, someone with interesting things to say who isn't employed by me."

She offered a curious smile, but then said, "In a roundabout way, I *am* employed by you."

He acknowledged the point. "Baby steps."

"Okay."

"Okay, you'll come?"

"Sure, why not."

She smiled, but then they heard voices approaching, the other restorers, and both of them looked forward again, in tandem, wanting to preserve this moment. And for just a second or two more, they enjoyed their private contemplation of Gozzoli's fresco and the question it raised, before the world came rushing back in around them.

Chapter Forty

Lombok, Indonesia — four months later

It was well after midnight and still the rain drummed relentlessly on the roof, and water dripped around the eaves and the night seethed with it. Every now and then, lightning would flash beyond the screen and illuminate the path down to the beach and the trees and the bushes slick with rain, but no thunder came.

Saul enjoyed it, and he'd written well tonight and reckoned he might get somewhere if the rainy season kept up like this. Reaching a natural break, he finally saved the document and sent it to himself, stretched, finished his beer, and casually clicked onto Google News.

He scrolled through the headlines—terrorism, Syria, Donald Trump—and then he stopped, scrolled back, focused. He read for maybe thirty seconds before he realized he wasn't breathing, soaking up the facts, scanning and rescanning.

When he did breathe, it was only to say, "Holy crap!"

Senator Robert Colfax had been found dead in the bathroom of his Oklahoma City hotel suite after a suspected heart attack. Saul clicked on a couple more of the stories, feeling the adrenaline buzzing in his bloodstream, looking to see if there were any more details.

No one seemed to be treating the death as suspicious, but he knew it had to be. Colfax hadn't been the whole story, he was sure of that, but he'd been the weak link, and one of the others—probably Emerson or Vicari—had decided to remove him from the picture before he caused them any lasting damage.

He opened the drawer in the desk and looked at the phones there, picking up the red one. He turned it on and scrolled through for Joel's number, but was mindful of Rosa sleeping in the other room, so he got up and stepped out onto the veranda before calling.

He could hardly hear the ringtone and put a finger in his other ear to block out the noise of the rain.

It rang for a while before Joel picked up, and Saul said, "Hey, Joel, have you seen the news?"

It was only as the voice came back that he realized it hadn't been Joel who'd answered, but a woman—and she didn't sound friendly. "I can hardly hear you! Who is this?"

"Er, I'm a friend of Joel's."

"Well, Joel's grounded right now. That's why I'm answering his cell phone. No phone, no tech, he's grounded—you wanna speak to him, you come to the house or write him a letter!"

Saul yanked the phone away from his ear and ended the call. His heart was racing more after being upbraided by Joel's mom than it had been from the discovery of the news. It was easy to forget Joel was sixteen and embarrassing to be reminded of that fact by getting through to his mom.

He walked back inside, glanced at the open news page, then walked on and stood in the doorway to the other room where he could just see the shadow of Rosa sleeping. It relaxed him to see her there, and by force of habit he wondered what he should do about Colfax, when he already knew that he didn't actually want to do anything.

The Hackstars had been cool for a while, but none of that stuff really mattered, not in the long term, and definitely not as he stood here looking at Rosa. He was finally living the kind of life he'd always claimed to be leading, finally writing a book, finally with a girl like her.

Joel Manning wouldn't be grounded forever, so if he wanted to keep looking into links between his dad and the late Senator Colfax, that was up to him. Saul was moving on.

He walked back to his desk, closed the page, and shut down his Mac. None of those people mattered to him anymore. He wasn't even sure why they'd ever mattered. He'd hated Max Emerson for a while, so much so that it amused him now to think of it, and he guessed that was because he'd envied him, resenting him for what he had and what he'd achieved. But standing here, with the rain rattling on the roof and a girl he loved sleeping in the other room, there wasn't a person in the world he envied, and he doubted even Max Emerson could claim that.

Acknowledgments

Thanks to Deborah Schneider and her team at Gelfman Schneider/ ICM Partners. Thanks to Emilie Marneur, Victoria Pepe, Monica Byles, and all at Thomas & Mercer. And thanks to "BB" for giving me an insight into the murkiest depths of high finance, one of the few areas of modern life in which fact is always stranger than fiction.

About the Author

Kevin Wignall is a British writer, born in Brussels in 1967. He spent many years as an army child in different parts of Europe and went on to study politics and international relations at Lancaster University. He became a full-time writer after the publication of his first book, *People Die* (2001). His other novels are *Among the Dead* (2002); *Who is Conrad Hirst?* (2007), shortlisted for the Edgar Award and the Barry Award; *Dark Flag* (2010); *Hunter's Prayer* (2015, originally titled *For the Dogs* in the USA), which was made into a film directed by Jonathan Mostow and starring Sam Worthington and Odeya Rush; *A Death in Sweden* (2016); and *The Traitor's Story* (2016).

47564233R00161

Made in the USA
Middletown, DE
28 August 2017